UNLEASHING DESIRE

BRIDES OF PROPHECY
Book 4

BROOKLYN ANN

Copyright © 2016 by Brooklyn Ann

Cover design by Brooklyn Ann

All rights reserved. No part of this book may be reproduced in any form or by electronic or mechanical means, including information storage and retrieval systems— except in the form of limited quotations or reviews— without permission in writing from the author.

The characters and events are fictitious and are used fictitiously. Any similarities to any real persons, living or dead, are coincidental and not intended by the author.

Published by Broken Angels, an imprint by Brooklyn Smith

https://brooklynannauthor.com

Dedication

Dedicated to Karen Ann
(06-11-62 ~ 02-14-09)

Acknowledgements

Thank you so much to those of you who made this book shine: Rissa Watkins, Layna Pimental, Bonnie R. Paulson, Shona Husk, Merrilee Remmick, and Bonnie Maestas.

And thank you to Bad Movie Club for saving my sanity.

Thank you to my friends and family for encouraging me. Thank you to my newsletter readers for keeping me going.

Special thanks to my son, Micah Turner and my love, Kent Butler, my favorite guys who take care of me.

Chapter One

It was a lovely morning for vengeance.

The rising sun shed its light upon the Romanian countryside, gleaming on emerald grass and dew-covered wildflowers. However, the picturesque view only merited a cursory glance.

Lillian cursed as she stumbled up the hill. She dug the heels of her hiking boots into the damp earth to keep her footing. With a firm grip on a finely carved oak stake, she approached the ruins of Castle Nicolae.

Even amidst the pinkish glow of the early dawn and the cheery melody of birdsong, the pile of gray rubble looked ominous. Lillian gulped a deep breath of morning air and suppressed a shiver as she pulled the castle schematic out of the pocket of her light summer jacket. According to the diagram, the chasm leading inside was right in front of her.

Her target lay below, in the bowels of the ancient fortress.

Shoving the schematic back in her pocket, she pulled out her phone and texted the AIU headquarters. *I'm going in.*

Her phone vibrated a reply: *Invalid number.*

Huh? Double-checking to make certain she texted the correct number, she tried again and received the same error message.

Mouth dry, Lillian eyed the castle. Was *he* somehow doing it? She shook her head. That would be ridiculous. It was probably the rural location. He shouldn't be able to mess with her if he was asleep.

By all reports, the vampire had been comatose for centuries, only waking once a year to feed. Last month, he'd killed the wrong person.

Thumb stroking the stake, Lillian growled through clenched teeth, "Your murderer will not go unpunished, Dad. Radu Nicolae will die today." Fierce gratitude flowed through her when the AIU director permitted her to take this assignment, despite her lack of experience. He must have understood that this was personal.

With grim determination, she groped along the cracked stone until she found the entrance, a narrow fissure in the rock.

Shadows closed over her as if encasing her body in ice. She pulled out her Mag Light, illuminating the treacherous tunnel with a bluish LED glow.

Though she tried to walk as quietly as possible, rocks and debris underfoot marked her progress with skitters and crunches. Darkness chased away the meager rays of sunlight as she descended further into the heart of the ruins.

After contorting her way down through the twisting passage, crumbled rock gave way to smooth stone steps coated in a fine layer of charcoal. There had been a fire here long ago.

Heart pounding in her throat, Lillian made her way down the stairs and found a clean chamber.

No ashy residue or cobwebs remained. A row of backpacks, ranging from new to old, lined one wall. An ancient prison cell dominated the other. She swallowed at the sight of the rusted iron bars. This must have been the castle dungeon. There was even a fireplace with a stack of wood beside it. A closer look revealed that most of the firewood consisted of sharp stakes.

Lillian shuddered, her palm sweating around her own stake. How many people had tried to kill him, only to die in this place? Choking vines of doubt wrapped around her lungs. If all of them had failed, what chances did she have of surviving? Rage singed the edges of the vines. So many deaths. She *had* to stop him.

At last, Radu Nicolae's slumbering form came into view. Lillian's lip curled with scorn. *This* was the big scary monster? The creature seemed already dead. It lay still, pale, and emaciated. Its cheekbones gleamed in sharp relief above a dark scraggly beard.

Her fingers trembled as she shone the light on the vampire's face. A gasp caught in her throat as she saw his hair. A shade of darkest chocolate, it lay like a silken waterfall in rich waves on the stone slab, incongruously beautiful compared to the rest of him. Without thinking, she reached out to touch those tresses, to see if they were soft as they appeared.

The sight of the stake in her fist made her snatch her hand back. Her stomach churned in revulsion at her insane impulse. *What was I thinking?* This monster killed her father. She was here to destroy it, not pet it.

Maybe it was another mind trick of his. Some sort of preternatural defense mechanism.

Gritting her teeth, Lillian set the flashlight on the slab so the beam pointed over the vampire's supine form. She removed the mallet from her pack and positioned the stake above his heart.

Shoulders vibrating with tension, she raised the mallet and paused to savor her vengeance.

She brought the mallet down.

Instead of crunching bone, her scream rent the air as those lashes lifted to reveal glowing black eyes. The vampire bolted upright.

Fangs gleamed in the darkness, and Lillian was yanked into the monster's embrace. The stake and mallet fell from her numb fingers.

The flashlight clattered to the floor, casting her and the monster in blackness. A feral growl rumbled inches from her ear, sending shivers down her spine.

Fangs pierced her throat, sharp pain exploding in her flesh. The sound of swallowing roared through Lillian's consciousness, heightening her terror.

He's killing me! Oh God, I failed, Dad. I'm so sorry…

Her life flashed before her eyes, along with a barrage of random, inane thoughts, like the mournful fact that she'd never have ice cream again.

Then the pain abated, and strange sensations crept in. His rhythmic sucking at her neck bled away her panic and tightened things low in her body. The vampire relaxed his grip on her ribcage. One hand stroked her back while the other caressed her hair. His rock-hard erection pressed against her body. Her clit throbbed. Moisture seeped between her thighs. Of their own volition, her hands gripped his shoulders, pulling him closer. Terror clashed with her body's arousal. What sort of magic did he have to elicit such an illogical response?

A low moan escaped Lillian's lips even as her mind screamed, *"No, I can't be enjoying this!"*

Then all was blackness.

Radu Nicolae removed his fangs from the Huntress's neck with a curse. Something was *very* wrong here, and he would keep this woman alive until he got to the bottom of it. As he gathered her into his arms, he mentally perused all that he'd seen in her mind.

The first indication that something wasn't right was her employers claiming he'd killed the woman's father. Radu remembered all the men he'd killed in the last century. This Joe Holmes had not been one of them. And even if he had killed the man, why did this company of Hunters send an inexperienced woman to kill him?

For centuries, the most skilled Hunters had tracked him to his lair, only to die under his bite. This Lillian Holmes was not a Hunter at all. She was a scientist, as had been her father. From what he pulled from her mind, they had been studying his kind, with no intention of killing them.

So, why, after her father disappeared, did her superiors pull her aside and lie to her? Why did they send her to hunt him, thus assuring her death? Radu's fingers clenched around the woman's arms. They'd *wanted* her to die. That much was obvious. And they presumed to *use him* as a pawn for that end. A growl of fury escaped his throat at the presumption of this AIU…this Abnormal Investigation Unit. Lillian whimpered, and Radu loosened his grip slightly.

They would pay. That much was certain. *Nobody* used him. It seemed he would emerge from his rest sooner than planned…and for that, he would need his strength. Radu licked the blood from his lips, savoring the sweetness.

Lillian would help him rejuvenate, but he would not be able to feed on her alone. What he had taken from her had revived him greatly. He flexed his muscles, enjoying the new strength coursing through his veins. It was enough for him to venture out and hunt for himself.

He frowned. He would also have to procure nourishment for Lillian. A definite inconvenience, but one that would hopefully be worthwhile.

Radu buried his face in Lillian's hair, inhaling the scent of strawberries that was almost as delicious as that of her feminine arousal. His cock stirred again at the memory. She'd wanted him, despite how hard she'd tried to fight her desire. Temptation flared to convince her to give in, but Radu shoved the thought aside. For now, it was enough to enjoy the warmth of a woman in his arms. It had been far too long.

As he awaited nightfall, Radu used the mental connection from feeding to probe Lillian's slumbering mind, absorbing her language, her emotions, and her memories. She was another American, from some strange, vast place on the other side of the world. He'd devoured a few of those, and learned the odd way they spoke.

Lillian's intellect astounded him. It was amazing how far science had progressed over the centuries. And the studies done on his kind...hell, this woman held more knowledge about what he was than he did.

And just as she'd demonstrated, she had no experience hunting vampires. She and her father had studied them. Images danced in his mind: blood dripped on panes of glass and then magnified to the point where it looked like nothing he'd ever seen before....Lillian smiling as she typed strange symbols on a screen that somehow transmitted to her father...Lillian and her father studying a black-haired infant in one of those steel and glass chambers before taking it to a cozy cabin, where Lillian sang and rocked it to sleep.

Radu frowned. He had also been taken from a cold, hungry place in infancy and brought into a warm, loving home. Along with...

Another of her memories came to him, sending the breath from his body. It was impossible! Files, pictures, and names that Lillian had read aloud skittered across his vision. Silas McNaught...Akasha Hope...*Razvan.*

There couldn't be any other vampire by that name.

Lillian knew of his *twin brother*!

Radu closed his eyes, his heart clenching like a fist in his ribcage. He hadn't seen Razvan in centuries, not since their parents were killed when their castle was put to the torch. Not since Razvan killed the woman he'd loved.

Lillian had information about Razvan's existence. She'd read his name from one of those pieces of paper that mortals had started using.

Radu would make her tell him his brother's location. It was past time for a reckoning.

As darkness neared, he lifted Lillian in his arms and carried her to the cell in the corner. He would not let this woman get away from him.

Chapter Two

Lillian awoke to the sound of splashing water. Her head felt like a lead weight as she lifted it from the…pillow? She leaned up on one elbow, opening her eyes. The sleeping bag slid off her shoulder, exposing her to the chill of the chamber. Reflexively, she pulled the cover back up to her chin…and that's when she saw the bars. He'd locked her in a cage.

Scrambling out of the sleeping bag, Lillian seized the bars and shrieked, "Let me out of here, you son of a bitch!"

The vampire sat with his back toward her, facing the fireplace, which was now lit with a merry blaze. The shadows were too chaotic to see what he was doing.

"You will not talk about my mother in such a manner," he said in a deep, forbidding tone.

Lillian nearly choked in outrage. "That's rich, coming from the bastard who killed my father."

He turned to face her, and her eyes widened. His face was lathered with shaving cream. The vampire pointed a wicked-looking old-fashioned razor at her. "I am *not* a bastard. My mother and father were wed. Furthermore, I did not kill your father, Lillian."

Her mouth opened, but no words came while she reeled in shock as his words registered. He spoke English, albeit with a thick accent and a rough voice, as if he hadn't talked in a long time. "How do you know my name?" she demanded.

"I saw *everything* in your mind when I drank from you." He smiled, dragging the blade across his chin with sure strokes. "And we will discuss many things I found there. But first, I must procure supplies and nourishment for you."

Lillian shuddered, disliking the effect his voice had on her. "I'm not taking anything from you."

His smile widened, black eyes filled with dark promise. "Oh, but you will. And I will take much from you as well. It will be enjoyable for us both."

Heat filled her face as she remembered his fangs in her throat and his erection grinding against her. To her relief, the vampire turned away to rinse the razor in a bowl of water before he continued shaving. The rasp of the blade and the crackling fire only emphasized the awkward silence.

Too soon, Radu finished. He turned to face her again, and Lillian gasped at his transformation. Though still full of sharp angles and hollows, his face had lost its sunken appearance. Now, framed with that lush, dark chocolate hair, that visage could give a model a run for his money...an evil model, anyway. Those long eyelashes and sensuous lips did nothing to mute the malevolence of his black eyes.

With predatory grace, he grabbed a long black coat, shrugging it over his lean, muscled form. Reaching into one of the newer backpacks left by the hunters he'd slain, Radu withdrew a protein bar and a bottle of water and approached her cell. "This should tide you over until I return with more fitting sustenance."

She ignored the items he held near the bars. If only she had her stake...though since vampires had superhuman strength, he'd probably just break her wrist. No, she wished she had a flamethrower.

His inky brows arched above midnight eyes. "Very well, but when I return, you *will* eat."

Lillian lifted her chin and mustered her most defiant glare. Radu's lips twitched, and he placed the food and water through the bars of her cell before disappearing from the room in a blur of preternatural speed.

Left alone, she collapsed to her knees and shuddered uncontrollably. He wasn't going to kill her. Her eyes darted from the sleeping bags to the food. Her trembling increased, despite the growing warmth from the fire. No, he wasn't going to kill her. What he had planned was much worse.

The vampire intended to keep her alive to use as a food source…and likely for sex as well.

The prospect of being raped was horrifying on its own. But being raped by an inhuman monster added a whole new dimension to the terror. Most revolting of all was that her body had responded to him.

Why? Although it had been a long time since she'd been with a man, surely she wasn't *that* hard up.

His earlier words suddenly rang in her mind. *I didn't kill your father, Lillian.*

Was it possible that he told her the truth? Radu was over a thousand years old, one of the oldest vampires documented by her organization. Vampires grew more powerful with age, so Radu had to possess incredible strength and other abilities…like mind control.

For all she knew, he could convince her that up was down and the sky was green. So what reason would he have to lie?

But if Radu hadn't killed her dad, then who did?

She didn't know how long she spent huddled in her cage, growing colder as the fire burned down. Trapped with nothing but her racing thoughts.

By the time she heard footfalls approaching the chamber, her head jerked up in a mixture of trepidation and anticipation for this to be over with.

Radu held a large sack in one arm and had a bundle of wood in the other, propped upon his shoulder. He carried the weight like it was nothing, a reminder of his inhuman strength.

"I've brought you food and more blankets." His voice slowly lost its husky rasp and took on a rich, melodious timbre. His face and body had also filled out, losing the rest of that emaciated look. From his healthy skin tone, it was clear he'd fed on some other hapless person.

He looked breathtakingly handsome. And Lillian hated herself for the observation. Radu dropped the firewood by the makeshift hearth and then knelt before her cage with the bag.

"Here." He pulled out a carryout restaurant box that smelled heavenly, along with utensils wrapped in plastic. Then he set down a small tub with an elegant logo that made her blink.

"You brought me ice cream?" She couldn't fight the disbelief in her voice even as she struggled to imagine him walking around in a grocery store like a normal person. How had he paid for everything? How did he even know how to shop in the modern world?

He nodded. "When I fed on you, I heard you thinking that you would never be able to eat it again." He rubbed his hand on jeans that he may have taken from one of his recent victims. Unbelievably, his lips curved up in a boyish grin of wonder. "It's very cold."

Infuriated with her maddening response to him, Lillian scooted back against the wall of the cage and crossed her arms. "I won't touch any of it."

A shiver rushed down her spine at the thought of him being in her mind.

He cocked his head to the side, and something that looked like hurt flashed in his black eyes. "Why not?"

She rolled her eyes and fought to not show fear. "Because you might have drugged or poisoned it."

His brows creased with confusion. "And why do you think I'd do that?"

She crossed her legs and hunched over smaller. "So you can knock me out and rape me."

He bared his fangs and growled what sounded like a curse in Romanian. "I do you a kindness, and you accuse me of something so despicable? I am not an animal. I am a man." He tapped his chest in primal emphasis. "I've never forced a woman in my entire life. Women clamor for a night in my bed." His teeth flashed in an arrogant grin before his brows once more drew together in anger. "First, you accuse me of murdering your father, now you accuse me of rape." The last word ended in a snarl, and his next turned into a roar. "What have I done to deserve such abominable assumptions?"

The metal bars of the cage dug into Lillian's spine as she tried to shrink further back, her heart in her throat at the sight of his glowing eyes and consuming fury. Licking dry lips, she spoke softly. "You drank my blood and locked me up."

"*You* tried to kill me," he countered, eyes narrowed as he pointed an accusatory finger. "Yet despite that, I am saving your life instead of killing you."

Lillian frowned in confusion. First, he was indignant at her assumption that he'd rape her, and now he was claiming to save her? "What do you mean?" she asked cautiously. Vampires were said to be manipulative. She mustn't forget that.

"You are a scientist, not an experienced Hunter, yet your employer told you a lie and sent you to kill a vampire as old and powerful as I am." He paced before her cage like a panther stalking its prey. "There is only one conclusion to be made from that."

Horror clawed her throat as Lillian digested his words. "Oh my God. You think they sent me here to die."

Radu nodded, his eyes full of sympathy and then anger. "They wanted to *use* me as their pawn. And it nearly worked." He looked like he wanted to say something else, then he shook his head and crouched in front of the cage, never breaking his hold on her gaze. "You've lost a great amount of blood, Lillian. Please, eat. And then we shall talk. I have many things to ask you."

Mind still reeling with the possibility that her own superiors had set her up to die, Lillian opened her mouth to argue, but to her humiliation, her stomach rumbled when he opened the carryout box to reveal some sort of noodle dish that made her mouth water. "What is that?"

"*Halushki.*" He held out the box and a plastic fork. "*Eat.*"

Her ravenous hunger, coupled with Radu's genuine anger at the idea that he'd drug her, compelled her to relent. Besides, she was too dizzy from blood loss and missing breakfast and lunch to be able to think straight about vampires and government conspiracies. Taking the box and a fork, Lillian took a bite and moaned at the taste of garlic, onions, and butter.

She looked up to see Radu closing his eyes in such abject pleasure that she blushed, feeling like a voyeur. Then those hypnotic black eyes snapped open, and he gave her that boyish smile again.

"When you eat, I can taste," he explained before pointing at her fork. "Take another bite, please."

For a moment, Lillian considered refusing. Why should she give him any pleasure when he held her captive? But her hunger, combined with her fascination at this new phenomenon, compelled her to comply. Watching Radu's blatant ecstasy as she chewed the food, her mind tried to work out a scientific explanation for his being able to taste her food. Transmitting thoughts via telepathy sort of made sense when observing electromagnetic brain waves. Was she somehow emitting a wave that sent a neural pulse to his taste receptors?

Radu interrupted her thoughts. "This ice cream. I want to try it." He held out the tub.

Normally, Lillian wouldn't dream of spoiling her dinner with dessert, but the stuff would melt if she didn't eat it soon. Setting down the half-finished haluski with a touch of reluctance, she picked up the ice-cold pint. The label was in Romanian, so she couldn't read it, but the picture made it look like vanilla. A safe choice.

It wasn't just vanilla. It was the best damn vanilla she'd ever had in her life. The flavor burst over her tongue like a revelation. Radu made a low sound that was more fitting to the bedroom than during a meal. Her loins tightened immediately.

Lillian bit her lip against the arousal. This had to be the most messed up situation she'd ever been in. Here she was, telepathically sharing a meal with a vampire she'd originally come here to kill. Getting turned on by him even as he had her locked up like an animal. *Can anyone say Stockholm Syndrome?*

Melting ice cream dribbled on her wrist, breaking off the thoughts. Not wanting such deliciousness to go to waste, Lillian quickly polished off the rest of the carton, ignoring the inevitable surge of brain freeze.

Radu suddenly groaned and pinched the bridge of his nose. "*La naiba*, woman, what is that?"

He was able to feel that too? Despite her own pain, Lillian couldn't help laughing even as she wondered how far the connection went. If she stabbed herself, would he experience that too? What about cramps? That brought on another gale of laughter.

"Brain freeze," she gasped between heaves of hysterical giggles. Served him right. "It happens when you eat cold things too fast, but I was only doing what you told me."

"I did not say to eat so quickly," he said with such a deep scowl that another burst of laughter exploded from her. "This is not something to laugh at. You have pain too."

"It doesn't last long." Even as she spoke, the pain faded away, leaving them both relieved…until Lillian realized she'd been laughing at a thousand-year-old vampire. She sobered immediately, justifying her actions aloud. "And for your information, it is perfectly normal to laugh in times of crisis. It's the brain's way of protecting itself from too much stress." And if this wasn't stress of the highest degree, she didn't know what was.

From the way his brows drew together in consternation, she inferred that he didn't understand half of what she said.

"You should let me protect you instead," he grumbled. "That way, there will be no pain."

"Protect me?" She fought a blush, reminding herself and him of the situation. "You said you planned to feed on me again."

He shrugged, indifferent to her disbelieving tone. "Yes, but I will take away the hurt next time, and I won't drink too much." His expression darkened as he changed the subject. "Now we talk. What do you know of a vampire called Razvan?"

Lillian blinked in surprise. She'd been expecting him to expound on his theory that the AIU wanted her dead. Should she answer? Why not? She didn't have much information anyway. "That was one of the vampires my father had a file on. But he burned it three years ago, for some reason." She frowned, mind turning over the information. Had what had been in the file gotten Dad killed? Did the AIU also have info on this Razvan? He hadn't been in the vampire database, but perhaps he was in a classified file above her clearance level.

"Where is he?" Radu interrupted her musing.

"Somewhere in the Northwest, but I can't remember exactly where." Desperation welled in her belly. She needed to get out of here, go through her father's things, and track down his killer. Find out if Dad had been to Romania, or if Radu told the truth.

"Northwest of what?" he demanded.

"The United States. It's a huge part of the country, so I'm not very helpful." Now that he'd brought up this other vampire, she had a lot of new questions, but… "Why do you ask?"

"Razvan is my brother."

Her jaw dropped. "You have a *brother*?" When he nodded, she frowned. "But vampires can't reproduce sexually. How can you have a sibling?"

"We were…what is the word you use? Raised by a man who was not our natural father. A vampire who Changed us when we became men."

"Oh, you were adopted." Lillian struggled to word her next thought carefully. "Do you think your brother may have killed my father, and the AIU confused him with you?"

"It is possible. We do look alike. And it wouldn't be the first time Razvan murdered someone." His eyes blazed at the last, making it apparent that the someone he referred to had been important to him. Brushing his hair out of his face, he met her gaze. "But I don't think your employer confused anything. If they'd meant for you to come out of here alive, they'd have prepared you better. Given you more information, better weapons. I know of the things mankind can use to kill."

The logic slapped her in the face. Why else would they allow an inexperienced scientist to attempt to take out an ancient vampire? And she wouldn't have even asked to be sent on this mission if Director Bowers hadn't told her that Radu had killed her dad. Then there was her sudden inability to contact the AIU headquarters once she arrived at the castle. Now the truth was clear as one of her microscope slides. She was an idiot for not seeing it in the first place. Was she truly a dumb blonde to let her desire for revenge cloud her reasoning? Or was it because she spent more time with cells and microbes than people?

"*They* killed my father," she said tonelessly as rage coiled inside her.

Radu nodded. "I think so." Before she was able to react, he reached through the bars and took her hand. Rubbing his thumb lightly across her wrist in an attempt of comfort, he looked down with an agonized frown. "My mother and father were murdered too."

Lillian's shock at his touch disappeared with his words. "By who?"

"A mob." Slowly, he withdrew his hand and clenched his jaw. "It was a long time ago… and it might have been my fault. Either way, there is naught to be done about it now." He looked up from where he crouched and met her gaze. "But for you, vengeance is possible. As I said before, I do not like being used. Therefore, I shall help you..." He bared his fangs in a grin. "Once you help me find my brother."

Chapter Three

Radu had to bite his tongue before he said anything more. What had possessed him to tell her about his parents? Much less his incapacitating guilt?

What did she think of him now? He tried to read her mind, but it had been too many hours since he drank from her…and he'd used the last of the power to find out what ice cream tasted like. Unfortunately, he couldn't drink from her until tomorrow at the earliest…and to be honest, it would be best to wait for the night after that. He didn't want to deplete her.

Instead of prodding him about his past, Lillian stared at him with such shocked disbelief that he had the urge to laugh. "You think *I* can take down a government agency? Do you have any idea how big and powerful they are?"

"They are humans." He let all his scorn flow into his words, tamping down a twinge of unease. Humans *had* managed to kill his parents.

"So am I," she countered. Her blue eyes flared in challenge.

Radu's lips curved upwards, despite himself. Yes, she was. Delightfully warm, delicious…and vulnerable. Yet that mind of hers held more power than she was aware of. The things she knew of his kind shocked him.

When Radu didn't remark, Lillian shifted in the cage with a sigh. "First, I want to find out why they killed my father and then tried to eliminate me."

"Did your father keep secrets from this AIU?"

A dry laugh emerged from her pink lips. "That's the thing. He had so many secrets that I have no clue where to begin. We had our own research projects separate from the AIU, and Dad had things going on that even I don't know about, like that file on your brother." A line formed on her smooth brow. "But the AIU's job was only to observe and study preternatural beings. They were a peaceful, passive organization."

"They aren't anymore," he reminded her, pointing at the stake on the floor. "You said he burned the file he had on my brother. I also saw other names in your mind. What about this Silas McNaught and Akasha Hope?"

He practically saw the thoughts churning in her brain, lighting on something when her eyes widened. "Akasha was a mutant of some sort, and my father had the opportunity to study her when she was in military custody. Another of his side ventures." A flash of discomfort flitted across her features as if she didn't approve of Akasha being studied. "He sent me all of his data…and he helped her escape." Her unease bled away, and she sounded more confident. "Silas is a vampire and involved with her somehow. Dad convinced Silas to give him some of his blood in exchange for him covering up the escape." Her frown returned. "But he wasn't operating as an AIU agent when he did that. It was a freelance job of sorts. Even the military was unaware he was there, aside from the sergeant that asked for his aid."

Radu nodded, impressed despite himself with Lillian's father's wit and willingness to help his kind. He recalled another of Lillian's memories. "What about the infant?"

Lillian's face went white as it had been when he'd drained her blood. "The infant?"

"I saw you and your father removing a baby from a..." He fumbled for the word. "Laboratory and taking it to a secret house by a lake. It had black curly hair and green eyes."

"Kiara," she whispered, somehow paling further. "If the AIU learned about her..." She shook her head. "No, then it would make no sense to kill either of us. They'd want our research. They'd also want the baby. Dad already placed her in a safe foster home because it was too dangerous for us to keep her."

Something about her tone alarmed him. "What is so special about this baby?"

"She's the daughter of Silas McNaught and Akasha Hope."

Radu's breath fled his body. "The child is half-vampire." How in the seven circles of hell was such a thing possible? Although his kind was able to engage in lovemaking, their wombs and seed were barren, much to his mother's heartbreak.

Lillian nodded. "A hybrid."

"And you and your father *stole* their daughter." Radu looked at her with new eyes. Was he foolish to ally himself with her? What kind of a woman was she?

She shook her head so rapidly that her hair formed a cloud the color of a sunset. "No! They don't even know about her!"

That was far from comforting. "Though the father's ignorance is understandable, how could a woman be unaware that she'd given birth?"

"Akasha didn't birth her. We used her eggs that Dad harvested when she was unconscious and then fertilized one with sperm cells I'd manufactured from Silas's blood." Lillian's eyes took on that look of zeal she imparted whenever speaking of her studies. "We implanted the embryo into a surrogate mother and monitored everything."

Although Radu didn't comprehend all the words she'd used, he understood her meaning. His own mother had been heartbroken that she could not bear children of her own. That was why their father, Alexandru Nicolae, had taken Radu and Razvan. How would Crina, his adoptive mother, have felt if the technology had been there to have children of her own blood? Radu would have either been devoured by wolves or frozen to death if that were the case. The woman who'd birthed Radu and Razvan had been unable to feed two extra mouths, so they'd put Radu outside to be offered to the spirits. Crina told him when he was a young boy. Alexandru had then stolen into the peasant's hovel and taken Razvan from his cradle, leaving behind a bag of gold.

Shame coiled in Radu's belly. During a spiteful argument, he'd lied and told Razvan that he was the one who was sacrificed. Either way, both twins were spared when Alexandru had taken them to give his bride the sons she'd so desired.

Shaking off the memories, he turned his ire back to Lillian. "Yet you kept this child secret from her parents."

"I didn't want to!" she said so vehemently that he believed her. "But Dad insisted."

"And do you plan on rectifying this matter?" he prodded. "Will you tell this mutant woman and her vampire mate that they have a daughter?"

Biting her lip, she nodded. "I only hope they do not kill me, especially since I have no idea where their baby is."

"I won't let them harm you." The severity of his vow gave him pause. Radu heaved a sigh, slightly ill with this talk of secret, scientifically wrought babies, and returned to the topic of his missing twin. "What did Razvan's file say?"

Lillian shrugged. "Dad almost slapped my hand when I tried to look at that one. He said it was too dangerous. All I know is that Razvan is often connected with reputed psychics."

Radu chuckled. "Wise advice. Even as a youth, my brother was clever and powerful." He frowned. "What are psychics?"

"People who can read minds like you…or do other things, like see the future."

He nodded as comprehension dawned. "Ah. We referred to those sorts as witches. We used to kill them on sight before they could use their powers to find out about vampires."

Yet his twin had been using them in his efforts to find him for the past seven centuries. In fact, one had been prodding for him only a few nights ago. But Razvan's efforts would never succeed as long as Radu didn't want to be found. After the deaths of his parents, his grief had been too great to bear facing the world.

Now, however, Radu was ready to face his twin.

"I still can't figure out why they wanted my father and me dead," Lillian said. "I need to get to our safe deposit box. Our house is out of the question, but his secret lab might still be uncompromised." She moved as if to stand, then slumped where she sat. "But I don't know how the hell we're supposed to get back into the states. Since I'm supposed to be dead, the AIU would be alerted if I use my passport, and you're so old you don't even exist on paper." She squirmed on her sleeping pallet. Her face was suddenly pink as strawberries and cream. "I need to use the bathroom. Will you let me out?"

It took him a moment to grasp her meaning. "You need to relieve yourself." Reaching in his pocket for the key, he unlocked the door and seized her hand in case she tried to bolt. "I will take you outside, but if you try to escape, you will not like the consequences."

Instead of humble acquiescence to his warning, she frowned up at him. "If we are to be working together, why keep me locked up in the first place?"

He cast her a cynical smile. "Forgive me if I do not quite trust you yet."

As Radu led her out of the chamber and up the cracked steps, he couldn't help but succumb to a thrill of pleasure at the warmth and softness of her flesh in his grip and the heady scent of sunshine and wildflowers emanating from her hair. Rampant lust roared through him that only his honor would suppress. However, that did not deter him from plotting ways to seduce her.

He grinned at Lillian's gasp when they turned down a corridor, and he hefted a heavy rock the size of two men to reveal a tunnel leading out into the night.

"That is much easier than the way I came in," she whispered.

He chuckled. "Yes, although I do appreciate the meals, I do not make it a habit of making it easy for Hunters to find me."

When they emerged outside, Radu led her to a copse of bushes. "I will turn around to grant you privacy, but if you flee, I *will* catch you."

Even in the darkness, he saw her crimson cheeks. Once she'd attended to her needs, she paused in the foliage. Radu's muscles tensed in preparation to give chase. Then he heard her heave a sigh and return to his side. His shoulders relaxed as relief and elation bubbled within him.

But when he turned to escort her back to the castle, Lillian stopped and placed her hand on his bicep. "Do I have to go back in that cage already? I'd really like to stretch and have some fresh air."

Her soft touch and imploring gaze made his chest tighten. "Very well."

Truly more time outdoors would benefit Radu as well. He'd only been steadily emerging from his hibernation for the past year. If he was going to be taking this woman to a strange country across the sea, he needed to become acclimated to this loud and busy place the world had become. His first venture to procure food for Lillian had jangled his nerves so severely that he never wanted to enter civilization again.

Yet, as Lillian and Radu walked in silence, side by side, he realized that being awake was not all bad.

"When will we leave?" she asked suddenly.

He halted his steps. "I do not know. It will take me some time to adjust to this new world. Much has changed since I went to ground."

Her blue eyes flashed with defiance. "You can't keep me locked up forever. I need to get out of here, avenge my father's murder, and find Akasha and Silas to tell them about their baby."

Before he formed a retort, she took off running into the underbrush. Heaving a sigh, Radu allowed her to run several paces before he took to the air and flew above her. He wobbled slightly, still growing used to flying again.

He landed in front of her, opening his arms as she crashed into him. "What did I tell you about running?"

She squirmed. "Well, I can't just give in like a stupid sheep."

Her movements against him made his cock harden painfully. He spoke through gritted teeth, clinging to a single thread of sanity. "While I admire your spirit, that does not change the fact that I'll have to keep you in your cage." *And safe from me.* "Now be still."

Lillian gasped as he rose into the air. Radu couldn't hold back a gratified smile as she clung to him tightly. His erection pressed against her thigh, her heat filling him with drugging need. From her intake of breath and crimson cheeks, he saw that she felt it too. But he didn't apologize. He was a man, after all.

By the time they landed, she was trembling like a mouse. Radu ran his hand through her hair in an attempt to soothe her. Not releasing her hand, he led her back into the castle ruins and down to his underground lair.

Biting back a chuckle at her mutinous pout when he led her back in her cage, he then set about making her prison more comfortable. Opening the bags he'd taken from Hunters who'd tried to kill him over the decades, he gathered up six more sleeping bags and tossed them into the cage to soften the hard stone floor. Another search through the castle and he found a chamber pot and a dusty chair.

Lillian turned her nose up at the chamber pot as he smirked and built up the fire to warm the cold chamber. Finally, she heaved a sigh of resignation and began unrolling the sleeping bags and laying them atop each other to make a bed.

"I have no idea how we'll get back in the states in the first place," she said.

The deep thought in her voice gave him pause. "What do you mean?"

"Borders are heavily guarded these days, and airport security is extremely tight." Her shoulders slumped with doubt. "Since you don't have any ID, the US wouldn't allow you entry. That is, if you would even be allowed to get on a plane from here. And if I boarded a plane, the AIU will find out that I'm still alive."

Radu had a basic understanding of what planes were, so he nodded. "We need new IDs, then." He'd seen a few of those small plastic rectangles with pictures and writing on them.

Lillian nodded. "And money and passports and…" She spread her hands helplessly. "Countless other things. I'm not sure if we can do this."

"We will find a way," he said firmly, settling back in the chair and watching her eyes flicker with rapid thoughts.

Suddenly, Lillian jumped up so quickly she nearly hit her head. "Oh shit, my phone!"

"Your what?"

"Open my bag. It's a plastic rectangle, light blue case." The urgency in her gaze compelled him to do as she asked.

He found the item she described and held it up questioningly.

"Destroy it," she whispered.

That was easy enough. Radu crushed the thing with a squeeze, splinters of plastic digging into his palm. Dropping the fragments on the stone floor, he smiled at her. "Why did you want me to do that?"

"They probably used it to track my location," she told him, fear reflecting in her large eyes. "They might have even had it bugged to record my voice, though hopefully it was muffled in my bag. I should search the rest of my stuff for bugs."

"Bugs?" he inquired, irritated at his lack of understanding so many words.

"Recording devices, so they can hear what I say."

"Ah, I am familiar with this recording." A few of the Hunters who'd tried to kill him had carried devices that absorbed spoken words and sounds and stored them on little plastic rectangles they'd called tapes. "Do they make them so small now?"

Lillian nodded. "May I have my bag so I can check?"

Radu raised a brow and searched the pack first, remembering her previous escape attempt. After removing an object that contained a knife and several other tools, so she wouldn't be able to pick the lock, he passed her the bag.

He watched her carefully examine each article of clothing, probing the seams with a tight look of concentration. Radu suddenly wished he could experience that intense, probing touch on his body. Unfortunately, she made it clear that she didn't want to touch him, no matter her earlier response. That didn't stop him from wondering if it was possible to change her mind.

"Okay, everything seems clean." She rolled her eyes. "I guess they didn't think I was smart enough or a big enough threat to make sure you killed me."

He smiled. "Now you may prove them wrong."

Her sculpted lips curved upwards for a moment, then her smile faded like a cloud covering the sun. "Will you please let me out?"

Her small hands clenched around the bars of the cage. Radu's gaze roved over her tousled hair, her heart-shaped face, haunting blue eyes, and lithe body.

Would you please let me in? He bit back the damning words and slowly shook his head. "Not until I regain my strength."

He reclined in the chair and closed his eyes so her beauty wouldn't steal his reasoning.

And that's when it happened.

The strange presence that had been attempting to probe his mind returned. This time, he seized it. His view of the fire vanished. In its place, he saw his brother slipping a betrothal ring on a woman's finger. *Razvan!* After seven centuries, his brother's face hadn't changed one iota. Still sardonic and full of mischief. Though the love in his eyes as he looked at his betrothed was new. Radu's shock of this vision of Razvan dissipated as he recognized the woman as the one who'd been questing for him.

"*You*," he whispered.

The redheaded woman gasped as he plunged further into her mind. In moments, he had her location, along with a few other details pried away. Radu broke contact enough to rise from his chair and turn to Lillian.

"We are going on a little trip, my pretty," he said aloud, more to the redheaded witch than to his captive.

In case Razvan didn't grasp the message, Radu turned his focus back to the witch and directed a clear thought at her. *I am coming, Brother.*

Chapter Four

Coeur d'Alene, Idaho

Razvan Nicolae, Lord Vampire of Spokane, paid the tab at the restaurant and helped Jayden into her coat. As they departed, smiles and congratulations were shouted at them for his public marriage proposal. Forcing a pleased smile wasn't too difficult, even if Jayden had just had a vision that shook the foundations of his world. His brother was coming.

Right after Razvan slid the diamond ring on Jayden's finger, her eyes had closed, and she'd collapsed in her seat. He'd quickly taken her outside, watching as she mouthed words that he was unable to discern. Until she opened her eyes and said, "Your brother is coming here…and I think he's still mad at you."

They'd headed back into the restaurant, pretending that she'd swooned from surprise at Razvan's proposal. Jayden did a far better job with the act, blushing and smiling like a true bride-to-be and holding out her hand to show off her new ring. Joy swelled in his heart. The woman he loved had agreed to share her life with him.

And now it seemed that he'd also be reunited with his long-lost twin. As Razvan led her out of the restaurant and into the Dodge Charger that he'd recently inherited, Razvan asked, "Why does Radu seem angry?"

"I don't know," she said softly. "Is there a chance he's still mad about what happened to Uta?"

Razvan closed his eyes, remembering the night he accidentally killed Radu's lover after discovering that she'd incited the villagers against them. "He could be. Or he may even blame me for worse."

"Should we go away?" Jayden asked. "Somewhere he can't find us?"

Razvan shook his head and fired up the ignition. "No. It has been far too long as it is. We need to face each other. I need to explain what happened." And learn why Radu had hidden from him all these years. When Jayden had located him beneath the ruins of their family castle, he'd nearly gotten on a jet back to Romania. Only his concern for Jayden's safety held him back.

When they returned to Silas and Akasha's home, the other couple waited in the front room, eyeing Jayden and Razvan eagerly when they came through the door.

Akasha took one look at Jayden's face and frowned. "What's wrong? Did he not propose? Or did you say no?"

Jayden shook her head. "No, nothing like that. I said yes, and I *am* very happy. It's just that I had a vision."

Silas's gaze whipped to her. "What sort of vision?"

Razvan answered for her. "Radu is coming."

The Lord Vampire of Coeur d'Alene surveyed him so intently that Razvan had the urge to double-check his shields. "You don't look as pleased as I would have thought after searching for him for centuries."

"I *am* pleased," Razvan insisted, reaching in his breast pocket for his pipe. "But I must face the fact that my brother is likely still angry with me, and that may put Jayden in danger."

"I see." Silas nodded in agreement. Only six months ago, Jayden had been abducted by an insane vampire. They all had reasons for wanting to be cautious. Silas turned to Jayden. "Tell me everything about the vision you had."

"I saw Radu sitting in a chair beneath the ruins of Castle Nicolae. He was awake, and he *saw* me." Jayden shivered.

"He *saw* you?" Silas's green eyes widened.

Jayden nodded. "He looked right at me and said '*you*' as if he recognized me. He must have sensed me searching for him all those other times. But this time, he grasped my mind. I felt searching for information, but I'm not sure what he learned, aside from our location and that I'm with Razvan."

"That would take a great deal of power." Silas turned to Razvan. "Was your brother always psychic?"

Razvan nodded. "Though not like this. Before, his abilities were as limited as mine. Mere parlor tricks. His power must have grown during his hibernation."

"Either that or Jayden's power is so great that she unwittingly acted as a conduit," Silas said.

Razvan nodded. Jayden's clairvoyant powers had been so strong that they'd driven her mad. When he first encountered her, she'd been trying to kill herself to make the visions stop. So it made sense that she'd been able to search Razvan's memories, and through those, latch onto the latent connection he shared with his twin to locate him over thousands of miles. She had no issues unleashing her powers. She needed aid in controlling and suppressing them.

As if reading Razvan's mind, Silas frowned and turned back to Jayden. "I think we need to continue with your lessons."

Jayden nodded and clung to Razvan's hand. "Radu has a woman locked in a cage. He's been feeding on her. After he saw me, he turned to the woman and said, 'we're going on a little trip, my pretty.' Then he turned back to me and said, 'I am coming, Brother.' I don't think that part was out loud."

"He is bringing a mortal captive." Silas stroked his chin. "I daresay that will slow him down. There's also the fact that with his being in hibernation for so long, he's going to be seen as a rogue vampire. Many lords may detain him, for that or for having a human with him."

Razvan scoffed. "They may try, but they won't succeed. My brother is as clever as I am. Perhaps more. Though you have a point about the mortal. If he thinks to bring her with him, that shall hinder his speed in arriving here."

"What are you going to do when he gets here?" Akasha asked.

"Hopefully, talk. There is much that needs to be resolved between us." He looked down a moment, willing himself to rein in his emotions. "After that, I pray we can be brothers once more."

"I thought Silas was the praying type, not you," Akasha said with an amused smile. "Either way, Silas and I have your back. Do you want to stay with us until everything is sorted out? I'll watch over Jayden while you deal with business and check on your vampires in Spokane."

Razvan raised a brow. "Shouldn't this offer come from your master?"

Her eyes shot violet sparks. "He's not my master, He's my husband."

Razvan grinned at Akasha's ire. He so enjoyed teasing her. "All the same, only the Lord of Coeur d'Alene has a say in who guests in his territory."

Silas took Akasha's hand. "My wife knows me well enough not to make an offer I would not extend. As for you staying with us, I insist. There is strength in numbers, and we can be certain that Jayden remains safe."

They had a point, but..."I cannot risk the Spokane vampires thinking me so weak I have to approach a younger vampire from a smaller city for aid."

"You'll be doing no such thing," Silas said. "We are helping you plan a wedding, after all."

Jayden smiled and threaded her arm through Akasha's. "That's right. I can't wait to look at bridal magazines with you, 'Kash. I'll need your help finding a dress, choosing which flowers I want, and so many other things."

Akasha rolled her eyes and lit a cigarette. "I'm going to need a lot of beer for this."

Razvan laughed at her tortured look. Aside from being a formidable human with her genetically engineered super strength, Akasha was a mechanic and most comfortable getting greasy under the hood of a car or guzzling beer and playing darts with the blue-collar men at the Powder River Saloon. Only Silas was capable of bringing out her femininity.

"Not too much beer," Jayden chided.

"Yeah, yeah." Akasha nodded impatiently, already heading to the fridge. "And for your information, I'm down to a six-pack a night instead of a case. Besides, we have an engagement to celebrate."

Razvan shook his head. If it weren't for Akasha's extremely high metabolism and resistance to disease, a case of beer a day would kill her. Still, it couldn't be healthy for her, and he was glad that Jayden was helping her to cut back.

After the women departed, Silas gestured for Razvan to follow him up to his office. Razvan lit his pipe, and Silas poured them each a finger of scotch before he sat down. "Your bride is not the only one in danger."

"I won't let him hurt Akasha either," Razvan assured him.

"I'm not worried about Akasha," Silas took another sip of scotch. "I was speaking of Radu himself. Aside from the fact that rogue vampires can be killed on sight, if he has shared what he is with a mortal woman, he could very well be arrested and executed for such a crime."

Razvan hid his shudder with a deep drink from his own glass. Grimacing against the taste of the liquor, he refused to allow Silas to see his fear. "Radu will find his way past anyone who interferes, I'm certain of it."

But did he? What if Radu was captured and killed just when Razvan had finally discovered his whereabouts? Just when he and his twin would, at last, be reunited.

That would be almost as tragic as the other thing he feared: That Radu would be so mad and dangerous that Razvan would have no choice but to kill his own brother.

Chapter Five

Lillian stared at Radu as his body jolted and his eyes looked past her at something far away. Then he swayed and slumped back into his chair as if all strength drained from his body.

"Are you okay?" she asked, unable to hide her worry. If something happened to Radu, she'd be trapped in the cage until she starved to death. She tried to tell herself that was the only reason she cared.

"My brother has a witch aiding him to find me. This time, I trapped her." Savage triumph gleamed in his black eyes. "I've found Razvan's location. Someplace called *Core-da-lane*, in the United States."

"Coeur d'Alene?" she repeated, shock reverberating through her at what that implied. "Silas and Akasha live there, according to my father's files. Somehow they must be affiliated with your brother."

Radu's brows lifted in surprise. Then he smiled. "That shall make our mutual goals much easier to accomplish."

"We still don't have a way to get into the United States," she said with a sigh, realizing that they had a big problem. "No passports or ID, remember?" Despair washed over her. What if she was trapped in Europe for ages until she found a way to enter the States illegally?

"ID is that plastic square with your picture, yes?" When Lillian nodded, Radu's lips curved up in a small smile as if pleased to understand something of the modern world. Then he sobered. "What is a passport? You keep mentioning those."

Lillian fished hers out of her bag and tossed it through the bars. "It's a sort of ID for traveling. You cannot enter another country without it."

"We will find a way." Radu picked up the passport and scanned it. "You are twenty-four?"

She nodded, wondering why that mattered. "How old are you?"

"I was thirty-five when I was Changed. And that was..." He silently counted, then translated the number into her language. "One thousand and six years ago."

The huge number momentarily stunned Lillian. She decided to change the subject. "How do you know your brother has a witch?"

"What else would she be to locate me from such a distance?" Radu paced in front of her "My father didn't believe in them, but my mother knew better. Our kind used to kill witches on sight. They're dangerous. And now my brother is actually going to wed one."

"She found you with her mind?" Lillian was unable to conceal her incredulous tone. "That sounds more like a psychic... though I've never heard of one being so powerful." She recalled the rest of what he'd said. "Wait, your brother is getting married? I didn't think vampires did that."

Radu fixed her with a pointed stare. "Why not? My parents were married. We're capable of love." His scowl deepened. "Though Razvan shouldn't be allowed to *have* a love after he killed mine."

Something in her belly tightened at his talk of love. He'd felt that for someone once. For a moment, Lillian wondered what Radu would be like when he was in love, but then her focus returned to the matter at hand. "You're not going to try to kill the psychic, are you?"

"It would serve justice." Radu shook his head. "But no, I am not one to kill innocents. Besides, it was Uta, the woman I loved, who sent the mob that killed my parents. But I'm not certain if Razvan discovered that before or after he killed her."

Whoa. Radu's girlfriend had sent a mob after his family? Lillian remembered the charred stones and blackened chunks of wood on her trek through the castle ruins. This Uta did not sound like a winner. Lillian couldn't blame Razvan for killing her. After all, she planned on avenging her own father. Yet from his tone and fierce scowl, Radu was clearly still angry with his brother for killing Uta, even though she deserved it. Maybe he was just angry about the lack of closure, or some sort of masculine principle. Or perhaps he still loved her, even after what she did.

Either way, Radu's centuries-long hibernation now made sense. Lillian's gaze lit on the stone slab he slept on. Radu felt guilty for the death of his family. Perhaps so guilty that he was only now ready to face his brother, though he still clung to a shred of anger and tried to place the blame on Razvan.

But she didn't dare say that aloud. Instead, she looked up at him. "Tell me about your family."

Pain slashed across his face, followed by a heavy look of weariness. "Another time, pretty one. Dawn approaches, and I must rest." He placed more logs on the fire and then slowly shambled back to the stone slab.

Lillian cringed as Radu lay on the cold hard surface. "Don't you want a blanket or something?" She grabbed one of the sleeping bags piled on her cell floor and held it up to the bars.

His head swiveled to face her, one brow arched. "Are you starting to care for me?"

Heat rushed to her face. Had that been hope in his gaze? "No, it's just that I figured that since you're ready to talk to your brother, maybe you're done punishing yourself."

Radu jolted up from the slab so fast her head spun. In the blink of an eye, he stood before the cage. His eyes glowed with unholy light. "You think I'm punishing myself?"

Reaching in his pocket, he withdrew the key to the cage. Lillian scrambled to her feet as he unlocked the door, but before she attempted to dart out, Radu entered the cell with a flash of speed and closed the door behind him.

With a gasp, she scooted as far back as possible, heart pounding with fear of what he would do to her.

"*This* is punishing myself," he said with an intent stare. "Lying next to a beautiful woman who does not want me to touch her."

With that, he lay down beside her, stiff as a board, and closed his eyes.

Lillian released the breath she'd been holding and stared at him in shock. She'd definitely struck a nerve. But why had he decided to come in here with her? What point was he trying to prove? She fought to uproot the tendril of warmth spiraling in her belly at his calling her beautiful. Although plenty of guys had said she was hot, they said it in a way that made her feel like an object. Radu, on the other hand, just sounded angry.

Perhaps he'd done this to punish her too. How the hell was she supposed to sleep with a vampire right next to her? She should have kept her mouth shut.

"Lillian," Radu said softly, eyes still closed. "I'm finding it hard to sleep with you staring at me. Lie down. I speak truly when I say I won't touch you."

"Then leave," she snapped.

"I think not." His lips curled up in a mocking smile. "You spoke truly when you said these sleeping bags are more comfortable."

For a moment, she considered waiting for him to fall asleep before she tried reaching through the bars to grab another backpack near the cage. Maybe there was a stake or other weapon in there. He had the key in his pocket. She could kill him and get out of this cage. The idea shattered as she remembered how easily he'd overpowered her before.

Then, the pained longing in his eyes when he spoke of his brother, with whom he'd finally be reunited, flashed in her memory. Her conscience railed. What kind of person would she be if she killed him when he was so close to seeing his brother again?

And of course, there was the most important matter. Her agency had lied to her, murdered her father, and attempted to send her to her death as well. If they found out that she was still alive, they would undoubtedly kill her. Having an ancient, powerful vampire on her side would improve her odds of survival.

With that decided, the invisible weight lifted from her shoulders and settled on her eyelids. Lillian tucked herself in a sleeping bag, trying not to notice Radu's smile at her compliance. Sleep claimed her immediately.

Lillian awoke in what seemed like moments later. The only way she inferred that some time had passed was that her left hand had fallen asleep from being at an odd angle for so long. Even more alarming was that sometime during the day, she'd scooted closer to Radu and was now snuggled against his back, her arm draped around his waist.

The fire had long since gone out, and the room was cold, so she must have instinctively sought his warmth. Lillian remained still, not wanting to wake him. His scent, a combination of smoke and some other tantalizing smell, invaded her senses. The heat of his solid body seeped into her chest and legs, emphasizing the chill at her back. His heartbeat was steady against her palm. Her eyes widened. Dad *had* been correct in his theory that vampires were living organisms rather than animated corpses.

The realization filled her with relief, though she didn't know why. Honestly, she shouldn't be surprised, given that she'd studied several samples of vampire blood with her father. She'd even named a few of the unique organelles she'd found in their cells.

The old movie myths died hard, she supposed. Lillian wondered what Radu would think of vampire movies. Maybe he'd like

Dracula, but what about *Twilight*? She bit her lip before her giggles burst out. Still, her belly shook and a snort escaped her lips.

Radu's hand squeezed hers. "Do not be afraid."

"I'm not," she said, all humor chased away at his touch. "I'm just cold."

"Then I shall warm you." Before she managed a protest, Radu rolled over and pulled her into his arms, covering them both with one of the sleeping bags.

The best idea would be to push him away, but as the heat of his body warmed her and his strength gave her a much-needed sense of safety, all she could do was close her eyes to hide from his gaze. Damn him for not turning out to be what she expected. Damn him for being so unpredictable. Damn him for feeling so good.

Thankfully, or maybe not so thankfully, her bladder intervened after a while. "Um, I need to pee."

Radu nodded, his chin brushing her hair. "The sun has not yet set, so you will have to use the chamber pot." He slowly released her and stood. "I will get the fire going again to give you privacy."

A chamber pot? Lillian's face flamed. She barely tolerated using a public restroom if another woman was in the next stall. But her bladder felt like it would explode any moment.

When Radu left the cage and headed to the fireplace, she took the ancient bronze pot, arranged the sleeping bag like a privacy curtain, and relieved herself. Carefully, she set the pot outside the cage door, hoping Radu would let her dump it soon.

Her eyes widened as the sight of the open door sank in. Had it been a mistake? Cautiously, she crept out.

Radu turned his head from the fireplace and smiled. "You may sit in the chair to be warm."

So he *was* deciding to trust her. Well, to a point, since she saw the tension in his shoulders, ready to spring if she tried to run. And now would be the best time to do so. He couldn't follow her out into the daylight.

But she'd accepted the truth. Even if she managed to escape him—which was doubtful, given his speed—she'd either be a broke and illegal immigrant or hunted by the AIU the moment she tried to use her credit card. *They* wanted to kill her. Radu did not. Besides, he was beginning to treat her more like an ally rather than a prisoner.

Accepting Radu's offer, she settled in the chair opposite from his. Heat from the fire wafted her way, calming her shivers. How had Radu been able to bear such cold? It had to be even worse in the winter. She rubbed her hands together before the flames and met his dark gaze. "Thank you for the fire." A thought struck her. "I thought vampires were completely unconscious during the day."

Radu smiled. "That's what we want you to think. Besides, I am tired of sleeping."

"I would think so." For some reason, that made her laugh. He'd been sleeping for centuries. The laughter only grew when he chuckled in understanding. And then they both roared with laughter.

As her giggles died off, Lillian wiped her eyes and caught Radu staring at her with an unreadable expression. She tamped down her nervousness. "Are we going to leave when the sun goes down?"

Radu shook his head. "No, but at nightfall, we will visit the village for supplies. I also want to explore the area and learn more before we proceed."

"And what are we going to do until then?"

Unbelievably, his lips curved in a flirtatious smile. "I have a few ideas."

A fresh wave of heat flooded her face. Did he mean what she thought he meant? Lillian cleared her throat. "I mean, if we're going to be traveling, we'll need money."

He nodded. "We can search the Hunters' bags. Also, you need to eat, and I need to feed."

Lillian's hand crept up to the place where he'd bitten her before. "Can't you go out and bite someone else?"

Something that may have been sympathy flitted across his features. "I'm sorry, but I need strength in case there are other vampires in the village." Slowly he reached forward, as if to touch her, then dropped his hand. "I won't take as much this time. And I can also make it painless."

Still holding her neck and fighting the memories of his erection pressing against her, Lillian shot him a hard glare. "If you can make it painless, why did it hurt before?"

"Because I wanted it to," he said mildly. "After all, you were trying to kill me."

"Are you going to bite me now?" Her voice came out tremulous. Would her body respond to him again?

Radu shook his head. "No. You should eat first. Before and after. Let us search the bags."

Together, they hauled the twenty backpacks and satchels to a pile near the fire. A tremor of dread crawled over her skin at the large number. "You killed that many people?"

"Not all of them," Radu said, and he unzipped one of the newer-looking packs. "I cleansed the memories of many and sent them away. If they found their way back here, well, I granted them a chance." He shrugged. "Others deserved their fate, I swear it."

Slightly relieved that not all these backpacks belonged to dead men, Lillian grabbed one and unzipped it. A few brown plastic packages caught her eye, and she grinned. "MREs." Much better than that protein bar he'd handed her when he first locked her up, though not as good as the noodles and ice cream he'd given her last night.

Radu looked up from his bag, holding what looked like a wallet. "What are those?"

"Meals Ready to Eat. Soldiers carry them." This one said *chicken enchilada*. Lillian dug into the package, pleased to see that it held a flameless heating element. Her stomach rumbled in anticipation as she heated the meal. Once it was done, even Radu's staring couldn't distract her as she devoured every bite.

After scooping the last bite of rice in her mouth, she glared at him. "What? Do you not like the taste? I mean, I've had better, but…"

Radu shook his head, shoulders slumped with dejection. "I can only taste your meals for a few hours after I feed on you."

Fascinating. Lillian guarded her expression. Did his ability to read her mind also wear off? Her thoughts broke as Radu set down the wallet and approached her. "Speaking of, it is now my turn."

Reflexively, Lillian drew back, but he closed in on her, enfolding her in his arms. She tried to remain rigid as he stroked her cheek and whispered, "Just a little this time, pretty one. I will not hurt you." His head dipped to her throat, his breath caressed the sensitive skin on her neck.

Lillian shivered and swayed forward. Razvan drew back and captured her gaze, seeming to peer into her soul. "No pain," he whispered before lowering his head and trailing his lips along her neck.

Frissons of pleasure made her gasp and hold onto him for support. His tongue laved her skin, making her knees weak. Then his mouth closed over her neck, his fangs pierced her flesh, drawing a cry from her lips. Sharp bliss shot from her neck all the way to the juncture between her thighs, her clit pulsing with every swallow.

Just as her hips bucked forward to press against his erection, Radu released her. Panting with longing, Lillian stood rapt and motionless as he bit his finger and trailed it across her puncture wounds. "You should drink some water," he whispered.

Still mute, she nodded and slowly backed away to fetch a water bottle from the pack with the MREs. He'd told her there would be no pain, but he didn't say it would feel so good.

"Are you still hungry?" Radu asked her eagerly.

Not for food, Lillian thought and then cursed herself as the vampire's brow rose. "No, but I still have room for the peanut butter and crackers from the package."

Thankfully, her snacking distracted him from talking about her unreasonable lust. They returned to the task of searching the bags, making separate piles for money, food, clothing, and tools. Every time Lillian put a cracker in her mouth, Radu closed his eyes and hummed with pleasure.

Lillian realized she enjoyed this odd phenomenon. The utter bliss on his face was captivating. Part of her wished she'd saved the MRE until now. She took another bite of her food, and he actually moaned, sending frissons of heat through her body.

She couldn't help but wonder what it would be like to please him in another manner.

Chapter Six

Phoenix, Arizona

Agent Stebbins made his way through the lab and down the hall of the AIU headquarters, trying not to notice the stiff, jerky movements of his colleagues as they stepped aside or nodded as he passed. Things had been tense since the new director took over, but no one was more nervous than Stebbins.

He'd been promoted to executive assistant after the former one had retired. *If* that was what really happened to the man. Agent Stebbins suspected that the former director's fate was most likely similar to that of the late Agent Holmes Senior. Or perhaps the fate of Agent Holmes Junior…whom he was to report on today.

He closed his eyes, unable to hold back sorrow for the young, eager scientist who everyone called "Junior" so as not to confuse her with her father. Quick-witted and diligent, she'd been following Joe Holmes's footsteps and quickly becoming one of the best field researchers in their department.

But because her father had been poking around outside his jurisdiction, both he and Junior had to be eliminated.

Before knocking on the director's door, Stebbins composed his features and shifted the file he carried under his arm as he wiped his sweating palms.

Director Bowers reclined in his ergonomic office chair overlooking the view of the Arizona desert. "Is operation Vlad complete?" he asked without turning around.

Shivering slightly at the sibilant voice, Stebbins replied. "Yes. The tracker remained stationary for over twenty-four hours within the target zone. Then it was either destroyed, or her battery died. Perhaps the, ah, *creature* found it on her." He breathed an inner sigh at remembering to call vampires by Bowers's preferred term.

Bowers chuckled. "They do have freakish strength. Which is useful in these cases." The director spun in his chair to face Stebbins, his gray eyes cold as gunmetal. "And what of the search of Holmes's residence?"

Stebbins resisted the urge to wipe his brow. "Nothing in the preliminary search, Sir. Not so much as a test tube or a computer."

Instead of being angry like Stebbins had feared, Bowers smiled. "That only proves that he was indeed aware of the consequences of his actions and either destroyed or hid the evidence. You did collect all of his personal effects, yes?"

"Of course," Stebbins said. "We have them secured in Storage Room 19."

"Good. I want you to assemble a team to sort through everything. I want bank statements, P.O. Box addresses, titles or rentals, and receipts. And if you find so much as a USB cable, I want to be notified immediately." Bowers tapped his pen on his desk.

"Yes, Sir."

Bowers smiled, like a grizzly baring its teeth. "And after you do that, I want a report on the progress of Operation Wrangler."

Stebbins swallowed despite his dry mouth and nodded. "Is there anything else you require?"

"No, you're excused." The director turned his chair back to face the window again.

Dread and guilt twisted in Stebbins's gut for his upcoming role in Bowers's newest initiative after taking the director's chair: capture a live vampire.

Under the old director, that wouldn't have been as bad. The AIU had secured a live specimen forty years ago, a male vampire who'd been burned by the sun. The vampire was photographed, blood samples were taken, and they'd questioned him before releasing him at dusk. Back then, the AIU's objective was to study vampires and other supernatural beings.

Now, under Bowers's command: the objective was to kill them.

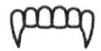

Radu found the silence unbearable as they sorted the objects and money from the packs. After centuries of quiet, Lillian's voice was welcome. More than welcome, she was intoxicating. He stared at the red-gold sheen of her hair, her rounded cheeks, the curve of her lips. He enjoyed conversing with her, learning more and more about her and the world every moment.

He found himself madly curious about her, the multitude of thoughts and memories he'd seen in her mind only mere tastes. While they awaited nightfall, there was nothing to do but talk. But of what? He thought of nothing but how she felt in his arms, the way she'd pressed against him and moaned, the scent of her desire.

But he also felt her resistance to her body's response. Though the hostility had vanished once he'd convinced her that he hadn't killed her father, something else held her back.

"Are you a maiden?" he blurted.

Her head jerked up from the pack she was searching through. "Excuse me?"

Though he cursed himself for being so forward, he pressed on. He had to know. "I can smell that you want me, yet you resist."

"You can smell *that*?" she gasped.

He nodded and repeated his inquiry. "Are you untouched?"

Lillian shot him a sharp glare before she sighed. "Kind of."

Radu frowned in confusion. "What do you mean?" He'd thought a woman either was or was not.

She heaved another sigh. "I had a boyfriend back in college. He kept pressuring me, and I finally gave in." Her blush deepened as she took a deep breath. "He was only…um, *there* for a second before he…couldn't anymore."

"He was impotent?" Radu asked, aghast.

"Maybe." She shrugged. "He broke up with me after that like it was my fault. Of course, now that I look back, he didn't really seem to like me in the first place."

He shook his head. "I cannot believe any man would not be fond of you."

"Well, *I* can't believe I'm talking to you about this!" Lillian said with crimson cheeks. She shrugged. "I do get plenty of compliments on my looks, but once a guy starts talking to me, I get all awkward. Other than my studies and experiments, I don't have much to talk about. And most guys don't like nerds anyway, unless for a one-night stand, and I just wasn't into that."

Radu cocked his head to the side at the unfamiliar word. "What is a nerd?"

She remained silent a moment, visually thinking out her next words. "Nerds are those who rely on their brains rather than brawn or social status. We are always buried in a book or some project. With me, it's science."

"So they fear your intelligence?" He spat on the floor, making his contempt known. "Cowards."

Lillian chuckled. "That's what I tell myself to feel better, but honestly, things didn't work out with other nerds either. My colleagues would get angry if I performed better than them. Others disliked my fascination for the supernatural. And the few times when a fellow scientist didn't care about any of that, there wasn't any chemistry."

51

Radu remained silent, hoping she'd continue. His patience was rewarded.

"Maybe my awkwardness with men is because I spent most of my life being too busy working on experiments with my dad." Grief haunted her eyes at the mention of her father before her lips curved up in a wan smile. "I can't decide whether he kept me busy because he enjoyed my company and my contributions to his work, or if he was trying to keep me with him because he was protective of me ever since Mom died."

Acute sympathy pierced Radu's heart. "Your mother died?" He'd been very close to both of his mothers, the one who'd birthed him—after he and Razvan had gotten to know her and she'd explained why she had to give them up—and the one who'd raised him. The pain of losing both were still raw wounds. He looked back at Lillian. "How did she…?"

"Cancer," Lillian said with a sigh. "She got sick when I was two or three. Most of my memories are of seeing her in a hospital bed, drawing her pictures, and waiting for her to get better." Her shoulders slumped. "She never got better. Several times she was able to come home, and I'd think that she would be able to finally do the things my friends' moms could do, but she always ended up back in the hospital. And when I was seven, she never came back."

Radu had no notion of what cancer meant, but he had witnessed people dying from a lingering illness. Some had been his mortal descendants. Watching his loved ones waste away had been painful, not only as a grown man but also as a vampire. He couldn't fathom how terrible such an ordeal would have been for a little girl.

Slowly, he crossed the chamber to her side and placed a hand on her shoulder. "I am sorry you lost your mother. I know what that hurt is like."

Lillian looked up at him, eyes wide and studying every detail of his face as if she'd never seen him before. "Yes, you would, wouldn't you?" She reached out slowly as if to grasp him, then her hand dropped, and she looked back at the pack she was inspecting. "We should get back to work."

Radu nodded and returned to his set of backpacks. How had the conversation shifted from seduction to grief? How had Lillian managed to turn what had been simple lust into some deeper, more poignant connection? Mind swimming with a multitude of thoughts, he focused on gathering money.

Radu sorted the coins and paper currency into different piles according to how they appeared. He did not know how much any of it was worth. In his day, people paid in gold, crops, and livestock. These coins of silver and copper and multicolored pieces of paper, etched in strangers' faces, mystified him. Lillian must have sensed his confusion, for she sat next to him, sorted a few coins and bills, and began to count.

As he watched her lips shape the numbers, her forehead lined with concentration, it took all his effort not to interrupt her. When she at last finished counting, Lillian rattled off the amounts. "We have two thousand lei, five hundred euros, two hundred pounds, and eleven hundred US dollars." She frowned and pointed to another pile. "Those might be rubles, but I'm not sure. We'll have to find a money exchanger if we want to exchange the lei for euros or dollars." She sighed. "And after that, we still need to figure out how to get new IDs."

"I may have an idea for securing such things," Radu said. Surely other vampires had a method for acquiring what was necessary to pass undetected through this modern world. He and Lillian would have to make contact with one of them. However, he wasn't certain he was ready to face another of his kind after so long. But he had to. Rising from where he sat, he gathered up the currency that she had said belonged to this country. "The sun has set. Let us go to the nearest țări, ah, village, and see if we can find more of my kind."

Lillian rubbed her arms and looked down at her feet. "Can we go someplace where I can take a shower? I'm filthy, and I've been wearing the same clothes for two days."

Radu smiled. "I have just the place. Take your bag and change of clothing…and those soaps we found in the Hunters' bags. You may bathe after our foray. I'm sorry, but I need more blood, and I do not want to drain you."

Her face paled at that, her female vanity forgotten, as she did as he suggested and then delicately fetched the chamber pot to be dumped.

His brows drew together at seeing her perform a servant's chore. "I'll dispose of that for you."

The tips of her ears turned red. "But—"

"No need to be embarrassed at what is natural." He took the pot from her hands. "Let me do something for you at least."

When they exited the castle, Radu took her in his arms to fly to the village he'd visited to procure her meal the other night. He tried to tamp down the raging desire combined with fierce protectiveness that flared up the moment her body touched his. It was only because he'd been many years without a woman. He didn't dare fathom that it could be any more than that.

Chapter Seven

Lillian clung to Radu as they flew, her belly seeming to try to crawl up in her throat at the sensation of being so high in the air. She wasn't afraid of heights, but this was too strange. Burying her head in his shoulder, she tried not to think about how far away the ground was.

Instead, she focused on the sensation of his firm body against hers, his intoxicating scent, and the deeply personal conversations they'd shared. He was right. She did want him. Heat flooded her face as she remembered that he was able to *smell* her. Not only did her body have to go haywire around him, but it also announced the fact to its very stimuli.

Frustration roiled within her. Why was she so attracted to him? Surely her biological clock wasn't ticking that fast. She was only twenty-four, and he was sterile anyway. Maybe she was just ovulating? No, it was more than that. Even though he was an ancient vampire who could kill her with one hand, he hadn't hurt her. He'd even treated her with kindness, despite taking her captive. Talking to her like she was a human, expressing empathy, and even apologizing when he'd had to feed on her.

Maybe her connection to Radu was because she now had nobody else. Her father was dead. She had no other living family. She'd lost touch with her friends ages ago as her work took all her attention. But now that the AIU had set her up, she didn't even have that.

A hard lump filled her throat as the enormity of her loneliness cascaded over her. Now her only friend was a vampire who'd imprisoned her because she'd tried to kill him. And here she was considering sleeping with him. Could her life be any more messed up?

They landed on the outskirts of a small town. Lillian clung to Radu a moment longer as she waited for her dizziness to abate. As he held out his hand to lead her into the town, she frantically patted her hair down, knowing she looked like hell.

The vampire wasted no time seeking his next meal as they came upon a man in an alley pressing a syringe into his arm. Lillian's stomach churned in disgust at the sight of him. Dad had recruited drug addicts from slums for some of his experiments as they wouldn't ask any questions because they only cared about getting money for their next fix. Again, she wondered what reduced people to such a pitiful state.

Radu used his vampiric power to place the man in a trance and struck quickly. Lillian shivered, remembering the intensity of his bite. In moments, Radu withdrew and gave the man a few of their Romanian dollars as she blinked in surprise at his act of kindness.

They walked down the narrow roads, passing ancient cottages and some old-fashioned buildings with red terracotta tile roofs before they reached more modern structures. As they saw a few men head out of a bar, Lillian wished she knew how to speak Romanian so that she could better help gather information on other vampires in the area. She watched him from the corner of her eye as he watched people walking by, listening to their conversations.

They wandered aimlessly for an hour until her stomach growled. Radu chuckled, leaned down, and nipped her neck, making her squeal in protest. He then led her into the fanciest-looking restaurant in the area.

"I wish to taste this meal," he whispered.

Rubbing her neck, she eyed the elegant furnishings of the restaurant doubtfully. "Shouldn't we save our money?"

"You deserve a good meal." His tone forbade argument.

The hostess glared at their shabby appearances but still escorted them to a table in a corner far away from other patrons.

Lillian bit back a laugh when the overhead lights revealed that Radu was nearly as disheveled as she was. No wonder their server turned her nose up at them when she delivered their menus and water.

Since she couldn't read the menu, Radu ordered for her, and she prayed that whatever it was would be edible. Her worry abated as she was served a savory lamb stew and some dish with mincemeat and rice wrapped in cabbage leaves.

Radu closed his eyes and hummed with pleasure with every bite she took, and then he persuaded her to have dessert.

"Did you learn what you needed to?" Lillian asked when Radu finished blissing out on her food.

He nodded. "There are no others like me here. We will have to venture further to find the Lord of the nearest city. When you finish your *Papanași*, we will procure a map, along with food and clothing."

Lillian looked down at the cheesy, jelly-coated doughnut and clutched her belly. "I can't. I'm stuffed."

Unbelievably, he pouted like she'd broken his heart. "One more bite, please?"

His entreating eyes held hers prisoner until she picked up her fork in surrender. "Oh, all right."

The moment she placed her fork in her mouth, he practically purred. Lillian shook her head, unable to repress her amusement at his delight.

They paid the bill with more of their lei, and Lillian hoped they had enough for whatever else they needed. Next, they went to a store and purchased clothing and then to another for food and snacks that didn't need heating or refrigeration.

Lillian stuffed as many of their purchases as possible into her backpack and held the other bags as Radu took her into his arms and they flew away from the village.

He landed in the forest near the castle, at the edge of a steaming pool. "You may bathe now."

Lillian stared in awe at the hot springs until Radu began stripping off his clothes. Then her attention focused solely on him. His skin gleamed in the moonlight, casting highlights and shadows on the ridges and planes of his lean, muscled form. Her eyes traced his broad shoulders, then down to his nipples and pecs, and lower still to his flat abs. Unable to stop, her gaze drifted lower to his...

Oh my God. Her heart sped up at the sight of the enormous length between his thighs. Face flaming, she averted her gaze, then looked again.

Radu waded into the water, giving her a view of a scrumptious backside before the water closed over his narrow hips and rose to his waist. "I will remain with my back turned to preserve your modesty."

"Okay," she squeaked, all the more ashamed for ogling him, and searched the bag for soap, shampoo, and a razor.

She stripped off her grimy clothes and waded into the pool. A blissful sigh escaped her lips at the heat of the water. Her muscles relaxed as the water went up to her chest. She opened her eyes to see Radu grinning at her.

"I do wish you would allow me to look upon you." His deep, accented voice was like a caress.

She managed a snort of protest. "I barely know you."

"We could know each other better." This time, there was no mistaking the hunger in his eyes.

For a moment, she considered it. A nerdy, workaholic, practically a virgin, making torrid love to a vampire in a moonlit hot spring.

Lillian shook her head. "I need to get clean." Before it got too slippery, she broke the little bar of travel soap in half and handed him a piece. Then she took a deep breath, turned around, and washed up, hoping he wasn't peeking. Shaving her legs was a little more awkward, but her constant glances over her shoulder revealed that he was behaving himself. As she dragged the razor up her thigh, she wondered why she bothered with this silly female vanity.

Once her legs were as smooth as she could get them, she tossed the razor by the edge of the pool and reached for the shampoo, but it wasn't possible without stepping too far out of the water. Radu laughed and strode through the water to grab it for her, treating her once more to the tantalizing sight of his naked body.

This time he didn't avert his gaze. He watched her as if in challenge as she tried to cover her breasts and maneuver the shampoo. Lillian shot him a glare and knelt in the water until it was up to her collarbone before lathering her hair.

Once her hair was clean, she dreaded leaving the pool's warmth. Especially when the night breeze chilled her wet hair. She looked around for Radu. He was nowhere in sight.

Suddenly, he rose from the depths of the pool, water sluicing down his lean form. He cocked his head to the side and peered at her as if he were trying to discern the secrets of her soul. "Shall we return to our lair?"

"*Our* lair?" she raised a brow, though the word struck an alarming chord within. "I thought I was your prisoner."

"No. You are my..." As he trailed off, his lips curved in a bemused smile. "I do not know what you are exactly. Perhaps I can call you friend?"

Her feet slid across the stony bottom of the pool as she walked closer to him as if pulled by a spell. "If I am not your prisoner, does that mean I can go?"

"No." He reached forward and grasped her shoulders, sliding his fingers along her wet skin.

"Why not?" she whispered. Her body thundered with the awareness that they were both naked and inches from each other.

"If I let you go, you would be in danger from those who wanted you dead. This AIU wanted to use me to kill you. Some of the other Hunters I've killed may have been sent by them as well." His eyes glowed black with rage. "If you die, they win. If you live, *I* win, and so do you." His grip on her arms tightened as he pulled her another inch closer. "There would be other dangers as well. As you said, you have no ID, no passport, and no way to leave the country without alerting the AIU. You do not speak the language here. Men could take advantage and hurt you. And there are wolves in the woods."

The stark reality of his words sank in, twisting her stomach in a knot and laying heavy in her throat like a lead weight.

Radu's eyes softened. "I did not intend to make you cry."

Damn, she was crying? Radu confirmed his words as he released her arm and gently brushed a tear from her cheek.

"I'm sorry. It all just hit me now. You're right. I don't have anywhere to go. I can never go back to my house, or drive my car, or go out for drinks with my friends." The tears came faster, and she sniffled. "But I didn't really have any friends anymore. They all drifted away because my work was so classified that there wasn't much I could talk to them about. I don't have any family left. No one will miss me. I have no one." Her words broke off in a whimper.

"You have me." His arms enfolded her, pulling her tight against his firm warmth. This time his voice and touch didn't seem lustful, just comforting.

Lillian relaxed in his embrace, taking a measure of comfort in the safety of his arms. Maybe he was right about that. Maybe in the forests of Romania, beneath the moon, with warm mist from the hot spring curling around them, this vampire was her only friend.

Slowly, her arms slipped around his waist, and she rested her head on his chest. They held each other in the steaming water. Lillian lifted her head to look up at him in wonder. How could someone so beautiful and so deadly also be so kind?

Radu's eyes met hers, searching and imploring. Giving her enough time to pull away, he lowered his head and brushed his lips over hers. Lillian rose up on her toes and tangled her hands in his wet hair, deepening the kiss.

When his tongue delved between her lips to slide across hers, electric desire arced through her body. A moan escaped her throat, and she pressed her body to his, feeling his erection against her belly. To hell with logic. She wanted him.

Grasping her waist, Radu lifted her, and she wrapped her legs around him. His hardness made contact with her aching clit, and she cried out. She lifted her chin to kiss him again and shivered as the night wind blew across her wet skin.

His lips caressed her ear as he whispered, "Let's get you inside and warm."

He carried her out of the pool, and they quickly dressed, gathered their bags, and flew back to the castle. Once back in the chamber, Radu bade her to sit by the hearth while he built up the fire.

Every cell of her being reverberated with need and anticipation. Would he kiss her again? Would they finish what had started in the pool? Or did he change his mind? The thought filled her with aching dismay. What if something was wrong with her that turned men off? What if—

Radu's strong arms wrapped around Lillian, pulling her against his firm chest before his lips came down on hers. The heat of his embrace warmed her more than the fire as her hands reached under his shirt to caress his smooth, muscled chest.

His hands did their own exploring, delving under her shirt, sliding across her back and shoulders before grasping the fabric and pulling the garment over her head. Then his palms covered her breasts, just resting there, as he closed his eyes as if savoring their shapes. His fingers sought her nipples, lightly flicking along their hard peaks.

Lillian tugged at his shirt, eager to have him bared to her again. Radu stripped it off with an impatient growl and then sank to his knees to kiss and suckle her breasts. Lillian moaned at the blissful sensation as she threaded her fingers through his damp hair.

He then unbuttoned her pants, tugging them down past her hips, taking her panties with them. Lillian's previous shyness was forgotten as she reached for his fly. When they were both naked, they froze, staring at one another in rapt fascination.

"You are beautiful, Lillian," Radu whispered.

"So are—" Her words broke off as he seized her once more.

His eyes glowed with hunger as he kissed and stroked her everywhere. When his fingers delved to the wetness between her thighs, Lillian gasped and nearly toppled on suddenly weak legs. Moaning from his ministrations, she wrapped her fingers around his shaft, taking primal satisfaction in his harsh intake of breath.

The fire crackled and popped as they explored each other. Somehow, they'd backed into her open cage. Lillian didn't mind. The sleeping bags were much softer and warmer than the cold, hard stone floor.

Radu's thumb stroked her clit, sending fresh jolts of ecstasy through her body. Lillian lightly squeezed his cock, suddenly needing to feel its length inside her.

"Please," she gasped.

Instead of lowering her to the bedding as she'd expected, Radu grasped her hips and lifted her as he had in the pool. She'd often thought this position looked incredibly erotic but never imagined it would be practical. A vampire's strength opened new possibilities. Lillian grasped the bars above their heads and wrapped her legs around his waist to keep her balance. Then the tip of him pressed against her entrance. Then inch, by inch, he impaled her.

Lillian moaned at the sharp intensity of this new sensation. It didn't hurt, but the fullness was so overwhelming that it verged on unbearable. She wiggled her hips, trying to adjust to him. Radu hissed through his teeth as he raised her and lowered her again…and then again.

The rhythmic motion increased the throbbing within. She wanted more. Grasping the bars, Lillian matched his thrusts, reveling in the stroke of his shaft inside her.

And then he thrust deeper, harder, reaching a place within that flared with molten awareness.

"Oh God," she gasped as her pleasure built and built at an exponential rate. She clung to the iron cage for balance as her hips bucked against him, her center pulsing until it peaked in bursts and waves.

When she thought she couldn't take anymore, his hands gripped her ass and guided her through the hypnotic motion until the climax overtook her in an excruciating crescendo.

He buried his face between her breasts and let out another low, savage sound of pleasure before she felt him pulse within her when he reached his own orgasm. Lillian's strength bled away. She released the bars and clung to his shoulders, panting as her climax ebbed to light flutters.

His hands moved up from her hips to wrap his arms around her in a tender embrace. He kissed her long and deep before withdrawing from her and lowering her to the floor. Lillian sank into the cushion of the pile of sleeping bags, sated and boneless.

Radu gathered her in his arms and heaved a contented sigh. "I hope I did not hurt you. It has been centuries since I've made love to a woman."

Lillian rested her head on his chest, listening to his pounding heart. "No. It was incredible."

"You were magnificent." His voice rumbled beneath her. "Next time, I want to savor every bit of you."

Next time. The tenderness between her thighs gave a tremor at his words.

For a moment, the enormity of what she'd done struck her. *I had sex with a thousand-year-old vampire.*

But then Radu pulled one of the sleeping bags over them like a blanket, creating a warm cocoon in the haven of his embrace, and her eyelids drifted closed.

She'd worry about that later.

Chapter Eight

Razvan's footsteps echoed as he paced through Akasha's shop. He lit his pipe, and the smell of cherry tobacco mingled with the old oil and grease, reminding him of a bygone era. Isuzu, Akasha's seal point Siamese cat, watched him contemptuously from his perch atop a Stingray Corvette. At least the feline didn't growl and hiss at him anymore.

Akasha rolled out on her creeper, the little light above her safety glasses nearly blinding him. "Would you stop pacing? It's driving me batshit."

"I apologize." He halted and sat on one of the stools. It wasn't like him to behave so nervously.

She flipped up the glasses and lit a cigarette before sitting up and rolling her shoulders until they made a cracking sound. "It's okay. I had no idea you'd become so attached to this baby."

He glanced back at the dark blue Charger on the jack stands. He'd inherited the car after Akasha's mentor had been murdered. Razvan hadn't known that Max liked him all that much. Yet the Charger had been bequeathed to him, along with the words, "that son of a bitch needs to learn how to drive." A lump filled his throat. "Of course I'm attached to it. Not only is it my first car, but I inherited it from a great man." Before he got overly sentimental, he inclined his head at her '73 Roadrunner on one of the lifts. "I wager you are pleased to be working on your own car."

Akasha grinned. "It's about damn time. Car d'Lane is only a week away, and of course, everyone and their dog wants their car done at the last minute. I'm sorely tempted to say no to anyone who's a daywalker." But she never would, and they both knew it. She loved working on older cars.

Razvan nodded. That explained the surplus of classic cars taking up every lift in the shop, relegating his Charger to mere jack stands. Every June, the townspeople polished up their classic cars for the annual car show. Akasha always drove her Roadrunner in the cruise down Sherman Avenue. Jayden would ride with her. Razvan and Silas would have to wait until dark before they were able to informally show off their cars.

Akasha broke into his musing. "Dude, you look really distracted. It's more than just the car. Are you nervous about the wedding?"

"Somewhat," Razvan confessed. "Jayden has already planned so many details that I've lost count. I hope I don't do anything to ruin it." He took another draw from his pipe. "But mostly, I'm worried about Radu. I swear I can sense him getting closer."

Akasha nodded. "That makes sense. You're twins, after all." A line of worry formed between her brows. "Do you really think he's going to be hostile?"

"I don't know." Razvan sighed. He remembered the utter wrath and fury in his twin's eyes the last time they'd seen each other. Razvan had been holding Uta, Radu's mortal lover in his arms. He'd accidentally broken her neck from shaking her in anger. Radu had burst in the door right after. Then they had fought bitterly until they'd been forced to flee from the dawn. Razvan hadn't seen him since.

So it was indeed likely that Radu would try to kill him. Yet Razvan still wished to see him again. The absence of his twin felt like an amputation. For better or worse, they needed each other.

Not wanting to elaborate, he rose from the stool and approached his car. "I must thank you again for making room for me in your busy schedule."

"No problem." Akasha crushed out her cigarette in one of the ashtrays scattered around the shop. "It's better than having your driveline fall out in the middle of the road. I still can't believe Max didn't keep an eye on those U-joints." She bent and picked up her ratchet and tapped it against her palm as she continued. "It's also in dire need of a tune-up, and I want to change the leaf springs, give it an alignment, and…"

Razvan shook his head. "Are you trying to bankrupt me?"

"No, I'm trying to keep your car in good condition," She tapped the ratchet harder on her hand. "Owning a classic car is a big responsibility, you know."

A drop of something flew from the socket on the ratchet and landed in Razvan's goatee. Immediately, the foulest odor invaded his nostrils. "Good Lord, woman, what is that?"

"What's what?"

"Something flew off your tool and landed in my beard."

Akasha lifted her ratchet and sniffed the socket on the end. Immediately her nose wrinkled, and she drew back. "Oh shit! I'm so sorry!" Her words broke off in a giggle. "It's gear oil."

"This is not amusing," Razvan said and strode over to her shop sink to try to wash it out while Akasha alternately laughed and apologized.

"You won't be able to wash it out," she said. "The smell sticks to anything for all eternity."

Razvan shot her a glare and kept scrubbing with degreaser soap. Then he tried the borax and then the dish soap before, at last, admitting defeat. "I'm going to have to shave," he grumbled. "Now."

"I really am sorry." Akasha scooped up her cat and gestured for him to follow her out of the shop.

They took Silas's car and drove to the castle on top of Cherry Hill, where the Lord Vampire of Coeur d'Alene resided. Even with the convertible top down, Razvan's eyes watered from the pungent odor of the gear oil. He darted out of the '68 Barracuda the moment Akasha parked in front of the massive garage. Isuzu followed behind him.

When Razvan burst through the door and started up the stairs, Silas and Jayden looked up from the dining room table.

"What's wrong?" Silas asked, bending to pet the cat.

Razvan pointed at Akasha. "Your wife *ruined* my beard. I need to use your razor."

Akasha blushed as she looked at her husband, finally looking truly repentant. "I accidentally flicked gear oil at him."

"Oh…my…" Silas breathed before looking back at Razvan with pity. "My razor's in the bathroom in the master bedroom."

"Thank you," Razvan said tightly, avoiding Jayden's gaze lest he see pity there as well. Unable to stand the wretched smell a minute longer, he ran up the stairs.

When he emerged, Jayden and Akasha looked at him with wide eyes before they both shook their heads.

"No mustache," his fiancé said. He couldn't tell if that was horror in her green eyes or a fight against laughter.

"Yeah, you look like a 70's cop," Akasha said. "Or a porn star."

That had him heading back up the stairs. Once Razvan finished and washed the shaving cream off his face, he froze, staring into the mirror at his hairless chin and upper lip.

He was looking at his brother's face.

Chapter Nine

Radu watched his twin writhe on the floor in agony as his body transformed. Their father had given them the opportunity to choose whether or not they wanted to become vampires. Razvan had been eager right from the start, salivating at the prospect of power and immortality. Radu hadn't been so certain. He loved the sunshine, was repulsed over the prospect of drinking blood, and most of all, immortality filled him with dread rather than delight. He and Razvan had been reunited with their blood kin only ten years ago. Radu did not want to watch them grow old and die while he remained forever young. He'd begged the vampire who'd raised them to Change his mortal family, but Alexandru had refused.

But Razvan had embraced the change. Radu had vowed to remain mortal, to stay away during his brother's transformation. But he couldn't. Their twin bond was too strong. He returned to the castle to find Razvan huddled on the floor in agony, sharp fangs growing in his mouth.

Ignoring Alexandru's warnings, Radu had clung to Razvan's hand. His pain was Radu's pain.

For hours, they remained together until Razvan's eyes began to glow with unholy light, and his lips curled back to reveal sharp fangs. Alexandru separated them as their adopted mother, Crina, brought a maid to Razvan's side. Radu watched in horror as his brother drank the woman's blood until Father forced him to stop. The maid was sent back to her room, and Crina helped Razvan to his feet and took him downstairs to the castle bowels to hide from the sun.

Alexandru turned to Radu. "I must retire as well. Dawn approaches. Please spend this day thinking of your decision, my son."

Radu nodded and trudged up the stairs to the bedchamber he shared with his brother. Not anymore. As he lay on his bed, loneliness consumed him like an ache. His gaze remained fixed on Razvan's empty bed.

By the time the sun dipped low in the sky, Radu made his decision. He couldn't let Razvan take this journey alone. They had to be together.

The dream faded, and Radu's eyes opened to the most beautiful sight he'd ever laid eyes on. Even in the meager light of the dying coals of the fire, Lillian's hair gleamed like the dawn he so missed. He inhaled her scent of sunshine and flowers and immediately relived the rapturous pleasure he'd shared with her last night.

The memories made his cock harden and ache for more. Lillian murmured something in her sleep and scooted back against him. Radu pulled her closer, savoring the feel of holding a woman. But as she made a soft, contented sound, he realized that it was more than that. He enjoyed holding *her* in particular.

Even stronger than the memory of their lovemaking was that of comforting her when she'd cried when she realized that she was alone in the world. Radu's heart ached for her. Though he was also alone, at least he had his twin. Even though he hadn't seen Razvan in over seven hundred years, he took comfort in knowing that somewhere out in the world, his brother was alive.

Lillian didn't have that comfort. Her family was dead, and the people she'd trusted had betrayed her. Radu had spoken the truth when he said she at least had him.

Though how long would she be content with that? Would she wish to remain with him for the span of her life until she grew old and died? Or would she eventually find other mortal friends and perhaps marry and have children? Or would she wish for him to Change her so they'd be together for eternity? Did he even wish to Change her? As she'd astutely pointed out, they barely knew each other.

However, Radu already genuinely liked her. Her quick wit and way of analyzing things charmed him. He loved talking with her, just to hear whatever new ideas she may conceive. Her honesty was admirable, even with uncomfortable topics. He loved her sense of humor. He loved...

Radu broke off the thought before he delved into dangerous territory.

For now, he and Lillian had their own missions to accomplish. They'd worry about their future later. One thing was certain. He'd do everything in his power to ensure her safety, no matter what happened.

Once more, memories of Razvan haunted his mind. He'd abandoned the sun, food, and the chance to sire children for his brother. Thrown away his humanity and become a monster. Now, after spending centuries apart, Radu wondered if his sacrifice had been worth it.

His dream made him realize that he must make haste to come out from hiding in this castle, and confront his brother.

Radu gently shook Lillian's shoulder. "Pretty one, it's time to wake."

She grumbled in protest before she suddenly gasped and stiffened in his embrace. Worry gnawed at Radu. Did she regret what had happened between them? He withdrew his arm, allowing her to move away if she wanted.

Lillian slowly rolled over to face him, clutching the sleeping bag to cover her breasts. "Is it night already?"

He nodded, unable to conceal his relief that there was no revulsion or accusation in her gaze at him having made love to her. "We need to go to Bucharest. I must speak with the Lord of the city."

Her eyes widened. "Bucharest?"

"Yes, and hopefully the United States after." He watched the multitude of emotions play across her face.

She glanced down, and her face turned crimson as she sat up, pulling the sleeping bag around her like a robe. "I need to get dressed."

Unmindful of his own nakedness, Radu rose and strode out of the cage to where their clothing lay strewn on the floor, a testament of their passion. As he bent to pick up her shirt, he took pleasure in the shy glances she cast his way. She enjoyed looking upon him. That much was apparent.

Still blushing, Lillian dove under the sleeping bags and dressed. He shrugged and took his time donning his newly purchased trousers and a black button-down shirt. While pulling coats from the shopping bags, he watched Lillian brushing her hair with unreasonable fascination.

"Do we have time for me to heat up an MRE?" Lillian asked as she pulled on her boots. "I'm starving."

Radu shook his head. "The nights are too short this time of year. We will both find our meals on the way."

He selected the largest of the backpacks he'd searched and filled it with all the money they'd sorted, as well as clothing, food, and water. Then he lifted a stone near the slab he'd slept on for so many years and withdrew his mother's jewel box. It was all he had of his parents. The rest of the castle had been looted. His father's sword, his coffers, everything had been taken.

Lillian watched him with an inquiring look as he stuffed the box into his pack. "Why the sudden hurry?"

Too embarrassed to admit that he needed to see his brother and had an inexplicable feeling that he should get to him as soon as possible, Radu gave her an alternate explanation that was no less true. "For one thing, I am strong enough and have ventured out into the world sufficiently to adjust to my surroundings and absorb the language. For another, I've been wondering if the AIU will send someone else, either to check and make certain I killed you or because they have other people to eliminate. I think it's best we be far away from a place they know about."

Lillian nodded, eyes strained with fear as she quickened her pace in packing her own bag. "Good point."

"There is one thing we must do first." And he prayed she would agree to it. "I must Mark you."

She frowned. "What does that mean?"

"I will feed you a few drops of my blood and say the ceremonial words to create the magic," he explained. "Other vampires will sense my Mark, and know that to touch you is to face my retribution."

A line formed between her brows. "How long does it last?"

"Forever," he said.

Her frown deepened. "I'll be bound to you forever?"

"Yes," Radu said. "But once we've settled everything with my brother and the AIU, if you want me gone from your life, I'll go."

"How does this Mark work?" she asked, eyes flickering with worry. "Will it mess with my head? Will you—"

"Do you trust me?" he interrupted.

She drew back as if struck, her features frozen in shock. Her lips parted as she looked like she was going to argue. But then she nodded, shoulders squared with resignation. "What do I have to do?"

An invisible weight lifted from his heart. She trusted him! Shoving away the elation, he concentrated on the sacred ritual that he'd been taught but never performed.

"First, I will say the words." Radu reached down and cupped her cheek, forcing all his power forth as he gazed into her eyes. "I, Radu Nicolae, son of Alexandru and Crina Nicolae, Mark you, Lillian Holmes as mine and mine alone. With this Mark, I give you my undying protection. Let all others, immortal and mortal alike, who cross your path sense my Mark and know that to act against you is to act against myself and thus set forth my wrath as I will avenge what is mine."

He thought of doing it in the traditional manner, by biting his finger and dripping his blood in her mouth, but then he had another idea. Closing his eyes, he bit his tongue, wincing at the pain. "Kiss me."

She hesitated a moment, bringing a spear of hurt to his chest, but then she rose on her toes, wrapped her arms around his neck, and pressed her lips to his. Radu slipped his tongue between her lips, tangling with hers. The moment his blood touched her tongue, the Mark blazed forth between them, filling him with heady magic. His cock hardened immediately.

The taste of iron mingled with hers of honey until his wound healed. Then all he could taste was Lillian. The scent of her arousal, heady and potent, awakened his lust. Holding her tight in his arms, Radu pulled her closer, needing more of her. He deepened the kiss, searching, tasting, savoring.

When he finally broke away, they both gasped with ragged breaths. Radu wanted to take her now, bury himself deep with her slick heat again and again. Alas, there wasn't time.

Recovering his control, he brushed another kiss on her lips. "As soon as we are alone again, I'm going to kiss you somewhere else."

Her cheeks pinkened once more, tempting him to forget about his mission and stay here one more night. But that sense of urgency refused to abate.

He took Lillian's hand, placated by at least a measure of contact. "We must go now." But as they headed out, he paused at the doorway and swept the chamber with a last glance. Hard to believe that after so long, he was finally leaving this place.

Each step through the tunnel weighed heavy on his mind even as his soul unburdened. And once they were outside, he had to turn back and give the ruins of the castle one final look. Although instead of a pile of rubble, he saw Castle Nicolae as it once was; tall and grand, a haven of safety and family, where his father looked after his sons and his vassals.

"This was my home for over a thousand years. I cannot believe I am leaving." Paltry words to describe the deep ache piercing his heart, but they were all he could muster.

"At least you can say goodbye." Lillian squeezed his hand in reassurance, eyes shining with understanding. "And who knows? Maybe someday you can come back. Maybe even rebuild, so you're not stuck in the dungeon."

Unlike her. Guilt penetrated his grief. "I'm sorry, Lillian. You are right. It is foolish of me to speak thus when you can never return to your own home."

"Don't feel bad," she pleaded. "I didn't mean to make you feel guilty or anything. Besides, it was my dad's house. I've never had my own home."

"You are as kind as my adopted mother." Crina would have liked Lillian, he realized. They had the same warm spirit and empathy. As they arranged their bags and prepared to fly, Radu vowed to give her a home of her own. Even if she did not wish to share it with him.

When she was secure in his arms, he took to the air. He stopped in the village to feed and procure a meal for Lillian before he flew towards Bucharest. He made it for an hour before his strength began to wane. He'd have to land before he risked dropping Lillian. When he lowered them to the ground, he saw that they were still miles from the city.

Already, he needed to feed again. But he didn't want to take from Lillian again and weaken her. Already she was far too pale for his liking. As soon as they reached the city, he would press her to eat more beef and fruit.

"I am sorry, pretty one, I cannot fly any longer. We must walk from here." Humiliation burned within him at admitting such weakness. Uta would have frowned in derision.

"It's okay." Lillian adjusted the straps of her backpack. "I don't need to be carried everywhere."

A measure of his self-recrimination ebbed away at her understanding. Radu began to wonder why he'd loved Uta in the first place.

They walked in silence through a field as Radu tried to determine how far they were from the city and how he would go about locating its lord. A dog barked somewhere close by, making them both jump. Radu met Lillian's gaze, and they both grinned before bursting into laughter.

He had no idea what was so amusing about being startled by a dog, but he couldn't stop laughing all the same. Lillian's shoulders heaved as she laughed, tears streaming from her eyes as she clung to his arm for balance. Joy warmed his body. Oh, how good it felt to laugh with her.

"What is so funny, rogue?" A voice, speaking Romanian, intruded on their hilarity.

Radu jerked upright to see a tall male vampire watching them. Four others fanned out behind their leader, ready to surround Radu and Lillian. Radu focused on each, sensing their ages and power. The one who had spoken was around three centuries old, the others only one or two hundred years old. All younglings compared to him. Lillian eyed them nervously, unable to understand their words but recognizing their danger.

"I am no rogue," Radu replied in their tongue as he thrust Lillian behind him and straightened to his full height. "I am Radu Nicolae, and I'm going to Bucharest to speak with the Lord of the City."

The first vampire's eyes widened. "You are the brother of Razvan Nicolae! The one he's been searching for."

The vampires behind him gasped before breaking out into whispers and mutters. Radu heard some interesting words in their snatches of conversation. *Prophecy…Queen…the thirteenth Elder.* What was this? The Thirteenth Elder was a myth. As for the rest, he had no notion. He would be certain to ask the Lord of Bucharest what the other words meant.

The first vampire held up a hand, silencing the others. "Who is the woman?"

Radu bared his fangs. It would not bode well to reveal that she was associated with an organization that studied and possibly killed their kind. "She is mine."

"It is forbidden for mortals to know about us." The Romanian vampire said coldly. "Our lord may well arrest you for this crime, so I hope she was worth it."

Radu held fast to Lillian and held the other vampire's gaze. "Then take me to him or her, and we shall see."

Chapter Ten

Lillian stayed close to Radu as the men led them out of the field. It didn't take a biophysicist to figure out that they were vampires. And although she didn't understand Romanian, she could tell that Radu had said something along the lines of "take me to your leader."

From the way the vampires looked at Radu—like he was a mythological figure—it was apparent that he was older and more powerful than they were. Even the lead vampire who'd done all the talking eyed Radu warily, despite the bravado in his voice.

The way they'd looked at her was far different. Suspicion, scorn, and hunger reflected in the four pairs of glowing eyes darting her way.

Radu's grip held her firm, with determination to protect her. The words he'd spoken before giving her his blood kiss repeated in her mind. *With this Mark, I give you my undying protection.* Even though he'd told her his Mark was permanent, those words conveyed the sense of true eternity and utmost severity. Almost like wedding vows. Lillian's mind swam. He barely knew her, yet he'd promised to destroy anyone who hurt her. A rush of warmth enveloped her body at something so poignant.

Shaking off her physical response, she wondered what exactly the Mark had done to her. Aside from an almost electric spark when she tasted his blood, she didn't feel any different. There was no compulsion to serve him like a bride of Dracula, or anything like in the movies. Only her previously established sense that Radu was an ally and her only key to safety at the moment. Never mind that her attraction to him burned like a wildfire threatening to grow out of control.

One of the other vampires glanced back with a leer, which she matched with a glare even as she pressed closer to Radu. What a strange turn her life had taken in the past few days.

Ever since Lillian had learned of the existence of vampires, she'd fantasized about encountering one in the flesh.

The reality was far from what she'd imagined, with one being her lover and protector.

Lover, her mind repeated, and her belly dipped in response. Memories of their torrid sex flashed in her mind so vividly that she almost felt the cold iron of the bars she'd clung to, Radu's tight grip on her hips, and the sensation of his cock thrusting inside her. He'd given her pleasure she'd only read about in novels. There was no way it had been as incredible for him. Though he'd said she was magnificent, despite her lack of experience. He'd said he wanted to savor every bit of her next time…

Lillian blinked as her awareness returned to her surroundings. *What the hell, Lil'?* her mind shrieked. *You're so overdosed on dopamine that you're in a foreign country, surrounded by vampires who are eyeballing you like you're a steak, on your way to face some head vampire who may or may not kill you, and all you can think about is getting naked with Radu again?*

Taking slow, deep breaths through her nose, Lillian fought to rein in her raging hormones. Radu squeezed her hand and gave her a sideways grin. Oh crap, could he tell what she was thinking?

As she, Radu, and their escort crested a hill, city lights came into view. If Radu had been able to fly further, would they have made it past this patrol? Or would they have encountered another group?

From Radu's satisfied expression—as if these vampires were doing his bidding—she supposed it didn't matter. At the bottom of the hill was a shadowy parking lot, with one streetlamp flickering dimly to reflect on a black car. The lead vampire said something to the other four, which made two of them nod and vanish into the night.

One of the remaining vampires opened the trunk and gestured for them to place their bags inside. Radu did so with a reluctant nod, and Lillian followed suit.

Then another got into the driver's seat, while the third opened the rear passenger door and gestured for Radu and Lillian to get in. The scenario reminded her of so many movies, where getting into a car with mobsters never ended well. She looked up at Radu and saw that his face had gone pale, his eyes wide.

"What's wrong?" she whispered.

Instead of looking at her, he turned to the leader. "Do any of you speak English?"

"*Nu înțeleg*," both vampires responded with angry frowns.

Radu then turned to her and spoke quietly through clenched teeth. "I have never been in a car."

"Oh." Of course, he hadn't. Cars didn't exist when he went into hibernation. "You'll be fine." She squeezed his hand, marveling at the fact that she was trying to comfort a vampire.

The lead vampire barked something in Romanian, clearly wanting to know what they'd said. Radu looked back at him with a smile and said something that was undoubtedly a lie. Then he slid into the backseat of the car, and only Lillian observed the tension in his jaw.

The other two vampires scooted in on either side of them, making what would have been a spacious backseat uncomfortably crowded. Lillian's heart beat faster as the chance for escape narrowed even more. The one who sat next to Lillian gave her a leering grin and spread his knees apart so his thigh pressed against hers.

A low growl made the hairs on the back of her neck stand on end. Radu's eyes glowed black flame as he bared his fangs and grabbed

Lillian, settling her on his lap. Such animalistic, territorial behavior should have turned her off, but she was just happy to be away from the man-spreading, pervy vampire. She'd dealt with that bullshit enough on public buses. Also, Radu's lap was comfortable, his arms around her the only safe and stable thing in the world as they rode with strangers through an unfamiliar city.

A few minutes later, the car made a left and drove down a mile-long driveway, winding through curves and past manicured hedge animals before it stopped in front of a mansion. Built of some white stone and with countless embellishments on the rounded arched windows and narrow columns, the palatial structure was done in a neo-romanticism style, or baroque, Lillian remembered from college. A marble fountain even graced the front lawn amidst manicured topiary.

The driver and front passenger got out and opened the back doors. Lillian slid off Radu's lap and waited for him to exit the car before following him out of his side, ignoring the lead vampire's offered hand. One vampire opened the trunk and brought out their bags, but instead of handing them back to Radu and Lillian, he kept them. The four Romanian vampires surrounded them as they escorted them to the massive house.

A butler greeted them warily before leading them into a massive study filled with antique furniture. The vampire who had to be the big boss of the city sat behind a desk, smoking a cigar. Though he seemed to be short and of slight build, the set of his shoulders and fixed jaw gave an air of age and power. His gray eyes roved over them with mild curiosity, though his brow rose slightly as he looked at Lillian.

A slight frown turned the corners of his thin lips, and he said something to Radu. After Radu answered, the head vampire's eyes widened, and he said something else, though this time he addressed the ones who'd brought them here. All four gasped and stepped back almost apologetically.

Lillian looked up at Radu. "What did he say?"

"He asked why I had a human with me when it is forbidden and—"

The head vampire waved his cigar and interrupted in English. "No need to translate for the lovely *muiere*. I speak English. American, yes?"

Lillian turned to see him looking at her with a much friendlier expression. "Yes."

"Come, sit." He gestured to two chairs in front of his desk before narrowing his gaze at the vampires who'd brought them here and returned to Romanian, the wave of his hand a clear dismissal.

The other vampires set down Radu's and Lillian's bags, bowed, and departed. Radu nodded at Lillian, and they sat to face the vampire who gaped at them. "Allow me to introduce myself. I am Ivan Vâlcu, Lord of Bucharest. Are you truly Radu Nicolae, the Lost Brother?"

"I am lost no more," Radu said. "I am going to meet my brother in the United States."

"That is joyous news. Those of us who know of Razvan's quest have long wished for this. But none so much as me. I was a friend to your father, Alexandru, and he would be heartbroken at your long separation." Before Radu opened his mouth to respond, he turned back to Lillian. "As I was telling your master, Razvan Nicolae has immunity, decreed by Delgarias, the Thirteenth Elder himself, so I cannot report you to the Elders, but I am curious as to why he wants a human woman to come to him along with his brother."

Lillian chewed her lip. Ivan spoke as if she should know all about the Elders, whoever they were, and what immunity meant. Even more strange was that he seemed to think Radu's brother was expecting her too. What had Radu said to him? She decided it was best to play along and let Radu answer.

Radu took Lillian's hand and trailed his thumb up and down her wrist. "Actually, Lillian needs to speak with Silas McNaught and his bride."

Ivan's eyes widened. "Razvan's protégée and the General?" He leaned forward and peered intently at Lillian. "Is it about the Prophecy?"

Lillian blinked but kept herself from asking what that was.

Radu's grip tightened on her hand. "Perhaps. It is not something we are permitted to disclose. But I assure you, it is very important." His tone was so mild that if Lillian didn't know better, she'd think he was completely on top of what was going on.

Ivan stared at them for a long time before he crushed out his cigar and looked at Radu. "What do you need my help for?" His accent thickened, indicating that he was upset with Radu's vagueness. "I assume that is why you've come."

Radu nodded. "We need identification and a way to travel to the United States without being detected by human authorities. Do you possess the power and resources to accomplish this?"

Oh, that was smooth, Lillian thought. Make his potential refusal look like weakness.

"Of course I do!" Ivan clenched his fists. "But I believe that if I am to spend such effort and money to help a vampire I barely met and a human whose presence violates our laws, I should know something about why I am doing so."

Lillian couldn't blame him for that. All the same, she prayed he would help them anyway.

Radu leaned back in his chair and smiled as if amused. "My brother will reward anyone who helps return me to him." He sounded so confident that Lillian had to fight the urge to give him a questioning look. "As for Lillian, her information is something that Silas will not be able to keep secret for long among our kind, so you will undoubtedly hear about it before long." His grin broadened. "The question is: will you believe it?"

"With all that has happened in the last few years, I would believe almost anything." Ivan's scowl deepened a moment, then suddenly, he chuckled. "You're just as evasive as your brother. Though you've given me no answer at all, I will help you. But only because Alexandru would have wished it. You and your pretty little human may stay in my home while I prepare the things you require, and of course, you are free to hunt in my city, so long as you do not kill anyone. That is forbidden these days, in case you missed the news during your long hibernation."

Radu released Lillian's hand, and rose from his seat. He bowed deeply. "My gratitude is beyond measure, Ivan Vâlcu. I owe you a great debt which I shall repay."

Ivan extended his hand and they shook. "I trust you will. Now we can take your bags to your room, and then we shall go hunt." His gaze flicked to Lillian. "And, of your *muiere* shall have a meal as well."

Lillian finally dared to speak. "Thank you."

"The pleasure is mine." He reached for her hand, but instead of shaking it, he placed a chaste kiss on her knuckles while Radu frowned.

And with that, Lillian and Radu had gone from supplicants and potential prisoners to honored guests of the Lord Vampire of Bucharest. And soon, they would have IDs, passports, and a hopefully covert trip to the States.

Lillian frowned as they followed Ivan out of the study and down a wide carpeted staircase, remembering all the things Ivan had said. Elders…the Prophecy…strange things happening in the last few years.

They also had more questions.

Chapter Eleven

Radu smiled as he saw that he and Lillian had been given one room to share. Just because the Lord of Bucharest had offered aid and hospitality did not mean he was trustworthy. Furthermore, Radu did not like the way Ivan's vampires had looked at Lillian. If she'd been placed in a separate room, Radu would have barged in to protect her.

After a servant set down their bags and left them alone, Radu thought of other reasons why sharing a room with her was appealing. His gaze swept over the large canopied bed with appreciation. Just as he was imagining all the things they would do in that bed, Lillian tapped him on the shoulder.

"Who are the Elders?" she asked.

"A group of twelve vampires across the world who make and enforce our laws," Radu explained tiredly. Despite several tense moments that might have been the deaths of him and Lillian with one misstep, his careful words had prevailed. Now all he wanted was a meal and a bed. However, she needed to learn about his world. "They existed in my time, but I've never met one." And from how he was raised, one never wished to.

"But Ivan said something about a thirteenth Elder."

He frowned, remembering all too well the way Ivan had spoken of him. "The Thirteenth Elder was a myth. Delgarias is said to be the first of us, taller than any man and with hair that shines like the night sky. He was used by elder vampires to frighten their younglings into obedience." Unease coiled in his belly. "Yet Ivan said my brother's immunity was decreed by the Thirteenth himself, so he must be real."

"Well, maybe he doesn't look as weird as the rumors say," Lillian offered. Her lips turned down in a thoughtful twist. "Did he mean your brother has immunity from the Elders' laws?"

Radu nodded. "It seems so."

Her frown deepened. "Then that would mean he can kill people. Do you think he does now?"

"I cannot say," Radu said quietly. Razvan had reveled in everything about being a vampire. He did love to toy with his food, but did he take his games so far? His mind shifted to other confusing things he'd been told. "I also do not know about this Prophecy that Ivan and his vampires spoke of. Yet it is clear that Razvan is in the thick of it." A deep sigh escaped his lungs. "I have missed much during my long sleep."

Lillian's features softened. "I'm sure you'll catch up quick. After all, you figured out how to get me ice cream that first night."

Radu couldn't fight back a smile in memory of how delicious the cold substance had tasted. And how overwhelming and chaotic it had been to navigate through the loud village and shops, and the complications on deducing how to purchase food for her. "Perhaps you can have more when Ivan takes us somewhere for you to eat." The thought prompted another, which bled away his good humor. "We'll have to ride in one of those blasted cars again."

She smiled up at him. "I'd bet money you'll like them better once you get to drive. Practically all men do. Now I'm going to head into the bathroom to get changed so we can meet Ivan down in time." With that, she took her bag into another room and closed the door.

He wasn't so certain he'd ever grow fond of those cages on wheels, but her words comforted him all the same.

When Lillian emerged, Radu sucked in a breath at the sight of her in a pale blue dress that emphasized her curves. Her bare knees make him salivate. He'd donned black slacks, a black button-down shirt, and a long black coat that was the closest thing to the cloaks he'd worn in his day. He had to admit he did admire the efficiency of buttons and zippers. Boots were also sturdier and much more comfortable.

One thing that was not an improvement, in Radu's opinion, was the city. The lights, crowds, and noises overwhelmed him to the point where he feared he'd go mad. Ivan at first brought them to what he called a "club" full of bright lights, loud music, and hundreds of mortals bouncing around in odd jerky moments. Ivan took one look at Radu's pained face and led them out to an inn across the street that was blissfully quiet, aside from the timeless animated conversations that imbued drinking establishments.

"My apologies, Nicolae. Such places must be overwhelming after your long rest." Ivan gestured for the server to bring them drinks.

"Yes, but I shall have to become accustomed to this new world," Radu said, biting back a smile at the furious glare Lillian fixed on Ivan.

She was very brave, his little friend. Though frail and mortal, she'd already faced Radu with vengeful determination when she'd tried to stake him, and now she had the courage to defend him from a vampire who was old enough to have been a friend to Radu's father.

He and Ivan sipped their ale, cooler and crisper than Radu had drunk a millennium ago, and watched for the perfect moment to seek a meal. Two men rose unsteadily from their seats and tottered out the rear exit. Radu signaled for Lillian to wait while he and Ivan followed them.

Minutes later, and much more refreshed, Ivan led Radu and Lillian to an eating establishment that was opulent as a palace. Radu took two swallows of her blood in the shadows before they entered the restaurant. One of the serving men looked at Ivan with recognition and deference before leading them to a table overlooking the moonlit river.

The next hour was full of bliss as Radu tasted new and exotic flavors of the dishes Lillian ate with gusto. His sense of taste was far more amplified than it had been before. The Mark, he realized. Was it possible to taste Lillian's food without having to feed on her every time? He resolved to try at the soonest opportunity.

Ivan offered to show them around the city, but Radu declined, grateful that Lillian displayed the same reluctance. This chaotic modern world had overwhelmed his senses, making him long for a quiet bed and the embrace of a beautiful woman.

"Very well, my friend. There are only a few hours before dawn. Curse these short summer nights. You and the lovely Lillian may rest while I meet with Yuri about making your identification. He is the best in the world. Tomorrow night, you will select your names, ages, and other information, and he will take your pictures."

The moment they arrived at Ivan's mansion, Lillian dashed up the stairs to their chamber and went into the bathroom. Peering over her shoulder, he saw that the room held a sink, a seat with a bowl of water that he realized was used for relieving one's bladder, and a large bathtub with taps to make water flow straight into it. He'd heard the Romans had such cunning pipes in his day and felt a pang of regret that he'd hidden from the world instead of exploring it. Had Razvan traveled in his long life? Radu imagined he did.

Instead of filling the tub, Lillian showed him how to twist the knobs to make water spray from a fount above. He fiddled with the knobs and stared in wonder at such a marvel until she turned around and lifted one honey-colored brow. "May I please shower in private?"

He regarded her with a regretful smile, preferring to watch her naked body beneath the spray, though he backed out of the room with a respectful bow. "Only if I have a chance to experience this shower when you are finished."

"Totally." She grinned. "I think you'll love it."

The door closed behind her, leaving him bereft of her beauty. To distract himself from imagining her naked, Radu explored the bedroom, pausing at a large black plastic rectangle on the wall that somewhat resembled the "phone" Lillian bade him destroy.

Slowly, he reached out and pressed a button on the side. Noise and images made him leap back with a curse. People dressed similarly to how they had in the old days and spoke to each other in strangely accented English, while words in another language, presumably his own, appeared on the bottom screen. Was this a window through time? Radu waved his hand in front of their faces, but they did not see him.

They were discussing a battle, he realized. A battle between five kings. When their conversation ended, and the people disappeared to be replaced by a view of a young woman walking on a castle parapet, Radu understood what he was seeing. It was a play, and the big rectangle on the wall was a device to allow people to watch plays from their rooms.

"Oh wow!" Lillian's voice tore his attention from the play. "Ivan gets HBO here?"

"Is that was this is?" He pointed at the box. "An HBO?"

She laughed, though not unkindly. "No, it's a television. The channel you're watching is HBO. Looks like a *Game of Thrones* marathon with Romanian subtitles."

"*Game of Thrones marathon*? That is what this play is called?"

Her grin broadened. "We call them shows, but yeah, they're basically plays. A marathon is when they show several episodes all night. Looks like we're on Season 2, but I'll explain that later when you're done with your shower."

Shower. The word reminded him of what Lillian had been doing. Radu's gaze shifted from the television to the sight of Lillian's warm pink skin covered by a towel that he longed to tear away. However, he did not want to touch her until he was clean, so he kissed her nose and went into the bathing room.

Stripping quickly, he turned on the tap and stepped into the tub. The water nearly scalded him. Hissing through his teeth. Radu turned the knobs until the water was pleasantly hot but wouldn't boil him to death. Standing under the spray, his muscles relaxed in the blissfully warm spray. Radu reached for the soap and washed his body, singing an old song he used to sing with his brother.

After washing his hair, he let the hot water beat down on his back and shoulders until the water began to cool. He turned off the taps with a smile. So the hot water *wasn't* infinite.

When he reentered the bedroom, he saw Lillian sprawled out on the bed wearing one of the T-shirts she'd suggested he buy the other night. And nothing else. The sight made his pulse rise and his mouth go dry.

"Sorry for taking your clothes," she said, looking down at the shirt. "I forgot to buy pajamas."

"I am not sure what those are." So many holes remained in his knowledge of these times. He trailed his finger along her bare calf. "But I do not think you will need the shirt either."

Her lips parted, and her pupils dilated like they had when she'd first allowed him to take her. Tension he hadn't realized was there eased in his shoulders. Her willingness to make love with him hadn't been a fleeting thing. And more importantly, his ferocity that night hadn't frightened her away.

For a moment, he paused, drinking in the curves and color of Lillian's lips, anticipating her taste. Was she better than Uta? He remembered endless days longing for the village woman, but he couldn't remember her kiss. Radu cursed himself inwardly for such foolish thinking. Uta was dead. Furthermore, Uta had gotten his parents killed… or perhaps that had been him. Either way, she didn't matter.

All thoughts of his traitorous lover vanished the moment Radu kissed Lillian, long and lingering, tasting the chocolate she'd eaten earlier along with her unique flavor.

Lillian was *here*. She was alive, soft, and warm in his arms. Slowly, he lowered her to the bed and kissed her neck, reveling in her hitching gasps as his lips grazed sensitive hollows. He slid the collar of her shirt down to kiss her shoulders as her fingers ran through his hair.

Slowly, he reached under the fabric of the shirt, sliding his fingertips up her ribcage to cup her breasts, delighted at the smooth heat of her skin. Impatient to see and touch her, he pulled the shirt over her head, gratified when she shifted and helped him unclothe her.

For a moment, all he could do was stare as she lay on the bed before him, her hair fanned out in a reddish-gold halo, her breasts round and full, her stomach flat, and the tantalizing blue scrap of fabric hiding her female center.

Then his hands were all over her, touching, exploring, finding every place that elicited a gasp or moans and following with his lips and tongue. By the time he slid her panties off to taste the secret place between her thighs, Lillian was wet with arousal.

Pride welled within him that he hadn't forgotten how to please a woman. Flicking his tongue across her slick flesh, he closed his eyes in bliss at her taste. Lillian writhed and whimpered against his mouth, encouraging him to lick and suck her more thoroughly, taking care to circle her sensitive bud in a rhythmic motion.

Her panting breaths grew more rapid every moment until her hips arched upward, and she cried out in bliss. Radu's cock hardened further with every cry as he gripped her thighs and continued to lick her pulsing center until she went limp and shuddering beneath him.

Giving her little time to recover, he rose and covered her with his body. Holding himself poised at her entrance, he took a moment to nuzzle her neck and enjoy the sensation of her heart beating against his. It had been so long since he'd had any contact with another person that the closeness was intoxicating.

Lillian's arms wrapped around his waist, her hips shifting under him, silently entreating. With painstaking slowness, Radu slid inside her, maddening pleasure rushing through him with every inch. Once he was seated to the hilt, he once more remained still, content to hold her and savor the sensation of being inside her.

The stillness was impossible to maintain as her hips twitched beneath his, seeking that magical rhythm once more. Radu obliged, moving in and out slowly, making them both gasp with every motion. Time melted away until all that existed was heat and sensation. They breathed in tandem, bodies moving together in an eternal dance.

Sweat beaded on his forehead as Lillian tightened around his cock in gripping pulses that increased in rhythmic intensity. Radu swallowed her cries of pleasure as her orgasm overtook her and spurred his own. Light flashed before his eyes, and the Mark flared between them until they became one body, one mind, their climaxes feeding each other in one continuous loop.

After endless ecstasy, they came back into themselves as the pleasure ebbed to a saner level. Radu blinked, his vision swimming with gold-tinged bliss as he rolled over and pulled Lillian's limp and trembling form into his arms.

For the next few hours, they reclined in bed, sipping wine and watching *Game of Thrones*. Radu reveled in the peaceful relaxation, even as he anticipated making love to Lillian once more. With the dangers they faced in their upcoming journey, who knew when they would next have time for something like this?

Chapter Twelve

Agent Stebbins cringed as the vampire's scream echoed in the reinforced chamber. He threw off the set of headphones, but the noise still seemed to penetrate the sealed room. One of the skylights had been opened above the cell. A technician above aimed a beam of sunlight directly onto the vampire by using a mirror.

Director Bowers sat beside Stebbins, watching the vampire writhe under the beam. The interest in his colorless eyes seemed more predatory than clinical. Stebbins wondered if Bowers was disappointed that the sunlight didn't immediately make the vampire burst into flames like in the movies. Instead, they developed a sunburn that progressively darkened until their skin smoldered, and then finally caught flame.

Vampires were more difficult to hurt than the stories implied. Crosses, holy water, or any religious implements only made a vampire smirk. That had been documented when the AIU had encountered their first subject. As had the fact that vampires did indeed have a reflection in a mirror.

A stake would work, or anything that damaged the heart. That much was already known from fieldwork, when attempts to secure a specimen resulted in agents having to defend themselves. Still, one must be careful because vampires healed so rapidly that some recovered from a bullet to the chest. For a moment, it appeared that drowning would also do the trick, but then the vampire revived a few minutes after the fact, the same as he had with poison gas.

Sunlight and fire appeared to be the only guarantees. And it had to be natural sunlight. UV light alone did nothing, nor did Vitamin D.

However, they were unable to pin down *why* sunlight hurt them. Something in their cells' organelles acted like a chloroplast, only instead of activating photosynthesis, the cells combusted. But which element of sunlight triggered the reaction remained to be discovered.

Stebbins tore his gaze away from the vampire's crimson face that mostly resembled that of someone who'd fallen asleep in a tanning bed. Except for the places the mirror's beam had shone directly onto his skin, leaving stripes of flesh, black and smoking, like meat on a grill. It kind of smelled like cooking meat too.

Stebbins's stomach churned with a threat to eject the yogurt he'd eaten for breakfast. Taking slow, shallow breaths, he focused on jotting down his notes.

Operation Wrangler had been a success so far. The field agents had canvassed the city of Phoenix, drawing up a list of people suspected of being vampires. The biggest indicator being that vampires worked graveyard shifts and were reputed by their coworkers to keep to themselves.

Subject Eleven, as the burned vampire was called—although he was only the second that the AIU had managed to secure in a lab—had been a surprisingly easy catch. A well-aimed shot with a tranquilizer dart, and the vampire had collapsed in the parking garage of the business complex where he'd worked as a nightguard. And it took little starvation and exposure to sunlight for the creature to admit that it was a young one, only transformed thirty years ago.

However, it would not tell them which vampire Changed him or the location of others. Bowers did not seem to mind as the starvation, sun exposure, and other tortures—tests, Stebbins inwardly corrected—yielded more data.

Unleashing Desire

Now, as the vampire curled up on the concrete floor, trembling and weak from smoking wounds, the research staff tried to determine what weakened Subject Eleven most: the sun or blood loss.

Either way, Stebbins was certain that the vampire was not long for this world. And that Bowers didn't care. Stebbins missed the former director more and more every day. He also missed Agent Holmes…and his daughter.

As if reading his mind, Bowers turned his cool gaze on Stebbins. "I'll want another one secured before the end of the month."

Stebbins nodded. They had several likely vampires compiled in their database. Bringing in another would be easy.

The problem was, he wasn't sure he wanted to.

Not that he had a choice. Once you were part of the Abnormal Investigation Unit, you were there until death…which could be arranged sooner if you displeased the wrong people. Stebbins thought of the sad fate of Lillian Holmes and shivered.

Lillian clung to Radu's hand as they boarded Ivan's private jet. For vampires, flying was a complicated prospect, as they had to keep the trips short enough to arrive at their destination before sunrise. The richest Lord Vampires had sunproofed jets, but very few dared to test their capabilities.

For this flight, they would first fly to Dublin, Ireland, under Ivan's escort and spend the day there before making their entry into the states on a private landing strip outside Bangor, Maine. The Lord of Bangor would be waiting with a private car to bring them to his home and shelter them for the day after they passed through the Port of Entry. Furthermore, Ivan had to contact the Lord vampires in each place to gain permission to pass through their territories.

If Ivan's grumbling was any indication, Yuri, the best vampire forger in Europe, had an easier time giving Lillian and Radu their new identities. Radu had balked at changing his name, but with the AIU having a file on him, a paper trail bearing his name would be almost as dangerous as Lillian's. Since his first name was common enough, he was allowed to keep it. So he grudgingly agreed to become one of Ivan's cousins, Radu Vâlcu. Lillian was now Lily Vâlcu because married couples invoked less scrutiny. They'd even been given fake wedding bands.

Lillian twisted the gold ring on her finger. Even though the name was fake, the thought of being Radu's wife made a strange shiver course through her body. Several times, she'd stared at her Idaho driver's license, thinking it was so surreal to be a native of a state she'd never visited. Even weirder for Radu to be a native of a country that hadn't even been discovered when he was born.

Yuri had also hooked them up with birth certificates, passports, and turned all the money they'd taken from the dead hunters into cash and Visa prepaid cards. If that wasn't enough for them to make it across the country to Coeur d'Alene, the money Ivan loaned them would be.

The jet's engine roared as it made its way down the runway. Radu's sharp intake of breath was quiet but Lillian still heard it, and observed his white-knuckled grip on the seat.

However, once they were in the air, he relaxed and stared transfixed out the window at the moonlit clouds below them. "I've never dared to fly this high," Radu told her with a smile.

"As long as you try on your own," Lillian replied with a light laugh. "I don't want you carrying me then."

He nodded, his gaze fixed on the window. Lillian leaned back in her seat and closed her eyes, content that Radu was enjoying his first plane ride.

She awoke when Radu tapped her on the shoulder, slightly embarrassed that she'd dozed off. It was all his fault, keeping her up half the day with his lovemaking. Memories of the blissful hours she'd spent naked and entwined with him threatened to overtake her reason. Quickly she shunted them away.

Yes, she and Radu were lovers for the duration of their mission, but that didn't mean they had a future. Hopefully, Radu would find a home once reunited with his brother. Though where would that leave her? Silas and Akasha might eliminate that concern once they found out that she'd been part of her father's experiments in creating their baby and keeping her from them. Lillian only prayed they'd spare her life when she helped them retrieve their daughter. If she could find out where the baby was.

And after that? Lillian Holmes had the education and credentials to secure a good job as a biophysicist at any lab in the country or abroad. Lily Vâlcu, on the other hand, had nothing. With her luck, she'd have to go back to school or spend the rest of her life flipping burgers. Unless she managed to persuade Yuri to forge a degree and whip up fake references.

Ivan gestured for them to rise from their seats and follow him out of the jet. Lillian studied the vampire's back, looking for any sign of tension or betrayal.

Not for the first time did she wonder why Ivan, who, aside from being a stranger to them, was powerful enough to kill her and Radu the moment they'd entered his territory, was instead doing everything in his power to help them. The way his eyes had widened, and the reverent awe with which he'd spoken of Silas McNaught and Razvan Nicolae was clearly the reason behind most of his motives, despite his talk of being friends with Radu's father.

The question was: what were Radu's brother and the vampire he'd made involved in that not only placed them above vampire laws but also inspired other vampires to bend over backwards to aid them? The thought of such power made Lillian's gut churn with unease. What if Razvan and Silas had some evil plan? What if she and Radu would be used as pawns to do something terrible?

And yet she didn't dare voice her worries to Radu. For one thing, his heart was set on seeing his brother again. For another, Silas and

Akasha deserved to know that they had a daughter. And who knew? Maybe being parents would dissuade them from doing anything bad.

That is, if what they were doing *was* bad. Lillian's frown deepened. What if it was something good? *Prophecy*. The mysterious word drifted across her mind like a cloud over the moon. Although she embraced the supernatural, prophecies were far too outrageous concepts for her to swallow. True, she'd encountered a few people in her studies that were truly precognitive, but never to the extent that they were able to foresee something that had a global impact. That sort of thing was for science fiction and fantasy novels…right?

"What is the matter, Lillian?" Radu interrupted her racing thoughts.

She opened her mouth and closed it. She couldn't tell him her speculations about the Prophecy in front of Ivan. Note while Radu was pretending he'd heard all about it. "Nothing, just wondering how many hours we have until dawn."

Ivan glanced at her over his shoulder and smiled. "About four hours. You shall have plenty of time to get settled in at Donovan's place and for Radu to hunt."

Lillian nodded, tamping down nervousness at the prospect of staying with yet another strange vampire. They would encounter several on their journey, and she may as well get used to it. Her trepidation vanished when they departed the jet and entered the customs line. A new fear took its place.

What if their fake IDs and passports didn't pass inspection? What if they were hauled off to some Irish jail, and Radu was burnt to a crisp by the sun? Breathing through her nose, Lillian fought to keep her face expressionless and not look suspicious.

To her surprise, Ivan greeted the customs guy like a long-lost friend and chatted with him while he only gave their passports brief glances. Radu smiled and took her hand as they followed Ivan through the airport and to a man who held a sign with Ivan's name written on it in bright blue marker.

The driver took their bags and loaded them in the trunk of his black car before driving them through the narrow streets and to an ornate Victorian townhouse.

Donovan, the Lord Vampire of Dublin, greeted them at the door. "Ivan!" he exclaimed with a grin before embracing the Romanian vampire. "It is wonderful to see you after so many long years."

Lillian bit back a smile at the vampire's shock of red hair and thick Irish brogue before he turned to Radu. "And you are the fabled lost brother?"

"I am," Radu answered levelly without elaborating.

Donovan's grin broadened as his green eyes met Lillian's. "And who is this wee morsel?"

"Mine," Radu growled.

The Irish vampire laughed. "Not much of a talker, is he?"

Lillian nodded and extended her hand. "I'm Lillian Holmes."

"Donovan Roarke." He shook her hand. "Welcome to Ireland. Although you will not be here long, I promise to do my utmost to entertain you during your short time here."

True to his word, Donovan nearly turned himself inside out in his attempt to amuse them. A servant took their bags as the Lord Vampire took them to a roaring loud pub with live musicians and dancers. Radu at first appeared tense with the noise until Lillian's food arrived. She dined on fish and chips that Donovan swore were better than what the English served and sipped hard cider that was thick and strong enough to make her eyes water.

But the fish was fantastic. Radu hummed along with her, making her lean over. "Can you taste it?"

He nodded and gave her an impatient look as if he wanted her to keep eating.

"How?" she whispered in his ear. "You haven't...you know, bitten me...since the night before last."

"I think it's the Mark," he whispered. "It brings us closer together."

Her face heated. *Damn it, I should be disturbed by that instead of thinking it's romantic.* Yet still, she bent and finished her food, smiling at Radu's pleased reactions to the flavors. She had to admit that it was nice that she didn't have to give her blood for him to enjoy tasting food anymore.

Donovan then grasped her hand and led her out to the dance floor, where she embarrassed herself while Radu hunted. They returned to the townhouse shortly before dawn and were given a small but cozy bedroom in the basement to hide from the daylight.

Unlike their guest room at Ivan's house, this one lacked a TV. But Radu and Lillian found other ways to occupy themselves.

Donovan awoke them a few hours before dusk, and instead of asking questions, he taught them card games until sunset. Then it was time to go to the airport, where yet another private jet was waiting to take them to the States. This time, Ivan did not come along.

This flight was longer and much more nerve-wracking than the one to Dublin. The sky was cloudless, and nothing but ocean lay below them, so all they saw out of the tiny window was endless blackness.

The fact that the pilot was the only other one aboard intensified the feeling of bleak isolation. The tension in Radu's shoulders and the pilot's white-knuckled grip on the control wheel reminded Lillian that a terrifying new element was also in play.

Even though they were heading west and thus fleeing the sun and the clock, the minutes raced by quicker with every mile they flew. If the pilot kept up his speed, they'd make it to Bangor an hour before dawn. Lillian imagined the sun behind them, deadly and orange, creeping at their backs. If they didn't make their time, Radu and the vampire pilot would burn, and there would be no one left to fly the plane.

After the longest eight hours of their lives, the jet finally touched down at the small private landing strip in Bangor. When they got off the jet, it was miraculously two hours before dawn. Hopefully, enough time to pass through customs at the Port of Entry and find shelter.

Lillian and Radu heaved simultaneous sighs of relief.

They were finally in the U.S. They'd won the race against the sun. Now they had to win the race across the country…and keep the AIU from finding them.

Chapter Thirteen

Five Days Later

Radu shifted in his seat of the car Lillian had purchased in Bangor, trying to ease the numbness in his backside from sitting for eight hours a night. To avoid pressing their luck with airport security, they'd opted to buy the car and drive across this massive country. The thing was older and nowhere near as comfortable as the ones they'd ridden in before. Lillian yawned beside him, keeping her tired eyes on the road.

A wave of protective tenderness filled him as he wished he could give her his strength. At this stage of the journey, there was no question that Lillian intended to stay by his side for the duration of this mission. And hopefully longer.

The first night after they left Bangor, Radu woke in a hotel room Lillian rented to hide from the daylight to see her lying beside him.

Tension bled from his body to be replaced by a pleasant warmth. Part of him was convinced that once back in her home country, Lillian would flee from him at her first opportunity.

"Why are you smiling at me like that?" she'd asked after opening her eyes.

"You stayed with me." He caressed her hair.

"Of course I did." She smiled up at him. "We're in this together now."

Together. The word did strange things to Radu's insides.

From that night on, their bond strengthened as Lillian taught him about this land.

Radu was eager to learn more about this new world that had been undiscovered in his day. He'd never imagined how vast the United States would be, and they were only passing through the top half.

Most of the journey had been pleasant, with Lillian showing him wondrous sights, like Niagra Falls, the Great Lakes—which he'd first assumed were large seas—and Mount Rushmore, a massive rock face with the visages of past presidents carved into it. Lillian had tried to explain the concept of presidents, men who were somewhat like temporary kings that the people selected to rule them. But Radu didn't quite understand how such a thing worked.

Still, he did his best to absorb everything Lillian told him about how her country worked, the good things, and the bad. He was delighted with the belief in freedoms of speech and religion but horrified with her talk of violence, hatred, and poverty. Those things were a constant with every time and place. And when she told him about her country's bloody history, he changed the subject, wanting a happier topic.

"What is American music like?"

She laughed and shook her head. "You know, it didn't even occur to me to try the radio in this thing when we bought it. The one in my car was broken, and I never bothered to get it fixed." She pressed one of the many buttons on a rectangular panel between them. The strains of some strumming instrument filled the vehicle. Then a man who sounded drunk started wailing in an irritating voice about a truck and a woman. Lillian laughed at the way Radu cringed. "Don't like country, huh? Well, if you press this button, you can skip to the next station. And that one will take you back. But the available stations will change as we pass through towns."

Radu amused himself toying with the buttons and making different styles of music come out of the things Lillian called speakers. He settled on a song with hypnotically fast drums, instruments that he couldn't identify, but sounded sweet and savage to his ears, and singing that was angry, yet stirred his passion.

Lillian glanced at him with a wry smile. "You like heavy metal?"

"Is that what it's called?" He drummed his fingers on the armrest and looked out the window. "I think I do. It sounds powerful. Do you like it?"

She was silent as she passed a slow-moving car. "Yeah. I had a metal phase in high school."

The landscapes they passed through were as diverse as the people, deep forests, spiraling mountains, cities of concrete and high glass towers, endless stretches of flat plains.

Some days they stayed with Lord Vampires, others in hotels, where Lillian blocked the windows from light when possible, and when she couldn't block out all the sunlight, he slept in the bathtub. One day they even risked having him sleep in the trunk of the car, which was more comfortable than a bathtub, but Lillian had been terrified that the cops would pull her over, search the trunk, and accidentally kill him. That was another downside to this modern world. Authorities were everywhere, and it seemed one couldn't sneeze without being ticketed or fined. However, one was allowed to insult the president all they liked, and no one would blink. In Radu's day, such a thing was treason, and one would be put to death.

Though Lillian wasn't stopped that day, the next night, their car was engulfed in the dreaded red and blue lights. Radu gripped his seat so tightly the leather groaned as the police officer inspected their false identification. He tried to make eye contact with the officer, but the man was too busy inspecting Lillian's driver's license and asking her why they were so far from Idaho. Radu bit back a growl of impatience. After an agonized wait where he was tempted to get out of the car and drain the cop to unconsciousness, they were at last released.

That ended his desire to rush the journey by riding in the trunk for the time being. Even so, a sense of urgency knotted in his gut. Some instinct screamed for them to get to Coeur d'Alene as soon as possible.

Since the days were so long, with an almost unbearable wait for dusk, even conversations and lovemaking couldn't fill those hours. So Lillian began teaching him to read English. From the mortals Radu fed on, he'd learned to speak the language, but the writing was something he had yet to decipher. She purchased a phone for each of them, another display of trust, and used what she called text messaging to match the correct symbols to make words. Lillian was a kind and patient teacher, never treating him like a child or mocking his mistakes. The more Radu read, the more questions he asked, and the more he learned about what he'd missed over his centuries of sleep.

The Lord Vampires they stayed with, at least, were not hostile. Though some regarded Radu with a measure of fear, while others practically bowed and scraped as if wishing to curry favor with him...or his brother. Lillian was eyed with a mixture of curiosity and disgust, making him remember that human paramours were forbidden. Thankfully, none dared insult her, especially once they learned she was to meet with Silas McNaught.

Radu eventually discovered the source of their fear of Silas and Razvan. Only last winter, they had slain a Lord Vampire who'd taken residence in the territory between theirs, along with all of her followers. Due to their immunity, they'd gone unpunished. Radu now understood why they appeared relieved when he and Lillian went on their way.

Now, as they drove through Montana, Radu began to wonder if his reunion with Razvan would be even more ominous than he already anticipated. What if Silas and Razvan were angry at him for intruding on whatever they were doing with this Prophecy?

Radu's fists clenched at his sides. It was *his* turn to be angry. Razvan's ire would have to wait. They had a seven-hundred-year-old score to settle.

Closing his eyes, he once more saw Razvan's powerful hands locked around Uta's slender upper arms, her head jolting back and forth as he shook her like a rag doll. Razvan's eyes locking on Radu's as he came upon them. Uta dropping to the floor with a broken neck.

Lillian made a small sound beside him, tearing him from the memory. For a moment, all he could do was stare at her. The fine-boned angle of her jawline, her high cheekbones, pert nose, and lush lips, that gleaming hair. A wave of primal protectiveness surged through him. What if Razvan hurt her too? His nails dug into his palms. He wouldn't let him touch her.

"Are you alright?" Lillian's voice pierced his anger.

He nodded. "I am only thinking."

"About this Prophecy?"

"Yes." The simple answer was best.

"I'd been wondering about that too." She kept her eyes on the road. "I mean, a lot of prophecies deal with things like the end of the world. Do you think your brother and Silas are trying to make something like that happen?"

"I truly do not know." Another disconcerting thought emerged. "What if we are part of this Prophecy?" There was magic in twins, according to many legends. And Lillian...there was something about her.

Her nose wrinkled with skepticism. "How so? I mean what would *we* do?"

"Some of the Lord Vampires who sheltered us think there is to be a war. Perhaps we are meant to take part in it. My father trained my brother and me in swords, pikes, and archery. And you," he pointed at her. "Your knowledge on technology and the workings of life itself would be a priceless asset in a war. You and your father managed to manipulate nature to create a life that should not have been possible. You may have—" He broke off as the implications of what Lillian and her father had done brought another possibility to light. "Prophecies often speak of saviors as well. What if that child—"

To his astonishment, she snorted. "No. Although Kiara possesses some unique attributes, there's nothing magical about her. And she didn't come from a miracle or anything. My father had planned her for years. She is a product of science, not mysticism, and there's no way ancient vampires could have predicted her birth."

The skepticism in Lillian's eyes made a smile tug at Radu's lips. "You don't believe the Prophecy is real, do you?"

"I don't even know what the Prophecy is!" she retorted. "And neither did any of the vampires who were so obsessed with it. But no, I don't believe in any prophecies. I believe in science."

"Why not?" Radu peered at her in confusion. "You've been dedicated to studying the preternatural…or 'abnormal,' as your former employer calls us. You believe in vampires. You believe in psychics…who can predict the future. Surely prophecies come from them."

"A little precognition is not the same as predicting the comings and outcomes of world-changing events," she said with an impatient frown. "I believe people are responsible for their own futures, and outside influences are random and not controlled by supernatural forces."

"Even though I and my kind are proof of supernatural forces," Radu countered. When she glared at him, he held up his hands and chuckled. "Very well, we will find out what this Prophecy is about soon enough. How many hours are left on our journey?"

She pulled over and dug out her phone from her purse. Her fingers flicked rapidly across the screen until a map appeared with a line tracing their route. "Less than six hours."

"Why don't we stop somewhere in an hour or two and stay until tomorrow?" he asked. "I want to arrive in Coeur d'Alene as early as possible tomorrow night."

"Why don't we just keep driving?" she asked. "We should get there a couple hours before dawn."

"Because, if either my brother or the Lord of Coeur d'Alene doesn't sense my presence in his territory immediately, one of their subordinates will and notify them. I want time to rest tonight, study the map, and come up with a plan that will be safer for both of us." He reached out and placed his hand on her thigh. "And I want one more night alone with you."

That intoxicating flush of pink imbued her cheeks. "Well, when you put it that way…" She slid her finger across the map and grinned. "Hey, there's a town called 'Hot Springs' a little over three hours from here, and it's two hours from Coeur d'Alene. I'll bet we can find a motel and have a soak before the sun comes up."

Radu closed his eyes in blissful anticipation of getting out of this accursed car and immersing himself in a pool of hot water with the beautiful woman beside him. "That sounds delightful."

They drove in silence as Radu watched the endless expanse of grassy flatlands pass through the window. Most of North Dakota had that same monotonous landscape as well. Radu preferred the forests best.

As if to emphasize the wisdom in stopping for the night, the bland terrain gave way to mountains and forests. From what he remembered of the road map he'd studied, Coeur d'Alene had a similar landscape.

They arrived in Hot Springs—the town—and pulled into a motel made up of small cabins surrounding the springs themselves.

The sleepy clerk eyed them balefully, but Radu didn't care as long as he took their payment and gave them lodging. Lillian gave him the usual story about their having been on the road for hours and that they were absolutely not to be disturbed.

"Fine," he grumbled, "but if you plan on sleeping all day, you'll have to pay for tomorrow as well."

"That's all right," Lillian said. This was almost always the case.

Radu locked gazes with the clerk, bared his fangs, and drank his fill before healing the puncture wounds and releasing the man's mind from the trance.

After the tired old man shuffled back to bed, Radu and Lillian took their bags from the trunk and found the small, somewhat ramshackle cabin where they would rest.

Throwing their bags on the bed, they wasted no time in finding the hot springs and soaking their stiff muscles. Then they enjoyed a leisurely swim in the pool before returning to the spring. Radu pulled Lillian into his arms and made love to her.

After they were sated, they bundled up with the towels and returned to their cabin, where they covered the windows with the blankets they'd brought, not trusting the curtains. Lillian then set up her camp stove and cooked a steak from the cooler and boiled water for instant mashed potatoes…which Radu enjoyed far less than real mashed potatoes.

But the steak more than made up for the inferior potatoes. It was so delicious that he had to lick the juices from her lips when she finished eating. Then she padded to the bathroom and brushed her teeth, filling his mouth with the taste of mint. Radu scowled before grabbing his own toothbrush. Lillian wished for him to care for his teeth as well.

Once they were settled in the surprisingly comfortable bed, Radu watched the windows carefully. If too much light made its way into the room, he would have no choice but to retreat to the bathtub. The dawn pressed around him in warning, though the room remained dark.

"Are you nervous about tomorrow?" Lillian asked as she stroked his hair, her gaze darting from the door to the windows anxiously.

"A man does not admit such a weakness."

"Nowadays, a man can say what he feels," she said in a chiding tone that he was growing accustomed to. "You don't have to do the tough-guy act twenty-four-seven."

Radu smiled and pulled her closer, tucking her head under his chin. "I am nervous," he admitted. How Uta would have laughed at him.

"And?" She prodded.

He took a deep breath. Such modern openness was difficult to become accustomed to. "Although Razvan killed the woman I loved, it is *my* fault our mother and father were killed because I told Uta what we were. I wonder if he's been searching for me all these years to kill me."

Her sharp intake of breath told him she hadn't considered that possibility. "What will you do then?"

"I cannot say. For what I've done, I deserve to die, but I want to live." His travels with her had resolved him to enjoy this new world. "I suppose I will have to fight him or flee like a coward and spend my days hiding from him and his witch."

"What about me?" she whispered softly, with a trace of fear.

"I will protect you." He held her tighter, his words fervent and wrought with intent. "And if Razvan kills me, I am certain Silas will ensure your safety. You are the key to him getting his daughter back. And if he won't, his wife will. All the Lords have said that Akasha has him wrapped around her finger. It is odd that he hasn't Changed her yet."

Lillian shivered. "I think I'm more afraid of Akasha than the vampires."

"I can understand that. The Lord of Chicago told me that she caved a vampire's face in with a slight push of her hand. They say she is stronger than our kind." He still marveled at such a possibility and almost dreaded meeting this woman as much as he anticipated it.

"She's the result of the military trying to create the perfect soldier." Lillian then explained fascinating phenomena like mutations, genetic manipulations, and other godlike powers that humans wielded at this time.

Radu felt a twinge of guilt for distracting her from her original question. Because he didn't know what he was going to become of her. Though he'd spoken what he believed would happen if he died, Radu had no notion of what their fate would be if he survived. Would Lillian want to spend the rest of her life educating him on how to dwell in this society? Or would she wish to leave him and live her own life once she'd assisted Silas and Akasha in securing their child?

Did he only want to keep her with him as a helpmate and a beauty to warm his bed? There were countless beautiful women who would gladly pleasure him. But he could only think of Lillian.

As Lillian's eyes closed, red gold lashes resting on her cheeks, a wave of tenderness clenched his heart, similar to when he'd first met Uta, yet much more intense.

Radu's breath fled his body as another question roared in his mind. Did he love her?

Chapter Fourteen

Lillian awoke to Radu kissing her cheeks.

"Wake up, pretty one," his deep voice rumbled. "It is time for us to depart."

She groaned in reluctance. "It's dark already?"

"No, but I can ride in the trunk until then."

A flicker of fear made her wake up all the way. "Do you have to? It's so dangerous. I'm lucky I didn't get pulled over that day."

"You said we're two hours away. I can bear the trunk that long." He stroked her hair in a clear attempt to soothe her.

"Why the rush?" Suspicion crept into her voice.

His gaze suddenly turned distant as he answered in a faraway voice. "I have a feeling, that's all. Besides, we need to find someplace to board while we look for Silas."

"Okay." Radu's instincts ended up being correct more often than not. Another concern arose. "What if he throws us out of his territory?"

Radu shook his head and favored her with an evil grin. "He won't. Not with the information you have. And he won't get it unless he provides me a sanctuary as well."

Her heart clenched with understanding. Radu would use her as a shield to keep his brother from killing him. Was that all she was to him? A tool to bend another vampire to his will...and a piece of ass on the side? A midnight snack?

Immediately, self-disgust filled Lillian at her unreasonable disappointment. She'd started out as a prisoner to him. Now they were partners who shared a cause. And the sex was incredible. There was no logical reason to deny themselves such pleasure.

And yet, she couldn't help but wish for more.

"Okay," she said, returning to the matter at hand. "But I need a shower first."

Once she was clean, she rummaged through her backpack, wishing they'd stopped at a Laundromat before this point. They might meet Silas and Razvan in mere hours, and she didn't want to look like a slob. Finally, she settled on a pale lavender maxi dress that was only slightly wrinkled. She'd never had time to buy makeup or anything, so she just brushed her hair out and braided it so it wouldn't get all windblown.

By the time Lillian emerged from the bathroom, Radu had all their things packed except for a sleeping bag, which he would cover himself with before they went outside.

"Okay, go into the bathroom while I open the door to back the car up closer," she told him.

When she went outside, she looked around to make sure no one was around to see them. Thanking the heavens for secluded rural motels, she backed the car almost to the cabin porch, angling it so the rear passenger door was as close as possible to the cabin's door.

Then she folded down the backseat to open the trunk compartment of the old Honda and moved their other bags out of the trunk, setting them on the floorboard and leaving the rear passenger door open.

After Lillian headed up the cabin steps, she carefully opened the door in case Radu wasn't ready. Covered head to toe in a sleeping bag, he would have looked comical if the situation wasn't so dangerous.

"I'm going to lead you down the stairs and then into the backseat, so you can roll into the trunk," she told him and placed her hand on his chest, his firm warmth seeping through the thick fabric into her palm.

"Okay." His voice was muffled. He'd come to like using that word.

Walking backward with her hand pressed to his chest, Lillian told him when to step, when to bend, and when to get into the seat. She shaded him with her body as he slithered in awkwardly and then rolled into the trunk. Then she pushed the seats back in place to secure him in the darkness before going back into the cabin to load up the rest of their bags.

As she checked the time on her phone, she frowned. It was only a quarter to seven. Sunset wasn't until eight-forty-five, and it would be at least another hour after that before it would be dark enough for Radu to be able to escape his cocooned prison. And it was eighty degrees outside, which meant that it *had* to be even hotter in the trunk from it baking all day.

When she returned the keys to the clerk, his eyes narrowed at her car…with its empty passenger seat. "Where's your husband?"

Lillian feigned an exasperated sigh and rolled her eyes. "He wandered down to that bar down the road. Now I gotta drag him out of there and pray we make it home in time, or the house sitter will freak. She has a party to go to." She gave him a "why me?" shake of her head and left the office.

"You okay back there?" she asked him.

Radu shouted something garbled that she had to ask him to repeat until she understood that he wanted music. Fiddling with the dial, she searched for the hardest rock station available. Almost everything out here was country. Finally, she found the classic rock station, which was the best Radu would get. Oh well, he needed to be exposed to the classics anyway.

Thinking of Radu suffocating back there made it hard for her to resist flooring the gas pedal to get them to Coeur d'Alene as soon as possible. But that wouldn't make the sun go down any faster, and she certainly couldn't risk getting pulled over for speeding.

She cranked up the air conditioning and blasted it until goosebumps rose on her arms, but she didn't dare turn it down, hoping that some of the cool air would reach her poor vampire.

As she reached another town, the radio station fuzzed out, so she switched to another. This one played both modern and classic heavy metal. One song, featuring a woman singer, sounded so beautiful and compelling that Lillian had to turn the volume up. When it ended, she sighed in disappointment.

The DJ's words made her sit up straighter. *"That was Rage of Angels, who vanished without a trace last December. Aside from some false sightings, no one has a clue where they went. Hailing from Coeur d'Alene, Idaho, the group hit it big in Seattle, inspiring a heavy metal Renaissance. Come back, Rage of Angels. We miss you."*

Lillian sucked in a breath. That band was from Coeur d'Alene too? What an odd coincidence. Home to rock stars and prominent vampires. It must be some town.

Every sign she passed that showed the miles to Coeur d'Alene in progressively smaller increments made her heart beat faster.

Soon she and Radu would encounter the vampires that all others spoke of with fear and reverence. And Akasha, a woman that Lillian was acquainted with only on paper from the notes and test results her father had sent her secretly. Lillian remembered reading those notes with fascination. Akasha was able to bench press five hundred pounds, maintain a running speed of twenty miles an hour for thirty minutes, metabolized elephant tranquilizers in less than three hours, and could snap a two-inch-thick steel chain like a twig. If only Dad had photographed Akasha so Lillian would recognize her instead of just sending Lillian the woman's genome data.

Back when Dad had first sent her the data, Lillian had found it astounding. Now that she was about to tell Akasha that they'd secretly used her eggs to create a baby and kept it from her without her knowledge, Lillian was terrified. More so than she feared Silas's reaction, even though he and Razvan had systematically slaughtered every soldier in the complex where Akasha had been imprisoned five years ago.

After all, fathers frequently learned about babies they were unaware they'd sired. Mothers, on the other hand? Not so much. And if Akasha was stronger than a vampire, how would it be possible for Radu to protect Lillian from having *her* face caved in?

Then there was the fact that Radu had neglected to tell her that there was the possibility his brother would want to kill him. Why the hell hadn't he mentioned that sooner? Maybe they should have stayed with one of the Lord Vampires who didn't want to hurt them and attempted to make contact in a more diplomatic manner.

Then again, she remembered how all of them seemed to be afraid of Silas and Razvan. So maybe they would have refused to protect them anyway.

Her worries, at least, made the miles pass quicker, that and the faint sound of Radu singing along to the radio. He really liked ACDC, she'd discovered.

As she crossed the Idaho border, the sky grew more cloudy. Perhaps if it would be overcast enough, Radu would be able to emerge sooner. Taking the first exit into Coeur d'Alene, Lillian blinked as she saw that four out of five of the cars driving down Sherman were '50s and '60s classics that looked brand new. If it weren't for the equally new Dodge ram and the '90s minivan in the other lane, she would have thought she'd driven through some portal back in time. Did this town have some sort of retro thing going on?

At least the sun had gone down, and the cloudy sky was brilliant pink and orange. Radu would be able to get out soon. Turning onto a side street, she saw cars parked nose to bumper at every block. No, there was some sort of festival going on, likely a car show.

Lillian drove down four more blocks before she found a place to park under the shade of a leafy maple tree. Peeking back at the sky, willing it to grow darker, she scrolled through her phone, looking for a hotel.

Everything downtown was full, likely for the festival, along with the fact that she'd recently learned online that Coeur d'Alene was a major tourist town in the summer. Her lips quirked up in an amused smile. She'd bet the local vampires loved that. So much new prey.

Lillian then found a vacancy at the Bennett Bay Inn. Apparently, the regular cabins were taken, so all that was still available were theme suites with hot tubs inside the rooms. Radu would like that. The only suites left were the Victorian room and the Galaxy Room. Lillian called and booked the Galaxy Room. Radu would get a kick out of the black lights and gaudy space-themed decor.

By the time she made her way up a gorgeous lake road and a steep winding hill to the hotel, the sky was dim enough for her to risk pulling the back seat open a sliver. "Do you think you can come out now?"

"Yes," Radu's answer was muffled but coherent. She pulled down the seats and saw that he lay atop the sleeping bag and just had a blanket over him.

Flinging off the blanket, he rolled out onto the folded-down seats and grinned at her, looking disheveled but not very sweaty, considering the situation. Stretching his lithe form as much as he could in the cramped backseat, he sat up slowly, black eyes intent. "My brother is close. I can sense him."

A cold chill rushed up her spine despite the warm summer night. She was not looking forward to this reunion. "Well, um, I got us a room. Did you want to bring in our stuff and make a plan?"

Radu shook his head. "I do not think we have time. I need to feed to be strong enough to face him, and there are too many witnesses here for me to bite the clerk." He gestured to a group of kids shrieking and splashing in the nearby swimming pool that was right in front of the office. "I need to find a human in seclusion or in a crowd...and you should eat soon too. It is past time you have a decent sitting-down meal instead of that junk you eat while driving."

Lillian cast a longing look at the cabins. Then again, with the noise of the playing kids and her stomach growling for a full sit-down meal, maybe it was a better idea to get out, explore the town, and stretch her legs. "There's a car show going on downtown. It's definitely crowded, and I saw some great restaurants down the road. It looks kinda fun. Want to check it out?"

"That sounds like it shall do." Radu slid into the passenger seat before popping open the glove box and pulling out a comb.

Lillian headed into the office to pick up their keys before unbraiding her hair and giving it a quick comb. She looked over to see Radu staring at her hungrily.

"I want you again," he said softly.

Gazing at his rich chocolate hair hanging rakishly over his dark eyes and his lean muscles visible under his white T-shirt, Lillian's belly fluttered. "The feeling's mutual." Shaking off the haze of lust, she fired up the car and backed out of the hotel driveway. "But first, we have things to do."

His face sobered. "Yes, we do."

As they drove back down the hill and along the lake road, some of Lillian's fear eased now that Radu was beside her.

"It is so beautiful here," he said, pointing at the pink and purple reflections on the lake.

She nodded. "A lot more gorgeous than where I grew up."

"Where was that?"

"Arizona. I lived in the part that was all desert, though we had a cabin by Lake Roosevelt for vacations almost as gorgeous as it is here."

"Was the desert like North Dakota?"

She bit back a laugh. It wasn't his fault that they'd only driven through the northern half of the country and he hadn't seen a real desert. "No, it's prettier than North Dakota. Really, it has its own beauty. Maybe someday when we're not hiding from the government, I'll have to show you."

Parking was somewhat easier to find now that dusk had fallen. Lillian and Radu joined hands as they headed down the block to the main street. Sounds of revving engines rumbled in their ears amidst echoing cheers, and the air was redolent with exhaust.

Then, as they reached Sherman Avenue, brightly painted Mustangs, Studebakers, Camaros, and countless other cars were either parked in lots with their hoods open for eager admirers or cruising slowly down the street while crowds cheered.

Glimpses of banners and overhearing snatches of conversations revealed that this event was called the "Car d'Lane." *Cute.*

Beneath the odor of gas, oil, and burnt rubber, Lillian's nose picked up the mouthwatering scent of roasted garlic and herbs, which made her stomach growl again. Unfortunately, it looked like there'd be a long wait before she'd get a meal there. But Radu needed to eat first before his eyes started glowing.

Live music poured from an overflowing bar called the Iron Horse. The people were packed hip to hip. Radu started to head inside, but Lillian shook her head. Too long a wait here too. "Is it alright if I stay out here and look at the cars? I don't want to get lost in that crowd."

For a moment, his jaw tightened as if he would refuse, then he nodded reluctantly. "Stay in front of the building. I will return to you as soon as I'm done feeding. And if you see anyone who even remotely resembles a vampire—in fact, if any stranger approaches you, get in here immediately and find me."

And just like that, the festivity of the evening drained away, reminding her of the danger of their situation. "If anyone looks at me too long, I'll be right behind you," she promised and meant it.

Radu kissed her quickly and pushed his way through the masses into the crowded bar. Lillian hoped all the restaurants in the area weren't as packed. Turning back to the street, she watched the gorgeous cars cruise by.

A dark green muscle car with white racing stripes and an emblem of the Roadrunner from Looney Tunes came down the road behind an old '40's pickup. A stunning woman with black curly hair was behind the wheel, laughing with a gorgeous redhead in the passenger seat. Lillian smiled as they drove by to hoots and whistles. It was good to see that this event wasn't just for men.

Suddenly, Lillian was practically pushed off the sidewalk by a group of staggering drunk frat boys. She opened her mouth to cuss them out, then rethought doing so. It wouldn't be a good idea to draw attention to herself.

Another group of people took up the sidewalk, keeping her from regaining her place. Lillian walked ahead of them before they ran her down. She'd meant to be unobtrusive, but not invisible. The moment a gap in the masses appeared, she took it, grasping the trunk of one of the potted trees for support.

Great. Now she was practically at the edge of the bar and almost at the corner of the street. But she still kept the front door in sight, so when Radu came out, she'd be able to see him. She found herself staring at a bizarre rusty iron sculpture of a giant rabbit wearing a saddle. For the longest time, she stared at it, wondering how the artist wove these strips of metal together…and why in the world he or she chose to put a saddle on the rabbit. This town was odd.

A dark motion flitted from the corner of her eye.

Lillian turned and saw Radu walking around the corner and towards her along the side of the building. He must have exited out the back and was making his way up front to meet her. She waved, but his dark eyes looked past her. She squinted at his white T-shirt. Why did it look different? When she started walking towards him, he still didn't look at her.

She frowned. Was he mad at her for not staying in place? Or had something happened in there?

"Radu?" she said in a more pitiful tone than she intended. "What's wrong?"

He reached out and grasped her upper arms with painful force.

"Ow! What are you doing?" She struggled, her stomach churning with unease. Something wasn't right.

"What did you say?" he demanded sharply. Something about his voice sounded off, but Lillian couldn't quite place it. Her gaze flicked to his jeans. They looked different too, somehow more broken in.

"I only asked what's wrong!" Still, she tried to pull from his grasp. "Radu, please! Let me go. You're hurting me!"

His grip loosened enough to quit hurting but not enough for her to get away. His handsome features twisted in an evil smirk. "That's what I thought you said."

And then it hit her. "You're not Radu," she gasped as her stomach plummeted. "You're Razvan." *Twins*. Radu hadn't told her they were identical. If she saw him again, she would slap him.

"You've heard of me?" The vampire's grin broadened as he led her into the bar. "Splendid. Now let's go find my brother."

Chapter Fifteen

Jayden sighed with relief when Akasha finally found a parking spot for the Roadrunner. Razvan had texted her and said he'd done a drive down Sherman in his Charger and had found parking near the Iron Horse. She texted back that she'd meet him there, and Akasha was going to meet Silas at the beer garden on 6th Street before taking another cruise with him in his Barracuda. Then they'd all meet up at the Powder River Saloon. But right now, all Jayden cared about was finding a bathroom.

Akasha grinned as she locked up her prized Roadrunner. "This was fun, huh?"

Jayden nodded. "Actually, I enjoyed it more than I'd expected."

Because of the intensity of her clairvoyant powers, Jayden had a difficult time coping with large crowds. The merest touch and sometimes proximity to someone triggered visions of a person's past. Only last year, her visions had been so overwhelming that she'd been unable to function properly. She'd been forced to drop out of school, lost her job, and then her home. After a month of living in her car, she'd been ready to kill herself to make the visions stop.

But then Jayden met Razvan, who not only became the love of her life. He'd also introduced her to Silas, another clairvoyant, who taught her to control her powers and shield herself from the psychic projections of others. Now she was able to function around people again.

Still, Car d'Lane was a huge event and extremely crowded, so Jayden had been hesitant. But she owed her friend big-time for accompanying her to try on wedding gowns, shop for flowers and venues, and sample cakes. Things the tomboy mechanic clearly found tedious, no matter how much she had tried to hide it. It was only fair for Jayden to tag along with her best friend to something she loved.

Akasha's violet eyes filled with concern as they walked down Coeur d'Alene Avenue to cross over to Fifth Street. "You haven't had any trouble, have you?"

Jayden shook her head. "No, my shields are stronger than ever, thanks to your husband. I have no idea how I'll ever repay him."

Unbelievably, Akasha waggled her eyebrows. "I think you talking me into buying that lingerie the other week already did the trick."

Jayden laughed, to the agony of her full bladder. "I bet it did! I can't believe you hardly had any!"

"I don't know shit about girly clothes. Beau used to help me with my shopping, but when he and the band moved to Seattle, I only got to go shopping with him when Rage of Angels was in town on tour or between albums. And now…" A cloud fell over her features, dimming her cheer.

Six months ago, the world-famous heavy metal band, Rage of Angels had vanished. Silas had assured Akasha that her friends were safe, and in another world, fulfilling part of the Prophecy. Jayden believed him because she'd seen them there too, in a vision.

But they didn't talk about that much, because it was too weird to wrap their heads around. All that mattered to Akasha was that Silas was convinced they'd return soon. Jayden had a feeling he was holding something back from them, yet she hadn't worked up the courage to confront him about it.

Anyway, she supposed it didn't matter since none of them could do anything but wait until Rage of Angels returned. And to be honest, right now, all Jayden cared about was getting to the bathroom and then seeing Razvan again. A wistful smile tugged at her lips at the thought of the vampire she was going to marry. He'd literally saved her life, helped her fight her inner demons instead of running away from them. And despite his sardonic exterior, he was the kindest, most generous man she'd ever encountered. With the threat of a less than friendly reunion with his twin and impending foretold war hanging over their heads, Jayden couldn't bear being separated from him for long.

"Do you want me to pop in the Horse with you?" Akasha asked when they reached the Beer Garden on Lakeside.

"Nah, I'll be fine. We'll see you at the Powder after the cruise," Jayden said, noting her friend's anticipation to see her man mirrored in her own eyes. That and her friend had been grumbling for a beer for the past two rounds through the cruise route. Jayden wouldn't mind a glass of wine herself. But first, she needed to pee.

Waving goodbye, she jogged the final block and a half to the Iron Horse, willing her shields to hold firm as she pushed her way through the crowd. The place was packed shoulder to shoulder. How the hell was she supposed to find Razvan in this mess? Jayden bit her lip as her bladder gave another twinge. She'd worry about that later.

The line to the bathroom was agonizingly long. Jayden squirmed as she took her place behind several women and scanned the bar. At last, she glimpsed a flash of long, chocolate brown hair. Yes, there he was, crossing the dance floor with a thunderous frown. He must really hate the live band. Not surprising, as Razvan was picky about his music.

Jayden waved, but he didn't seem to see her. Just as she lifted her hand again, the woman behind her tapped her on the shoulder.

"It's your turn, but if you don't go, I will."

"Sorry." Jayden dashed into the bathroom, resolving to find her fiancé when she was done.

Once she emerged from the restroom, her luck turned for the worst. Razvan seemed to have disappeared. For a moment, she was tempted to drop her shields enough to detect the Mark between them but immediately rejected the idea. This place was too chaotic. She searched the bar twice for Razvan, but he was nowhere in sight.

Fine. She'd text him outside and breathe the fresh air as well as keep an eye out for him. Jayden pushed her way out of the crowded bar. After all the noise and people, she looked forward to the much more peaceful Powder River Saloon, even if it *was* smoky.

All of the tables outside were full, so Jayden stepped out on the sidewalk and leaned against one of the sculptures that had recently been added downtown. This one was a big rabbit wearing a saddle. It wasn't the weirdest or ugliest one around, and it was well-crafted, but it was far from her favorite. She liked the one that looked like dandelion puffs the best.

Just as she pulled her phone from her pocket to text Razvan, she saw him pacing up and down the sidewalk, his features drawn with anxiety. He'd been looking for her too.

"Razvan!" She shouted and ran to him.

When she grasped his arm, she sucked in a breath and drew back at the shocked look in his eyes.

"Witch!" he growled in a much thicker accent than she'd heard from him. Seizing her arms, he lowered his face to hers. "Where is Lillian?"

Her shields shattered then, and Jayden's jaw dropped with the realization that this wasn't her fiancé. Razvan's missing twin had come as he'd promised in her vision. "Radu..." she whispered. Trying to control her panic, she forced herself to sound calm. "I don't know who Lillian is."

His eyes narrowed. "Then where is my brother? You know *him*."

For a moment, she debated on lying. In her vision, Radu had seemed angry with Razvan. The last time the brothers had seen each other was when Radu had tried to kill his twin. Then her phone chimed with a familiar notification tone.

Radu's gaze darted down to her purse. "Is that him?"

Before she formed a response, he seized her purse with lightning speed. Taking her phone, he fumbled with the screen as if trying to figure out how to operate it. When his brows drew together, it was clear that he'd read the text.

"He has taken my Lillian." Still holding her arm, he tugged her down the road. "But I have you."

"Wait!" Jayden struggled in his grip. "Razvan was supposed to meet me in that bar. If we just go back, I'm sure we can work this out."

"No. I was just in there." Radu said through clenched teeth. "His message said he just left the bar and is contacting Silas and taking Lillian somewhere secure to decide what to do with her. He wanted you to meet him at Silas's home, but that's not going to happen."

"Why not?" Jayden's worry grew. "Didn't you come here to see him?"

"I did, but not to walk into a trap." Radu scowled. "If he wanted to face me honestly, he would have remained here."

As he continued to lead her down the sidewalk, Jayden tugged against his grip, though it was futile. "Then what are you going to do with me?"

She saw a cop parked across the street and considered yelling for help. Her mouth closed. It was forbidden to bring mortals into vampire issues. Even if Radu cooperated, he'd likely be arrested and then burn to death in a jail cell. Razvan wouldn't thank her for that, and the Elders would kill them all. Their immunity only went so far.

"I do not wish to stand out on the streets like a vagabond. We will go to the motel, send my brother a message, and then all will depend on what he does with Lillian." Abruptly, he stopped in front of the Zipstop and marched to a man who'd just finished gassing up his SUV.

Capturing the man's gaze in the way she'd seen Razvan do when he fed, Radu said softly, "You will take us to the Bennett Bay Inn."

The Bennett Bay Inn? Jayden blinked. She and Razvan had stayed there during Memorial Weekend, along with Akasha and Silas. Razvan had loved having a hot tub in their suite and now wanted to install one in the warehouse in Spokane where they lived.

As the mesmerized man drove down Coeur d'Alene Lake Drive, she rode beside Radu quietly in the back, hands bunched into fists in her lap in an effort to resist reaching for her phone and calling Razvan. Radu stared at her the whole ride, eyes narrowed in accusation as if all this was her fault.

When the driver reached their destination, Radu leaned forward, bit his neck, and drank deeply. After healing the wound, he spoke a soft command. "You will return to the gas station and forget this drive."

The man nodded and drove away like a zombie. Jayden shivered. He was even better at that hypnotism trick than Razvan. Radu pulled a key card from the pocket of the same brand of jeans his twin wore and opened one of the cabins.

He stopped so suddenly that Jayden crashed into his back. "What is this?"

Jayden scooted around him as far as his grip allowed and glanced at the glowing stars and outer-space decor. "It's the Galaxy Suite. Did you not see it before you guys booked it?"

"No, we went down to eat and left our bags in the car." The corner of his mouth twitched upwards with a wistful smile as he looked at the hot tub. "She chose this for me."

From the intense longing in his eyes, it was clear that he was head over heels for this woman. Jayden would bet money that Lillian was the strawberry blonde that she'd seen in her vision. At that time, the woman had been locked in a cage, a bite mark visible on her neck. Clearly, things had changed between her and Radu since then.

"Is Lillian another vampire?" Jayden ventured after he closed the door behind them. Perhaps Radu had Changed her already.

"No. She's a scientist," he answered tightly before pointing at a chair beside the bed. "Sit."

A scientist? Jayden bit the insides of her cheeks as she plunked down. Did he have any idea how dangerous it was for a vampire to associate with that sort? The only thing worse would be a government agent or a reporter. But Jayden held her tongue for the time being. No sense in pissing him off by asking him if he knew what he was doing. Besides, there were more urgent matters at the moment.

Although she'd been holding her shields thick and tight all day, Jayden dropped them for a fraction of a second.

Radu stood in the doorway of his lover's cottage, agony and fury roiling within at the sight of Razvan holding Uta's dead body, her blue eyes staring sightlessly at the ceiling, her long blonde hair sweeping the floor. A red haze of rage tinged his vision as he fought his brother with fists and fangs.

Fleeing the dawn and awakening to the castle in flames, his mother and father screaming. Radu tried to save them, but the rays of sunlight scorched him through the holes in the stone walls hewn by village masons. Flames licked at him from other paths. His mother's screams dying away, smoke filling his lungs until—

"Get out of my mind, witch!" Radu roared, slamming Jayden back into awareness.

"I'm sorry, I can't always control it," she answered honestly, even though this time she'd intentionally probed him to see if he meant to kill her or Razvan. But Radu's pain and anger from his past were too intense to read his present intentions.

"What now?" she asked before he turned that rage on her.

Instead of replying, he took out her phone and fumbled again with the buttons. Since the phone chimed back seconds later, she gathered he'd texted Razvan. Jayden's muscles quivered with the urge to dive for her phone.

Radu scowled at the screen, making a shiver run down her spine. Razvan looked just like that when something had displeased him. Even the stiff set of his shoulders was identical. Although she'd known Razvan had a twin, seeing it in person was unnerving.

"What did he say?" she asked, desperate to break this awkward silence.

"He refuses to meet here because of the humans. He wants us to meet him at the lord's home." The scowl deepened as his accent thickened. "Does he think me so stupid as to walk into a trap?"

Jayden shook her head, even though she wasn't sure whether or not Razvan was planning exactly that. "He is your brother. He knows you better than anyone."

"Hmmph." He cast her a glare that would have broken her heart if it had come from Razvan before bending back down to the phone, texting awkwardly once more.

Her gaze traveled the gaudy space-themed room in bemused disbelief.

Radu glared at the redheaded witch sitting primly next to the bed that Lillian was supposed to be in. She looked back at him with no fear. Why wasn't she afraid? What plot had Razvan and the Lord of Coeur d'Alene concocted? What would they do with Lillian?

Again the memory of Uta dead in Razvan's grip slapped him in the face. If Razvan had so much as bruised Lillian, he'd kill him.

Radu's fists clenched in impotent rage. Why in the name of heaven had he not insisted on bringing Lillian in that bar with him? What idiocy had possessed him to let her out of his sight? And what had his brother and the red-haired witch been doing so close by? He cast the witch another glare. "Have you and Razvan been tracking us this whole time?"

The woman shook her head. "I only traced you to your family castle."

"Why didn't Razvan come to me there?"

"Because he—"

The phone made another sound, longer than the last chime, playing a song.

The witch's eyes widened, and she gave him an expectant look.

It was a phone call, he realized, remembering that one could speak into these phones, as well as send written messages. Swiping the "accept call" circle on the phone, he put it to his ear. "Brother—"

"I am not your brother." A voice cut off his words. "I am the Lord of this City and not only are you trespassing, you have also taken one of those who are under *my* protection."

Radu bared his fangs, his suspicion of a trap rising. "Silas."

"Ye've heard of me." The lord vampire's accent was lyrical like the Lord of Dublin's, but held a rougher flavor...and a far more forbidding tone. "Then you should be aware that if you do not present yourself to my home in twenty minutes and talk with your brother—who has been looking for you for a very long time, I might add—and request permission to guest in my territory, I and mine will have no choice but to surround the hotel and take you by force."

"Do that, and I will snap your witch's neck." He smirked as that drew a flicker of fear from the witch's green eyes. "Just as Razvan did to the woman I loved."

"You will do no such thing," Silas said mildly. "Not when we have your current..." he paused as if to think of the right word, "paramour."

The ball of ice Radu's gut spread to his chest. "How do I know she is unharmed?"

Suddenly, Lillian's voice spoke in his ear. "I'm okay, Radu." Just as abruptly, Silas's voice came back on the line. "See, we only want to talk. Lillian—" Radu gnashed his fangs to hear a strange vampire speak her name— "says she has something to tell me, but she refuses to say what it is unless she is returned safely to you. We can make her tell us." Radu growled in warning as Silas continued. "But I would much rather handle this civilly. And Razvan wishes for Jayden to be safely returned to him, so—"

There was a clattering sound, and then Radu heard his brother's voice growl, "Put Jayden on the phone, Brother. We let your woman assure you she is unharmed. I *will* have the same."

Gooseflesh rose all over Radu's skin at the sound of his twin's voice. He hadn't heard it in seven centuries. He sounded the same in many ways, it was the sound of Radu's own voice after all, and yet Razvan's accent had faded. Become more...American.

Part of him longed to tell Razvan how much he had missed him, and how sorry he was. The other part of him wanted to rage at him for killing Uta. Instead, he crossed the room and pressed the phone to the witch's ear.

"Razvan?" Jayden's voice trembled with longing. "He didn't hurt me, he—"

Radu jerked the phone away and put it back to his ear. "Is there somewhere neutral we can meet?"

Hushed voices echoed in his ear before Silas's voice came on. "We can meet in the mountains. Wait thirty minutes, and then fly northeast until you see a campfire. But be certain it is us before landing."

"I will be able to tell. I Marked Lillian." If only he was not too overwhelmed to sense it when she had first disappeared. But he sensed her now. Her essence pulsed to the north. Fairly close. "Will you feed her before you go?" Humiliation roiled within to be asking for a boon from his brother's ally, but there was nothing to be done about it. Lillian had been hungry when he'd left her to hunt.

"Of course we will, providing that you treat Jayden with equal care."

"Agreed," he bit out and slammed his thumb on the "end call" icon.

After he placed Jayden's phone in his pocket, something else occurred to Radu. Why hadn't Lillian told Silas who she was? Would it have helped her cause, or did she have reason to believe it would place her in danger?

Whatever reason she had, Radu would keep silent for her sake. Now he had to focus on holding his part of the bargain with Silas to ensure Lillian's safety. He turned to Jayden. "Are you hungry?"

Jayden gave him a startled look before shaking her head. "No, but I am thirsty."

He gave her a curt nod and filled a plastic cup with water. After he handed it to her, he sat back down in the chair to wait for the longest half hour of his life.

Waiting to see his brother whom he'd hidden from for seven hundred years. Waiting to see if Lillian was truly unharmed.

Chapter Sixteen

Lillian sat between Akasha and Razvan in a cramped Toyota pickup that smelled like oil and grease. A logo that read "Resurrection Wrenches" was emblazoned on the sides.

Akasha darted curious glances at her, tinged with hostility. Ahead of her, Silas McNaught drove a sleek black 1968 Barracuda convertible up a winding mountain road. They'd taken two cars because they expected to be carrying two more people down the mountain. But as prisoners or guests, Lillian didn't know.

Closing her eyes, Lillian leaned back in the seat, grateful at least to no longer be driving. Memories of how she'd gotten into this crazy situation washed through her mind.

Razvan had at first dragged her into the Iron Horse, and they'd searched the crowded bar to no avail before Razvan gave up. Lillian had wanted to keep looking, desperate with hope to see Radu and resolve all of this, but Razvan had made her get into his '67 Dodge Charger and driven her to a modern castle on top of a hill, rapidly texting while handling the wheel. She'd been convinced he'd roll them off the hill at any minute, especially when his phone buzzed with a reply. Whatever it was made him slam his brakes and curse in Romanian.

Lillian had shivered. He sounded exactly like Radu when speaking their mother tongue.

Before they made it to the front door, two other classic cars pulled up behind Razvan's. One of them was the dark green Roadrunner Lillian had seen in the car show. That was why she and Radu had encountered these people so quickly. They'd been part of the damn car show.

"My brother has taken Jayden," Razvan told the black-haired vampire who emerged from the Barracuda. "And I've taken his woman."

Lillian stiffened. That must have been the text that Razvan received on his way to the house. Did that mean that Razvan had taken her first? Either way, Radu now had Razvan's fiancé while she was stuck here. Now they were even. Hopefully, that meant they'd work out a peaceful swap.

"I see," the vampire said with a slight Scottish accent. Pale green eyes flicked over her with curiosity before he turned back to Razvan. "And you hope to negotiate a trade?"

Razvan nodded. "I asked him to meet me here, but he refuses, thinking we intend to trap him."

"Of course he thinks it's a trap!" Lillian wouldn't bite her tongue any longer. "You guys killed the last vampire who moved into this area, along with all of her people." She whirled on Razvan. "And you—"

She broke off as the woman who'd driven the Roadrunner marched up to her, purple eyes blazing with fury. It had to be Akasha. "The Lord of Post Falls was psycho! She murdered my mentor and tried to kill Jayden. Damn right, we killed her."

The vampire grasped her shoulder. "Easy, Akasha. It sounds as if this woman heard the news from another Lord Vampire. They would spin the truth in such a way." He extended his other hand to Lillian and introduced himself, even though she'd already guessed who he was. "I am Silas McNaught, Lord of Coeur d'Alene. And who are you?"

"Lillian." She wasn't about to tell them her last name. Not when she was standing before the woman who her father had experimented on without her consent. The woman whose eggs he'd used to create a baby with Lillian's help. True, that would have to come out soon, but not until she had Radu at her back. "I came with Radu to find Razvan, and there are things I need to tell you and your wife, but I won't say anything until you return me to Radu. Besides, Razvan was the one who—"

Silas raised a brow and interrupted. "I could *make* you tell me."

Lillian sucked in a breath and tried to step back, but Razvan held her firm.

"But we will play nice for now, since Razvan also wants his fiancé back," Silas said. "Shall we go inside and work out a compromise?"

Razvan jerked her into the castle, which looked like a modern mansion on the inside, where they proceeded to argue with Radu over the phone.

Jayden must have been the redhead who'd been riding with Akasha. Razvan's fiancé. Lillian remembered the rage in Radu's eyes when he'd spoken about her. *He should not have a love, not after he killed mine.*

A cold shiver snaked up her spine. What if Radu did something to Jayden out of revenge? Where would that leave Lillian?

She shook her head. No, even when Lillian had been an enemy trying to kill him, Radu hadn't harmed her, aside from biting her. She refused to believe that he would be able to bring himself to kill an innocent woman.

Willing herself to stay calm, she turned her attention back to the argument.

"He cannot spell very well," Razvan grumbled as he glared at Radu's response.

Irritation once more loosened Lillian's lips. "That's because he's just learning to read English! Not to mention the fact that he only learned about phones less than three weeks ago. He hasn't had time to learn everything."

To her surprise, Razvan's features softened into abject grief. "I'd forgotten. I apologize."

Silas heaved a sigh, took the phone from Razvan, and called Radu.

Throughout the whole exchange, Akasha paced through the dining room, smoking a cigarette and drinking a beer. Lillian's gaze shifted between her and Silas, recognizing which features Kiara had inherited. Now that the moment had come, how was she going to tell these two that they were parents?

Her spit dried in her mouth at the thought.

"What the hell are you looking at?" Akasha demanded.

"Nothing." Lillian forced her gaze back to Silas's conversation.

After a long, tense moment, Silas nodded in agreement to whatever Radu said and directed him to meet them in the mountains. He then turned to Lillian. "You will ride with Akasha and Razvan and follow me. We will stop for food on the way."

Lillian's stomach churned at the thought of food. Her appetite had fled the moment she'd encountered Razvan. But she nodded anyway, eager to be returned to Radu. Then they piled into the pickup for yet another road trip. Lillian would be happy to have a break from all vehicles.

Akasha stopped at a place called Zip's and ordered them burgers and fries and extra napkins. Lillian thanked her and nibbled on fries while Akasha practically inhaled her burger. Fighting back her stomach's protests, Lillian managed to eat half of her food while yearning for the nice sit-down dinner she'd anticipated with Radu. Could he taste what she ate now, or was he too far away?

A pang of longing speared her heart so sharply that it was difficult to breathe. When she'd been with Radu, Lillian didn't feel awkward and undesirable. He never made her feel like an object or like she had to hide her intelligence. He made her feel safe, valued, and wanted. She missed his childlike curiosity, his unabashed wonder at the world that made her take a second look at things she used to take for granted.

Fists bunched in her lap, she looked at the vampire who was identical to Radu on the surface, yet so different on the inside.

"You're not going to kill him, are you?" she asked quietly.

His black eyes, so like Radu's yet so full of pain and worry, studied her for an eternity before he replied. "I don't wish to, but if he forces my hand..." He shook his head and sighed.

"He thought you were searching for him to kill him."

Razvan shook his head so rapidly that he had to be sincere. "No. He's my brother. It would be like killing a part of myself." His brows drew together. "Not that I don't want to pummel him half to death, though."

"I hope you do," Akasha said from the front. "Your asshole brother abducted my best friend! I am sick and tired of my friends vanishing." Before Lillian could protest that she was pretty sure Razvan had abducted her first, Akasha continued. "Not to mention the fact that he totally ruined my drinking night. The guys at the pub are probably worried that I wrecked the Pretty Hate Machine."

Lillian frowned. Akasha did not strike her as the motherly type. Maybe she shouldn't say anything about the baby. No, she had to tell them. And pray they didn't kill her for playing a part in the deception.

Razvan chuckled. "Your compatriots will forgive you, I'm sure. And how do you know my brother is an asshole? You haven't met him yet."

"Because *you're* an asshole." Akasha grinned at him before turning her attention back to the road.

Ignoring the insult, Razvan's dark eyes narrowed on Lillian. "And just how *did* you find my brother and end up accompanying him here? With your American accent, you're clearly not from Romania, where Jayden tells me he's been hiding all these centuries, right under my nose."

Unable to help herself, Lillian glanced at Akasha, who was thankfully watching the road as they ascended higher up the mountain. Razvan followed her gaze. "I think you should clear things up with your brother before I explain." She folded her arms across her chest, refusing to say anything more.

Razvan's lips curled in a sardonic smile as he steepled his fingers together. "I look forward to it. But for now..." He jerked her purse out of her lap. "I think I'll look for clues."

Lillian lunged for her purse, but the vampire held up a hand in warning as his other hand withdrew her wallet. He studied her passport before withdrawing her driver's license and chuckling. "Lily Vâlcu? I wager that is fake. I assume my brother is also the proud owner of an Idaho driver's license?"

She nodded. "His says Radu Vâlcu."

"While I understand him needing to fabricate identification to enter the country, why do you? You're human. You should already have identification." That intent gaze held her frozen in her seat. "Unless you're a criminal or have some reason to hide your identity."

"I'm *not* a criminal," she answered his first speculation honestly.

His lips curved in a knowing smile. "But you do have something to hide."

"Later," she said through clenched teeth.

"Very well," he said in a silken voice threaded with steel. "But you cannot fault me for being curious."

At last, Silas's car turned down a narrow road that was even darker due to the canopy of trees. Akasha's truck followed behind, jolting on the uneven dirt and rock.

Lillian caught her breath as they parked in a clearing, and Razvan led her out of the car. The summer night air had cooled, making her regret choosing a light summer dress. Rubbing her upper arms, she followed Razvan and the others as they gathered firewood and lit a blaze. Akasha hefted a log that should have taken three lumberjacks to carry, then grabbed an ax from the bed of her pickup.

As Akasha attacked the log with impressive speed, Lillian stepped towards the warmth of the growing fire and watched the skies for signs of Radu.

Silas met Razvan's gaze as he fed more kindling to the blaze. A sword hilt protruded from a sheath on his back, making Lillian nervous. "Are you alright, Nicolae?"

Razvan nodded. "I'll be better when Jayden is back in my arms." He looked up at the moon, features drawn and pensive. "It's been seven hundred years since I've seen him. I can hardly believe this night has come." His voice darkened with bitterness. "How dare he hide from me so long only to barge in and steal my woman?"

Lillian stood, furious. "You took me first!"

Silas shot a glare at Razvan. "Is that true?"

Instead of replying, Razvan looked up at the sky.

Suddenly, she felt Radu's presence like a caress before a dark shadow obscured the firelight. He landed twenty feet away, a gorgeous redhead in his arms. Lillian fought back a surge of jealousy as Razvan growled the same sentiment.

Akasha quit hacking up firewood and crossed the camp to join her husband.

"Lillian," Radu said, gripping the other woman's shoulder, so it was impossible to flee. "Are you unharmed?"

"Yes. They fed me on the way too." She wished she could run to him right now.

Razvan held Lillian's upper arm and looked at his fiancé. "Jayden?"

The redhead's gaze flicked over Lillian before meeting Razvan's eyes. "I'm okay. He offered me food, but I wasn't hungry."

"Enough of this," Radu growled. "Give me Lillian, and I will return your bride to be."

"Are you going to try to kill me after?" Razvan asked wryly.

"That depends," Radu answered stiffly.

Akasha heaved a sigh and slapped the handle of the ax against her palm. "Oh, for fuck's sake, quit bullshitting and make the trade already!"

Radu raised a brow at her but released Jayden the minute Razvan let go of Lillian's arm. Lillian met Jayden halfway and impulsively held out her hand. "I'm Lillian."

The redhead shook her hand with a nervous laugh. "Jayden."

For a moment, they paused, regarding one another with wary curiosity.

"Do you really think they'll kill each other?" Lillian asked.

Jayden's brows drew together with worry. "No, but..." she shook her head. "They better not."

Before they had time to speak further, both were seized by each twin and pulled away. Radu thrust Lillian behind him, and Razvan did the same with Jayden.

As the two brothers closed the distance separating them, Silas and Akasha watched from the fire, not interfering.

Razvan threw the first punch. "That's for hiding from me for seven cursed centuries."

Radu flew backward with the force of the blow but recovered his stance before going down. In a blur, his fist connected with Razvan's jaw. "That is for killing Uta." He swung again. "And that is for taking Lillian."

"Well, you took Jayden!" Razvan snarled, punching his brother in the gut.

"You took Lillian first!" Radu lunged forward, fangs bared.

A silver blur arced between them, making both leap back. "That is enough!" Silas roared, wielding his sword. His Scottish accent went thick with his ire. "Ye both said ye wished tae talk, so sit doon and *talk*, for God's sake!"

The twins glared at each other, shoulders heaving with angry breaths.

Silas turned to Radu. "Five hundred years ago, Razvan entreated me to search for you. I did eventually discern where you were, but I did not tell him because I knew you didn't want to be found."

Radu cast Silas a sideways glare, but that was nothing compared to the virulent snarl that trickled from Razvan's throat.

Jayden stepped closer behind Razvan and addressed Radu. "When I searched for you, I saw Razvan's memories. He didn't mean to kill Uta. It was an accident."

Radu flinched but held his brother's gaze. Lillian wished she could come forward and contribute to the effort of calming the enraged twins, but her throat was too dry and tight to speak.

"What took you so long to stop them?" Akasha whispered to Silas, loud enough for everyone to hear.

"I had to let them get a few punches in," he told her in a patient tone. "My sisters thrived on their scuffles. And my uncles were even worse than these two." Pain slashed across his features, visible in the flickering firelight.

Lillian's chest tightened in sympathy for this vampire who clearly still missed his mortal family after countless centuries.

Razvan and Radu's glowing gazes intensified. They sidestepped the sword and lunged for each other again.

And hugged.

Lillian stumbled on a rock before realizing she'd been rushing forward to try to stop them from killing each other. Now she froze, slack-jawed at this about-face. Jayden met her gaze across the clearing with equal astonishment in her green eyes.

The brothers continued to embrace in silence, their twin bond rendering words unnecessary. A lump formed in Lillian's throat when the brothers parted and Radu turned to face her. A tear ran down his cheek, glistening in the firelight.

Silas sat by the fire beside his wife. His sword lay across his lap, thankfully not needed. "Now, are ye both ready tae talk sense?"

Side by side, the twins walked to the fire, sitting on one of the logs that Akasha had dragged over. Lillian and Jayden followed, each taking her place next to the correct brother this time.

As Radu and Razvan faced each other, Lillian hoped they'd resolve everything without further violence…or kidnappings.

She also hoped they took their time.

Because then it would be her turn to talk.

Chapter Seventeen

Radu stared at his brother, that face identical to his own, yet with eyes so different. In fact, they resembled each other more than ever since Razvan had shaved. Radu started to wonder why he'd done that. Razvan had always been fond of his beard. Then his speculation halted in a wave of hope and relief just to be standing before his twin at last. For seven hundred years, he'd felt like a vital organ had been torn from him. Now the key to being whole again was in his grasp.

McNaught's wife broke the agonizing silence, purple eyes narrowed on Razvan. "Did you really take Radu's girlfriend first?"

"Yes," Razvan answered, without breaking Radu's gaze. "I thought he came here to kill Jayden out of vengeance for Uta. But I did try to find him at the bar first."

"Not very hard," Lillian grumbled.

A low growl trickled from Radu's throat at the memory of Lillian being taken from him.

"You *ass*!" Akasha said before Radu was able to speak. "A lot of this drama could have been avoided if you'd just talked to him first, you know, like a grownup." As Radu nodded, Silas's bride turned an annoyed gaze on him. "And you. Why did you make things worse by abducting Jayden? She could have called Razvan, and you could have settled things easier."

"You three are infamous for killing an entire coven of vampires," Radu said drily. "Forgive me if I wanted a measure of, what do you call it? Insurance."

"*They* started the war first," Akasha countered as she placed another log on the fire. "And we didn't kill all of them. We took some prisoners."

"That's enough, lass." Silas set his sword aside and pulled his wife in his arms. "Let the brothers resolve this on their own."

Radu inclined his head in silent thanks and respect. Despite all the fearsome rumors about the Lord of Coeur d'Alene, Silas seemed to be a just and practical ruler. Against his original judgment, he was already beginning to trust him.

Razvan met his gaze, the pain in his voice spearing his heart. "Why did you hide from me, Radu?"

The fire popped and crackled, emphasizing the tense silence as Radu struggled to speak.

"It was all my fault that they died." He didn't need to specify who *they* were. "If I hadn't told Uta what we were, she never would have incited the villagers. I tried to save them!" His voice cracked, and he dug his nails into his palms to maintain composure. "I ran into the castle, but Mother and Father's chamber was engulfed in flame, and I couldn't…I couldn't…" He choked on the lump in his throat. "You must have wanted to kill me."

Razvan shook his head. "Never. You are my brother and all I had left in the world. To lose you tore a hole in my heart." His eyes glinted with moisture. "Though to find out that you were intentionally hiding from me made me want to thrash you. First, I thought you'd perished with Mother and Father, then I thought you'd been injured to the point of incapacitation or that you were captured."

"I couldn't bear to face you." Radu's fists swiped away his own tears. "I couldn't bear to face myself."

"I am sorry about Uta," Razvan said quietly. "It truly was an accident. When she laughed in my face as she told me about the mob that would attack the castle, I was struck blind with rage. But I didn't mean to kill her. I only wanted her to call them off. And if she wouldn't, she was yours to deal with."

"When I saw her dead in your arms, I wanted to kill you." Radu bent and found his own stick to poke at the fire. "Then when I learned what she had done, I was furious because I wanted to kill her myself. I'm sorry I was such a fool. If it were not for me, our parents would still be alive."

"Stop saying that!" Razvan seized Radu's shoulders and pulled him close until they were face to face. "If it weren't for Father's arrogance and overconfidence in his power, the villagers wouldn't have listened to Uta in the first place. Even then, from what I learned, the attack was likely already planned."

Selfish as it was, Radu grasped at the slightest thread of absolution. "What do you mean?"

"For centuries before we were born, Alexandru lived openly among the people. He made them pay him tribute. And when the Elders commanded all vampires to live in secrecy, he should have taken us all far away for at least a century before returning home. Aside from a brief tour of the country, he instead kept us in the same village that fostered legends of his own making. Even the lowliest of humans would have deduced the truth." Razvan's voice was thick with scorn for the vampire they'd both adored. Disdain for their father burned in his black eyes as he looked at Radu. "In fact, it is possible that if it weren't for us fighting after the incident with Uta, we might have perished as well." He shrugged. "So you may have saved us. Either way, I can't tell you to let go of all your guilt, but I can tell you that I do not blame you for something you did not intend to do. Did you tell your lover or those villagers to storm the castle with masons and torches?"

"No, but—"

Razvan held up a hand. "Then you did not kill our parents. Besides, Father was the *Voivode*. It was his duty to look after the villagers...his people. If he'd been vigilant as he had been of old, then our castle never would have been attacked. But he'd grown lazy and complacent."

For the longest time, Radu gaped slack-jawed at his brother. For centuries, he'd thought Razvan hated him. For centuries, Radu had hated himself, unable to face the world, repeating apologies to their parents every night until the words took on a meaningless chant.

Yet all this time, Razvan had placed the blame on their father. And even as guilt curdled in his gut for thinking ill of the vampire who'd raised them, Radu saw reason in his brother's words. Alexandru *had* spent more time visiting other Lord Vampires and paying court to the Elders than keeping an eye on the villagers. In fact, he'd ceased holding court a hundred years before the mob attacked. Instead, he allowed a mortal noble to rule over the village. *"What do I care about human affairs?"* he'd sneered when Radu had asked him about it.

Taking a deep breath before he drowned in memories, Radu met Razvan's gaze. "Do you forgive me then?"

"For our parents? There is nothing to forgive." Razvan's brows drew together. "For spending centuries in hiding while I searched the world for you, not knowing whether you were alive or dead? That will take some time." He looked down and dragged his boots over the dirt and pine needles on the ground. "Do you forgive me for killing Uta?"

Radu nodded. "But not for taking Lillian." He wrapped his arm around her shoulders, pulling her against him, savoring her warmth. "We were already looking for you, and when I came upon your woman, I was going to have her lead me to you if you hadn't already taken mine."

"Ass," Akasha murmured again across the fire, glaring at Razvan.

Radu smiled. This woman may be abnormal and frightening in her strength, but he was already beginning to like her. He met Silas's gaze. "I apologize for invading your land and taking one of your people. I had meant to present myself to you immediately, but my brother's actions caused me to overreact." Reaching in his pocket, he withdrew a thick sheet of paper. "I do not have a Lord or a territory to call my own, but here are writs of passage signed by every Lord Vampire whose territory we passed through on our journey here."

Silas rose from the log and took the paper. His eyes widened as he scanned through the list. "You drove here all the way from Maine?"

Radu and Lillian both nodded.

"Why?" Silas, Akasha, and Razvan asked simultaneously.

"Plane tickets are expensive," Lillian said to her sandals.

Silas frowned at her. "Not as expensive as the cost of fuel to drive here, much less food and lodging." The vampire's voice lowered with command. "Try again, lass."

She heaved a sigh and pressed closer to Radu. He tightened his grip on her shoulder. "I didn't feel comfortable passing through airport security again."

"Or being indebted to more than the two Lord Vampires we already owe," Radu offered. That much was not only reasonable, it was also the truth.

Akasha ignored him and continued to peer at Lillian with suspicion. "You have a fake ID, and you drove across the United States to avoid security? You're hiding from the authorities, aren't you?"

Lillian twirled a lock of her hair around her finger and nodded.

"*Which* authorities?" Akasha asked.

Radu eyed Silas curiously, wondering if he'd object to his woman doing the questioning. His mother would have never presumed to interfere when his father held an audience. Was Akasha's vocal involvement another sign of these new times, or did she and Silas rule this city jointly?

Lillian's answer was so soft it was nearly a whisper. "The AIU."

"Why? Are you a psychic or something?"

She shook her head. "No. I was one of their agents."

Akasha charged to her, grasping her upper arms with painful pressure. "You're with the fucking AIU?"

"Not anymore."

Slowly, she released her. "Are they after Silas or me? Is that what you're here to tell us?"

Lillian shook her head rapidly, rubbing her arms. "No. You're not even in their databases." Dad had made sure of that.

Silas pocketed Radu's writ of passage and crossed his arms over his broad chest. "All the same, *does* the AIU have something to do with what you said you came here to tell me?"

"Yes." A fine tremble had overtaken her body. She was so not ready for this.

Radu stroked her shoulder. "Would it be permissible for Lillian's news to wait until tomorrow? She is exhausted from driving and hasn't had a decent meal in days. I promise we will come to you right after nightfall."

"No," Akasha said. "The faster you talk, the faster you leave."

Silas sighed. "Look at the lass." He pointed at Lillian. "She's clearly exhausted from her ordeal."

Lillian warred between relief at his consideration and embarrassment that her weariness was that obvious. Akasha met her gaze and stared pointedly at her for the longest time.

Finally, she shrugged. "Fine."

Silas turned back to Radu and nodded. "See that you keep your word, else I will come looking for you. We'll put out the fire, and I'll take you to your car."

This time, Razvan opted to ride with them in Silas's car while Jayden rode with Akasha down the mountain. A twinge of happiness flowed through Radu at the chance to spend a few more minutes in his brother's company.

He held Lillian's hand as she looked out the window in silence, either because she was hesitant to talk to Silas or because she wanted to give him time with Razvan.

There was so much to be said, but right now, they didn't need to speak. For the moment, Radu was content to merely be in his brother's presence. The twin bond pulsed between them as if they'd never been separated.

Even then, Radu wasn't so big a fool as to believe that their conflicts had vanished.

But tonight, all of that could wait.

When Silas made it down the mountain, Lillian directed him to her car. After he parked behind the old Honda, he eyed her through the rearview mirror. "I very much anticipate hearing what you will tell me." His voice held an implicit warning that she better hold to her promise to give him her news tomorrow…or else.

Razvan craned his neck to smile back at her. "I am looking forward to it too." His gaze flicked to Radu. "Silas and I have a penchant for interesting females. I am pleased to see that they seem to hold the same fascination for you. Until tomorrow, Brother."

In tandem, they reached out and clasped each other's hands, both becoming whole for an interminable moment.

When he got in Lillian's car, he heard her stomach growl. "I thought you said they fed you."

"They did, but I was too nervous to eat much."

Radu snarled in remembrance of the panic he'd experienced during her abduction. Damn Razvan. How was it possible to loathe and love someone at the same time? Perhaps Lord McNaught had been right when he'd said such was common with family. "We will have a meal before we return to the hotel."

As it was after midnight, all the downtown restaurants were closed. But eventually, they found a twenty-four-hour diner in the town. Lillian devoured a chicken fried steak and mashed potatoes as Radu closed his eyes and tasted the rich flavors. Experiences such as this were his favorite effect of Marking her. He found his own meal in the parking lot.

"What was it like, seeing your brother again?" Lillian asked as they left the restaurant. "And why didn't you tell me you were twins? I thought he was you when he came out from behind that bar."

"I thought I had..." He foundered, now only remembering referring to Razvan as his brother. "If I omitted that information, I apologize. As for your first question, I confess that seeing him was different than what I'd expected. In some ways, I felt like we were never apart. Yet, at the same time, we are both different men. We both speak a new language, and his accent is more American than mine."

Lillian nodded as she watched the road. "That was my first clue that he wasn't you."

They parked at the hotel and brought their bags into their room. Lillian kicked off her sandals and flopped in the chair, where Razvan's woman had sat glaring at him earlier. Lillian's presence seemed to right a great wrong.

He peered at the stars and planets decorating the walls. "This room is interesting."

"Yeah, they have theme suites. I got the Galaxy Room because since I introduced you to science, I may as well expose you to science fiction." She peered at him shyly beneath her gold lashes. "Do you like it?"

"I think I do." And though a tendril of humiliation for his ignorance slithered through him, he asked, "What is science fiction?"

She grinned and stripped off her dress. "I'll tell you later. Right now, I'm dying to go for a swim before the sun comes up. I think we have about three hours left before we're cooped up in the room again."

Radu's mouth went dry as his gaze devoured her lithe body. As he reached for her, she donned her bathing suit and tossed him his swimming trunks. As they swam, Radu noticed that she seemed pensive and nervous. After her fifteenth lap around the pool, he climbed out and sat on the edge, looking up at the stars.

"You're afraid to tell Silas and Akasha about their baby," he said quietly.

"Terrified," she replied before splashing him.

"They seemed reasonable," he offered. Well, McNaught did, anyway. "And Razvan is the one who Changed Silas. I'm sure he will keep his youngling from harming you if need be. After all, you brought me to him. But I do not think they will hurt you. Not when they will need you to help them retrieve their daughter."

"A daughter who was brought into the world without their knowledge and consent," Lillian said bitterly. "A daughter who was created from Akasha being held captive and experimented on by my father. A daughter who he gave to strangers instead of returning her to her parents." She sighed and pushed back from the edge of the pool to float on her back. "They'll hate me."

Radu thought about what his brother had told him. "Razvan blamed my father for the attack on our home, not me." He himself could not quite accept his absolution. "Silas and Akasha should not hold you at fault for what your father did. You yourself said that creating the child was his idea. And I imagine he gave you little choice in helping him." He slipped back in the water and took her in his arms. "You're shivering. Let's go inside and warm up in the hot tub. Thank you for choosing a room with one." Though of all the hotels they'd stayed at, none of the hot tubs compared with the warm spring near his family castle.

"Are you sure?" she asked. "You should be able to be out another hour or two."

"We need time to cover the windows, and you need to be warm." Lifting her, he carried her out of the pool and back into the eccentric room.

Lillian sank into the hot tub with a blissful sigh that made his cock twitch with arousal. Radu had always had a penchant for beautiful women, but none had excited as much as this one. Tamping down his desire, he instead brought out the sleeping bags and blankets for the windows. There weren't many. Yet another reason to approve Lillian's selection of this room. After he covered the door, he joined Lillian in the tub, gratified at the hungry way she stared at his bare chest.

The steaming water was paradise after the cold swim in the pool, both healing balms against his ordeal of being shut in the blazing hot trunk of the car yesterday. Seeing that worried, brooding look return to Lillian's eyes, Radu attempted a distraction. "You were going to tell me about science fiction."

She smiled and regaled him with tales of ships flying through space to other planets and sagas called Star Trek, Star Wars, and Dune. "Of course, we haven't found life on other planets yet, but NASA— that's the National Aeronautics and Space Administration— keeps trying.

"Wait, are you saying that people really do go up in space?"

She nodded and began to talk about the first rocketships, the moon landing, and other unfathomable achievements. Radu shook his head. Would he ever fit in this new, advanced world? And how could he hope for Lillian to accept him, backward and ignorant as he was?

Radu silenced her with a kiss, sliding her bathing suit off her slick, damp flesh.

At least there was one way they fit together.

Chapter Eighteen

Akasha paced in the living room, smoke trailing behind her like exhaust as she glanced at the door. Silas sat on the couch, polishing one of his swords. She doubted Radu or Lillian would miss the not-so-subtle warning.

Razvan perched awkwardly in the recliner, puffing on his pipe, and looking ready to jump up to answer the door at any second. Watching him with his twin brother last night had been so surreal. Akasha had grown dizzy watching the identical vampires go from beating the crap out of each other to hugging and apologizing.

Even she was unable to hold back tears at the emotional reunion. Razvan's centuries-long pain of missing his brother had been a gaping wound that was apparent to anyone who knew him for more than a day.

Still, the issues between the brothers were far from unresolved. Maybe Jayden would give them family therapy. The red-haired psychic had done wonders with Akasha's inner demons. And then there was the mystery of Radu's companion, who seemed to have come here more for her and Silas than for Razvan's sake, yet was also clearly terrified to say why.

"What do you think she has to tell us?" Akasha asked Silas again. A thought gave her pause. "Do you think she has information about Xochitl and the band?"

Silas had previously Marked all four members of Rage of Angels on orders from the Thirteenth Elder, and Jayden had a vision of them in another world with two moons, so at least Akasha received confirmation that they were alive. But she didn't like to dwell on that creepy place and even weirder prophecy. She just wanted her friends back.

Silas shook his head. "Lillian said her news had to do with the AIU. I wonder if Agent Holmes failed to eliminate the evidence of your capture like he'd claimed."

Crushing out her cigarette in the ashtray on the coffee table, Akasha hugged her arms. Memories of being strapped to a table, hooked to a catheter, and being prodded with needles made a silent scream crawl up her throat. True, Holmes had helped her escape and covered up all traces that she'd been held by a rogue military unit, but she still loathed him for treating her like a lab rat.

"That wouldn't surprise me," she managed to say. "But why would she come to tell me? And why'd she look so scared of us?"

Razvan tapped out his pipe. "Maybe she's been experimenting on my brother." His eyes narrowed. "Jayden said she was a scientist."

Akasha shivered. That explained why Radu sent Jayden on an errand right before sundown. Who knew what the AIU did to psychics? "If she thinks she's going to turn any of us into lab rats, she has another thing coming." She blew out smoke. "I wonder why she's on the run from the AIU, though."

"I don't know." Silas cocked his head to the side, his preternatural hearing picking up something. "But we are about to find out."

Akasha heard a car door shut and headed to the fridge for another beer. If Lillian had bad news, she'd need a cold one. A twinge of shame nagged her as she cracked open the can of Coors. After a really bad bender, she'd promised to cut back on her drinking, and Jayden had been helping her. But right now, the stress was too high. At least Jayden wasn't around to give her a disappointed look. Silas indulged her in everything, so he wouldn't scold her.

When Silas opened the door and led Lillian and Radu inside, Akasha couldn't stop staring at Lillian. There was something familiar about her eyebrows and the curve of her jaw. When they sat on the couch, Razvan left the recliner to sit with his brother.

Some silent communication passed between them, as if Radu had pleaded for his brother to take his side with whatever Lillian would say. Shaking her head, Akasha took a swig of beer, wondering if she was reading too much into things. Either way, the palpable emotion of their reunion was too much to bear looking at for long.

"Would you like something to drink?" Silas asked. "We have beer, wine, coffee, juice, or tea."

"Water would be nice," Lillian said softly, as Radu nodded in agreement.

Silas went to the kitchen and poured two glasses. After he handed the couple their water, the only thing besides blood that a vampire could drink in large quantities, Silas sat in the recliner.

Akasha was too anxious to sit. Taking a swig of her beer, she met Lillian's blue eyes. "What did you want to tell us?"

"First, I'll tell you who I am. My ID says Lily Vâlcu because the Lord of Bucharest said Radu and I would draw less attention if we posed as a married couple. But my real name is Lillian Holmes."

Holmes. Now the quasi-familiarity of this woman's face made sense. The memory of the AIU Agent pointing a gun at her as he unfastened her restraints echoed in her mind. *"If you try to get violent with me, I will shoot you and worry about saving my own skin. I don't want to, though. I like your spirit. But I'd like to see my daughter again, and with one murder under your belt, self-defense though it was, I feel I should be cautious."* Those blue eyes that had stared down at her through thick glasses were the same as Lillian's, as was the arch of her eyebrows, though his had been bushier. Joe Holmes's hair had been white, but it might have once been strawberry blond.

"Agent Holmes is your father." Sneering accusation imbued her tone.

"*Was*," Lillian's features contorted with grief. "He was murdered last month."

"Oh *shit*," Akasha breathed. "I'm sorry to hear that. I mean, I wasn't exactly fond of the guy, but he did help me escape and got the military off my back. But still…" She paused and backtracked. "Did he tell you what he did to me?"

Lillian nodded. "I know he ran tests on you and took samples of your blood, skin, and hair, and I understand why you'd be angry about it, but he truly never meant you any harm. He didn't even tell the AIU about you or Silas or Razvan. He kept all of his specimens and samples in our private lab."

"He only told you?"

"Just me." Though something like doubt flickered in her eyes. "He sent me encrypted files of all your test results."

"Who murdered him?" Akasha tried to sound nonchalant as fearful suspicion crawled all over her skin.

"The AIU." The terror in her eyes implied that she was telling the truth.

Silas gasped and leaned forward. "What? From what I understood, he was one of their highest-ranking agents and their best biophysicist. Why would they kill him?"

"I think it was because he often did research and experiments on his own without reporting it to the director, like his studies on

Akasha." She sighed. "Or maybe he found out something they didn't want him to know. Ever since the new director took over, things had gotten kinda weird there."

Akasha's jaw dropped as she digested Lillian's words. "So, the AIU is after you because you know they killed your dad?"

Lillian shook her head. "They're not after me yet. They think I'm dead. That's how I met Radu. They told me *he* killed my father and sent me to stake him."

"They sent you to die," Razvan said as Radu nodded. "To send anyone to the lair of a vampire as old and powerful as Radu can be nothing other than an assassination attempt."

Holy shit. Lillian's own agency had murdered her father and then tried to off her too? What the hell had they been doing to deserve that?

Razvan looked back at Radu. "Why *didn't* you kill her? Although you've always had a weakness for a pretty face, I would think you'd not be merciful on someone trying to drive a stake through your heart, no matter how comely they may be."

Radu's eyes glowed with unholy fury as he spoke in his thick accent. "I will not be used."

Silas leaned forward, setting his sword aside. "Is that why you're here? To take shelter with us?"

"No," Lillian said quietly, her gaze flicking back and forth from Akasha to Silas. "I mean, I hope you will take us in, but you might not after I tell you what my father did." She looked down at her feet. "What I helped him do."

Akasha quit pacing and suddenly wished for Lillian's silence to continue as dread pooled in her belly. Whatever it was, it couldn't be good.

"Go on, lass," Silas prodded, concealing his impatience.

Lillian's wary gaze met Akasha's. "He didn't just take samples of your blood and skin. He also took your eggs."

Akasha's heart stopped as her mouth went dry. There was only one reason he would have wanted with her eggs. Her lungs constricted, and she struggled to breathe.

"You mean—" Silas began, but Lillian turned to him.

"And he and I used your blood to manufacture sperm cells," she told Silas. Sucking in a shaky breath, her eyes darted between them as if expecting one of them to pounce. "It took us a few tries to make a viable embryo, but last year, we pulled it off. We paid a surrogate to carry the fetus, and, well…"

Black spots danced in Akasha's vision, a dull roar in her ears almost overwhelming Lillian's next words.

"You have a daughter."

Suddenly, Silas's arms snaked around Akasha's waist as her vision went dark. She didn't even see him get up from the recliner. As he sat back down and pulled her on his lap, she blinked. "Oh fuck, did I faint?"

"Only for a second." He held her tight.

She turned to face him, seeking an anchor in his strong arms and steady gaze. "Did she fucking say that we have a kid?"

"A baby." His face was paler than usual, green eyes suspiciously misty as he looked over her shoulder at Lillian. "How old is she?"

"Six months." Lillian blushed but didn't look away. "I didn't think it was right to keep that from you, so when Radu allowed me to live and asked for my help in bringing him here, I knew it was right to tell you. I named her Kiara since you both have Gaelic roots."

"Damn right you should have told us!" Akasha growled. "Why didn't you before? I mean that's not something you—"

"Where is our daughter?" Silas growled.

"I'm not sure. Dad took her to a foster home a few weeks before he died and wouldn't tell me where," Lillian said, then lifted her chin. "But I can find out, and I will help you get her back. That is, if you want her."

"*If* we want her?" Silas's Scottish brogue deepened with his outrage at the question. "Of course we want her. She's our child! Besides, if the AIU finds out about her, she'll spend the rest of her life locked up."

Our child. The concept ricocheted through Akasha's brain like a firing squad had taken up residence in her skull. *I'm a mother...I have a daughter.*

"Oh fuck," she muttered. "Oh fuck, oh fuck, oh fuck."

The image of a black-haired infant with Silas's eyes flickered through her mind along with the strident echo of an infant's wail.

She couldn't process this. She couldn't...

Just then, the front door opened, and Jayden walked in. Her eyes narrowed at Lillian and Radu on the couch before taking in Akasha and Silas's stricken faces. Her shock at the news shifted to concern as she looked at her friend. "What's wrong?"

Razvan answered with a broad grin. "Silas and Akasha just found out that they're parents."

Chapter Nineteen

Lillian clung to Radu's hand so tightly that she was surprised she didn't hurt him. Right now, Silas's piercing gaze had shifted to his wife as she rocked in his arms and cursed. But she'd never forget the outraged accusation in their eyes when she'd told them the unfathomable secret that had been kept from them.

Akasha slowly slid off of her husband's lap. "I need another beer."

"I'd like a tot of scotch, as well," Silas said and followed her into the kitchen.

Jayden remained frozen by the door, mouth agape.

Lillian peered at Razvan. "Are they going to kill me?"

His lips curved in a wicked smirk. "For telling them about their bundle of joy? I doubt it. Though if your father hadn't already been killed…"

Radu gasped. "Razvan! You shouldn't say something so cruel."

Razvan laughed and inclined his head toward Lillian. "I apologize, Miss Holmes."

"Let me guess," Lillian said drily. "You're the evil twin."

The vampire put a hand over his heart. "You wound me."

Jayden finally recovered enough to cross the room and perch on the arm of the couch. "He's not so much evil as he is a button pusher."

Razvan scowled at his fiancé before turning back to Lillian. "Well, my brother may be more charming with the ladies, but he has a nasty temper." He pulled Jayden into his lap. "I assume you'd like to know what you missed while you were out?"

"Please," Jayden leaned back against him and held Lillian's gaze. "What's this about Silas and Akasha being parents? I thought vampires were infertile."

"Apparently anything is possible with science," Razvan said. "My brother's lovely pet mortal was employed with the AIU until they tried to kill her for reasons she's still trying to deduce. Though the fact that she and her father engineered a baby from Akasha's eggs and Silas's blood may be one of them…" Razvan proceeded to explain what Lillian had told them in a far more cheerful tone than the situation merited.

Akasha and Silas returned to the living room. Some color had returned to their faces, though both still looked like they'd been hit with shovels. Ice clinked in Silas's glass of scotch as his hand shook. Akasha gulped a beer like it was a cure for the plague. She caught Lillian's look and scowled defensively. "No need to look at me like I'm a drunk. I've been cutting back. But after dropping a bomb like that on us…"

Lillian held up her hands in surrender. "I wasn't…"

"Bullshit," Akasha cut her off. "Though I can't really blame you." Suddenly her expression shifted. "Kiara's a nice name."

"Thank you," Lillian replied, relieved that at least Akasha didn't seem mad at her for usurping that parental right as well. "I got sick of dad calling her 'Subject Alpha.' She deserved a name."

"Do you have any pictures?" Akasha's eyes filled with hope.

"Not on me. I'm sorry. But I do know where those are kept."

Akasha gave her a wan smile. "Do you think she's safe?"

Lillian nodded. "Dad and I kept her at his vacation home in Roosevelt until he believed that it wasn't safe anymore. Then he told me he placed her with a nice foster mother. Dad didn't say where the woman lives, but I trust his judgment. The surrogate he'd chosen was wonderful. She took special care of herself throughout the pregnancy." She heard herself babbling, but she wanted nothing more than to fix this. "Anyway, if I can get to his safe deposit box, I'd bet anything that Kiara's location is in there. And, possibly, whatever reason the AIU had to kill him and then later come after me."

Silas nodded and took a minuscule sip of his scotch. "First, we need to find out if the AIU knows about our baby." He pulled his phone out of his pocket and sent a text. "One of my people has access to their systems. Before we do anything, I need to have him take a look."

Lillian gasped. "You have someone on the inside?"

"Our kind has always monitored those who monitor us." The vampire's phone chimed. As Silas eyed the screen, he frowned. "Damn, I'd forgotten that Bryan is out of town at a convention. But he'll be here tomorrow."

Akasha stepped closer to Lillian, eyes wide with shell shock. "You don't think they know about her, do you?"

There was no need to clarify who *they* were. "I'm not sure," Lillian said sadly, wishing she had more of an assurance. "But my father took careful precautions."

The woman's purple eyes went cold with fury. "I'll kill them if they hurt her."

Lillian leaned back in alarm even as relief washed over her. There was the protective instinct. Perhaps Akasha was capable of being motherly after all. As for Silas, beneath the surface of his stunned expression, intermittent sparks of joy became apparent.

"A bairn," he said softly, "I never imagined I would have my own."

"Me neither." Akasha guzzled the rest of her beer and crushed the can in her fist like it was paper. "But I'm not about to let my daughter be raised by a stranger."

"I won't have it either. Our bairn must be reared by her true parents." Silas growled. Suddenly, his brows drew together with worry. "Is she healthy? What traits did she inherit from us?"

Breathing a sigh of relief for the topic shifting to more comfortable ground, Lillian rattled off the results of her and Dad's studies. "Like a vampire, she has an elevated white cell count, but she has more red cells than a vampire has, and they're shaped more like her mother's. She also doesn't have as many archaeocytes, and she has a smaller mixture of both mitochondria and vitochondria."

"Archaeocytes? Like a sponge?" Akasha lit a cigarette and sat on the edge of the coffee table. "Which of us has those? And what's vitochondria?"

Lillian blinked. For some reason, she hadn't expected Akasha to know what archaeocytes were, much less which species those cells were found in. Though Dad's notes on her had said that the mutant was intelligent, coarse manners aside.

"What's an archaeocyte?" Silas asked at the same time.

"Archaeocytes are totipotent cells, which means they can change to any type of cell that is required. Vampires possess them in abundance, which is how they heal so fast, and they likely also contribute to their inability to age," Lillian explained. "Vitochondria are cells unique to vampires only. They metabolize the blood and send chemical signals to the archaeocytes. But they also act like chloroplasts in that they respond to sunlight, only instead of triggering metabolism, sunlight kills them. I named them myself." She couldn't suppress a surge of pride in memory of that accomplishment. "As for traits inherited from her mother, Kiara has an abundance of IPCs, induced pluripotent stem cells, and is already showing signs of Akasha's strength." Noticing their perplexed frowns, Lillian realized she'd lapsed into that clinical speak that drove people crazy. "Um, and she seems to have your curly hair, Akasha, and green eyes like you, Silas."

Their expressions softened, and they looked at each other and smiled with such intimate warmth that Lillian felt like a voyeur.

Then Silas's smile vanished. "Is she vulnerable to the sun?"

A lump formed in her throat at the worry in his eyes. "Somewhat. She sunburns very easily, but she doesn't combust as you would. Of course, that may change after puberty. Dad and I were very careful with exposing her to sunlight, since we still haven't narrowed down why it makes vampire cells ignite." Taking in a deep breath, she added, "She's also slightly anemic, but we designed a formula with iron supplements and other nutrients to keep her in good shape."

"Do you think the family that your dad gave her to has enough of it?" Akasha asked.

"Probably. We made a year's supply of formula." But Lillian had no idea how much Dad had given to the woman.

Silas's frown deepened. "I don't care how nice the woman is. Our daughter belongs with us."

"Yes." Akasha's eyes blazed violet flame. "I never wanted children, but damn it, she's mine, and I won't let anyone else do my job as being her mom."

"I agree," Lillian said firmly. "I begged Dad to tell you two about her, but he refused, saying it was too dangerous."

"Too dangerous for him, maybe," Akasha muttered. Rising from the coffee table, she marched to the kitchen. Lillian heard the sound of the fridge opening and closing and the crack of a can opening. As Akasha reemerged with a can of Coors and lit a cigarette, she heaved a sigh and plopped on Silas's lap. "I can't believe we have a kid. We need to figure out how to get her back, how to take care of her…how to deal with all of this."

Razvan spoke up. "Perhaps we should give you some privacy to absorb this shock. My brother and his woman can stay at my home, and we can return tomorrow when Bryan comes."

Akasha nodded. "If you don't mind."

Silas pointed at Lillian, eyes severe. "But she is not to be out of your sight. I want you to watch her at all times."

"Of course," Razvan said the same time Lillian rose from the couch.

"Wait a minute." She glared at the vampire. "Do you think I'm untrustworthy?"

"I'm not well enough acquainted with you to make that judgment." Silas eyed her mildly, though his tone held a dangerous undercurrent. "But you are the key to us getting our daughter. I am not about to take any risks. Besides, you said the AIU tried to kill you, so think of Razvan guarding you as a protection measure."

"What about Radu? I already belong to him because of that Marking thing he did. Why can't he watch me?" And did Silas mean she and Radu weren't allowed to be alone together? To her embarrassment, a wave of disappointment washed over her at the thought of not being able to make love with him.

Silas shrugged. "I do not know him either."

Radu scowled but remained silent. His brother did not.

"Don't worry, my dear," Razvan smirked at her. "Radu can watch you as much as you want when you're in your bedchamber."

Both brothers grinned as Lillian's cheeks flooded with heat. What was wrong with her? For the last few years of her adult life, she'd been practically a virgin and had only cared about her next study. Now she'd turned into some kind of sex addict, anticipating the moment when she and Radu would next make love.

As if reading her thoughts, Radu pulled her closer to him. "I will watch her *very* thoroughly."

Akasha snorted while Jayden gave Lillian a sympathetic half-smile.

Razvan took his fiancé's hand and bowed to Silas and Akasha. "We'll leave you two alone now. And tomorrow, we will do all we can to help you recover your child."

As Lillian and Radu turned to follow Razvan, Akasha put a hand on Lillian's shoulder.

"Wait." Her usual take-no-shit demeanor had dissolved, leaving behind an entreating vulnerability. "Thank you for coming all the way here to tell us about our baby. Even though I sounded like I wanted to rip your head off, I do understand why you were unable to tell us sooner. And thank you for offering to help get Kiara back. If the AIU knows about her, you'll be putting yourself at risk." Her eyes widened in surprise at voicing the name of her child. "Again, Kiara is a beautiful name. I suck at naming things, so if it's okay with Silas, we might keep it."

Silas's expression remained carefully noncommittal, indicating that was another matter best discussed privately.

After they left the house, Razvan gave Lillian his address and asked her to follow him in her car.

"Why Spokane?" she asked, not in the mood to deal with another Lord Vampire.

"I am Lord of the city," he said, grinning at her and Radu's surprised expressions.

Radu clapped him on the back. "Well done, Brother."

Razvan shrugged. "I had to do something once I had given up looking for you."

Once more, an invisible shroud of sadness and regret enveloped them both.

"I'm sorry," Radu said in a voice barely above a whisper.

"Don't be. I enjoyed many adventures and joyous sights during my travels." Razvan embraced his brother and drew away with a grin. "Now, let's go home, and I'll have one of my people fetch Jayden and Lillian something to eat."

Home. The word tugged at Lillian's chest while Radu looked like he'd been struck between the eyes. As they were staying with his brother, the word held far more weight for him.

Following Razvan and Jayden's Charger to Spokane, Lillian's heart sank as the trees gave way to tall buildings and storefronts. She'd rather enjoyed all the green. This city was much larger than Coeur d'Alene, with countless one-way streets going to yet more buildings. When they stopped at a dilapidated warehouse, she at first thought Razvan had car trouble or something. But then, one of the massive doors rattled open to reveal a vast garage.

Lillian parked her little Honda beside the gleaming Charger, wondering if she would have to follow suit and get a classic car of her own to fit in with these people.

The warehouse looked even more decrepit on the inside until they rode in a rickety wooden elevator to the basement. Suddenly, they were transported to an opulent living space with gleaming hardwood floors, plush rugs, leather furniture, and brightly colored tapestries.

Razvan clicked on warm overhead lights that weren't too dim or bright and gave them a quick tour. Jayden showed Lillian their guest room while Radu pored through Razvan's record collection. Apparently, his twin shared his affinity for hard rock and metal music.

Pulling out his phone, Razvan dialed a number and rattled off orders to someone to bring food from some restaurant that sounded Italian.

Unlike Silas, who sounded like an old-world lord when he issued commands, Razvan sounded like a scary mob boss. Looked like one too, when a cringing subordinate delivered takeout cartons of what had to be the most heavenly smelling pasta in the universe.

Razvan took the food and paid the vampire courteously enough. But he still radiated a vibe that made Lillian want to finish his sentences with, *"You'll be sleeping with the fishes, see?"*

Jayden gave the vampire more gracious thanks and led Lillian to a dining area that gleamed and smelled new. For a while, Lillian lost herself in the sumptuous flavors of garlic, butter, perfectly *al dente* noodles, and the creamiest Alfredo sauce to ever touch her tongue. Radu made a noise from the other room, and she smiled, knowing he enjoyed the meal as well.

"Your place is beautiful," she told Jayden as she reached for another buttery breadstick.

Jayden grinned. "Thank you. I've been furnishing it for the past few months. You should have seen it before. It wasn't much better than the upper floor."

"Really?" Maybe Radu hadn't been the only one living in self-penance.

"Yeah. Razvan's fairly new to Spokane, and you know men, they always put off home improvement stuff." She grinned as the sound of Jimi Hendrix played from the other room. "Except his music collection. He's pretty obsessed."

Lillian returned her smile. "Radu seems to have the same taste."

"Wow," Jayden said as she finished her pasta. "It's crazy, isn't it? Them being twins?"

"Yeah. They're so alike, yet…"

"So different," they said together and laughed.

"What is so funny? Razvan asked as he and Radu came into the kitchen.

Jayden and Lillian exchanged smiles. "Nothing."

To Lillian's surprise, Razvan didn't press her or Radu for more details about Akasha's baby or the AIU's homicidal house cleaning. Instead, he regaled them with tales of his travels throughout the centuries. His gaze held Radu's, patently eager to paint the experiences vividly enough for his brother to live them too.

Then, before dawn, the twins went out to hunt while Jayden talked about her wedding plans. Razvan may be sardonic and slightly sinister, but this woman was clearly head over heels for him.

"How did you two meet?" Lillian asked.

"I asked him to kill me, but instead, he kept me and offered to help me." Jayden grinned and pointed at one of her countless bridal magazines. "What do you think of these bridesmaid gowns?"

Lillian's jaw dropped. "*What?*"

Jayden laughed. "I'm psychic, but back then, I couldn't control it, and—oh, our gentlemen have returned."

Razvan swept Jayden into his arms. "If you'll excuse us, Jayden and I haven't had a moment alone in the last two nights. We are going to bed early. Good day."

"There's food in the fridge and cupboards if you get hungry," Jayden called over Razvan's shoulder before they disappeared from the room.

Radu sat next to Lillian and trailed his lips along her neck. His breath whispered against her sensitive flesh, making her shiver as he spoke. "You look tired. Perhaps we should go to bed too."

Lillian caressed his thigh, heat pooling in her belly. "Another rule of the modern world. Never tell a woman she looks tired. That indicates she's not looking her best."

He chuckled and scooped her up. "Then I shall have to show you how beautiful you are. Every inch of you."

He carried her into the large guest room down the hall and kicked the door shut before laying her on the bed.

Sliding her sandals off her feet, he kissed up and down her calves and ankles before working her skirt up to her thighs. Once he'd removed her dress and kissed his way back up to her neck, he leaned back and studied her face. The combination of delight and desire in his eyes made her pulse quicken. Never before had a man looked at her like that. Like she was a gift waiting to be opened.

"Turn around," he whispered.

Lillian obeyed and lay on her stomach. As his hands massaged her tight shoulders, she moaned in bliss.

"I thought you'd be stiff from driving," he said as he kneaded a particularly painful knot.

"Aren't you stiff too?" she asked. Hell, he'd ridden in the trunk.

"Yes." He leaned over her so his hair brushed across the bare skin of her back. "But not from the car." His hips dipped down, and he ground his hardness against her backside.

She giggled at her inadvertent suggestive question even as heat radiated from her core. Only thin layers of fabric separated him from her.

His hands delved lower, rubbing her back until she felt like melting into a puddle beneath him. By then he'd shifted to straddle her, and every brush of his erection against her made her bite back whimpers of need.

When his hands moved from her body, and she heard a rustle of fabric, Lillian peeked over her shoulder to see Radu taking his shirt off.

God, yes, she thought as her gaze devoured his sleek, muscled form. When he reached down to unzip his fly, she sucked in a breath in anticipation, slightly disappointed that she couldn't crane her neck back around far enough to see more.

Seconds later, his fingers caressed her hips before sliding her panties down. She didn't know it was possible for him to take his pants off that fast. Breathless, she arched her hips up slightly and waited for him to enter her.

Instead, his fingers idly trailed across her buttocks, then along her hips and the backs of her legs. Then he lightly caressed her inner thighs, getting closer and closer to the source of her aching need but not quite grazing her heated flesh.

By the time Radu finally touched her wetness, Lillian gasped as electric bliss jolted through her core. Feather-light, he stroked her until she arched against his hand, needing more.

At long last, he shifted his hips against hers, the tip of his erection pressed to her slick entrance. Slowly he filled her, inch by inch, until she was light-headed at the fullness of him. Whether being careful not to hurt her, or to prolong the pleasure, Radu kept his thrusts slow and deep.

Drowning in pleasure and need, Lillian's thighs quivered at the intoxicating rhythm.

Reaching beneath her hips, his fingers found her clit and stroked it in tandem with his thrusts. A low moan escaped her lips as she undulated against him, craving his spellbinding touch.

She moved faster against him, silently pleading for more. Radu answered with a vengeance. Cupping her sex, he quickened his thrusts, delving deeper inside her even as he increased the intensity of his strokes.

The orgasm rose up like an earthquake as her clit, and some spot deep inside her simultaneously erupted with pulsing ecstasy. Lillian cried out, and still, his fingers and cock continued to mercilessly build her climax to higher peaks until she was blind from pleasure.

A low growl trickled from Radu's throat as his cock spasmed within her. Then he collapsed on top of her, both trembling from the aftershocks.

"Wow," she panted when he withdrew.

By the time he cradled her in his arms and tucked the covers over them, Lillian almost didn't care that she was homeless and a virtual prisoner.

Not as long as Radu was with her.

Unleashing Desire

Chapter Twenty

Silas leaned back in the recliner, watching Akasha pace around the living room, alternately sipping her beer and puffing on a cigarette. Strange how shock affected people differently. His wife couldn't sit still while he felt as if he'd been struck between the eyes, and his muscles turned to custard.

A bairn. Shockwaves continued to reverberate in his skull at the earthshaking concept. Although Silas had seen visions of Akasha holding a baby with their combined features, he'd always assumed they were mere vivid wishful daydreams and not true psychic portents.

Yet Agent Holmes and his daughter had achieved what was supposed to be impossible: spawning a child that was half-vampire. Even more impressive was that the original mutation Akasha's father and his fellow soldiers had been subjected to was supposed to render them as sterile as vampires. Yet somehow, her father had remained fertile. Akasha was a miracle, now the feat had been repeated in her daughter.

Their daughter. His blood ran through her veins. The blood of the long-lost clan McNaught. An aching lump formed in his throat even as his heart seemed to swell.

"Are you okay?" Akasha asked suddenly. "I'm sorry, I've been a self-centered bitch only freaking out for myself. This has got to be a bombshell on you too."

Slowly, Silas nodded. "Aye." Swallowing past the tightness in his throat, he resolved to be honest with her. "I hope you don't hit me for saying I am happy about this. I mean, not the circumstances that brought it about, but the fact that we have a child."

All right, not completely honest. He held back from telling how he would have loved to see her belly swell with the growing life they'd created together. To see their baby's tiny form on an ultrasound, to feel her kick beneath his hand on Akasha's stomach.

Unable to stop himself, he smiled. How she would have hated being pregnant. His elder sister had complained about her ungainliness and being unable to ride.

Akasha shot him a mock wounded look. "Just because I've decked Razvan a couple times doesn't mean I would ever hurt you." She cocked her head to the side. "What are you smiling about?"

"Imagining you trying to work on a car with a big belly," he answered cautiously. His lass had a temper, but to be fair, she had only struck Razvan when he'd portrayed himself as a threat to others. So her tough demeanor displayed more nobility than she'd likely care to admit.

Instead of being angered by his remark, Akasha laughed, a low, throaty sound as rare and precious as pearls. "Oh man, that *would* have sucked. It would have thrown off my dart game too."

Emboldened by her amusement, he dared to ask, "Now that we're alone, how do you feel about us having a child?"

She shook her head and tossed back the rest of her beer. "I'm still trying to process it. I mean, I'm mostly glad that I didn't have to go through the pain in the ass of pregnancy…and if someone had forced me to do so, I would have gotten rid of it immediately." She darted a glance at him to see if he was angry with that sentiment, but when he gave her a firm nod of support, her shoulders relaxed, and she continued. "And the fact is, I still didn't have a choice, and you didn't have a choice."

"But," he prodded.

Her features shifted to that unyielding protectiveness he'd seen earlier. "But that doesn't change the fact that she now exists. Our daughter. And though I'm pissed at Holmes and Lillian for creating her without our knowledge and consent, and I'm scared shitless that I'll be a terrible mom, I— I think I love her already." Her lips curved in a lopsided smile that made his heart turn over. "Isn't that silly? Loving someone you only learned existed tonight?"

"Perhaps, but I know exactly how you feel." His arms already ached to hold his child, to sing her to sleep, to help her take her first steps...Damn it, that lump in his throat returned.

Akasha reached out and brushed her knuckles across his cheek, the depth of her love for him reflecting in her magnificent purple eyes. "At least I'm positive that you'll be an amazing father." Her lower lip trembled slightly as worry creased her brow. "Do you think we'll get her back?"

"Aye," he said firmly. "I refuse to entertain thoughts otherwise. Besides, we have countless allies and resources at our fingertips."

She nodded, chin lifting in determination. "We will get our baby." Her eyes widened with awe at the word. "Oh my God. We're going to be parents." Shaking her head, she went into the kitchen for yet another beer.

As if sensing his concern about her habit, she regarded him solemnly when she returned to the living room and cracked open the can. "I'm going to have to cut back on these even more, but not tonight." Her gaze flicked to the ashtray on the end table.

"No more smoking in the house either, starting tomorrow. Actually, I should probably try to quit those fuckers altogether."

Silas nodded, relieved that he didn't have to say it. Though her vices often worried him, he'd never managed to muster the courage to seriously talk to her about them. He'd been too afraid of losing her. Jayden had been right when she'd called him an enabler. "And we'll need to get a crib, set up a nursery, buy diapers…" He sighed and leaned back in the recliner.

Akasha sat on the couch and lit another cigarette. "We're not doing it all pink and girly, are we?"

He laughed. "I can't really picture it. Maybe the McNaught plaid and crest? And you can make a mobile of hanging wrenches and sockets?"

Her giggle warmed the depths of his soul. "And posters of Mopar muscle cars." Suddenly, her expression sobered. "What *do* you think of the name Lillian picked out for her? You've been quiet on that front."

Silas took a deep breath and spoke through a sudden ache in his heart. "That was my great aunt's name." He shook his head at the coincidence. "It's like it was meant to be."

"With all that crazy Prophecy stuff, maybe it is." Crushing out her cigarette, Akasha rose from the couch and curled back up on his lap. For a long moment, they clung to each other, drawing strength and comfort from the indestructible bond of their love.

"I think we can do this," she whispered as her fingers curled around his hair. "I really think we can do this."

"Me too." Silas hugged her close. "If we can fight battles against soldiers and vampires, surely we can handle colic and tantrums."

"I don't know." She chuckled. "That sounds even more daunting." With apparent reluctance, she slid off his lap. "Anyway, let's invoke one of our privileges of being childless for now and go out and get some pizza. I'm starving, and you need to feed."

They headed to Moonlight Pizza, the only pizzeria open past midnight. Ran by some of Silas's vampires, the place was popular with college students, graveyard shift workers, and of course, drunks wanting to fill their bellies after the bars closed.

Silas fed on one of the latter who had stumbled out of the building. He got a slight buzz from the alcohol-soaked blood. When they entered the restaurant, the vampires at the counter, Sam and Jo, inclined their heads respectfully. Yet wariness widened their eyes to see their lord darken their door.

He regarded them with a gentle smile to reassure them that they were not in trouble. Akasha also smiled brightly at them before meeting Silas's gaze, her purple eyes dancing with amusement. He didn't have to tap into his Mark on her to see that she was thinking the same thing: How would his people react when they learned about Kiara?

Holding tight to the secret, for now, Akasha ordered a pepperoni pizza to go, along with hot wings and an order of cheesy garlic breadsticks. When she wasn't distracted with her work, his lass could eat.

Then they returned home, the baby discussion resumed as if both were bursting with ideas after the short venture.

"We're going to have to come up with a birth certificate somehow, unless Holmes made one," Akasha said between rabid bites of pizza. "You know, so she can go to the doctor and school, and oh shit, how are we going to handle school? Or a doctor, if she has so many genetic anomalies?"

"Dr. Greenbriar might be able to help. Or that Post Falls vampire who surrendered to us last winter, Jessica. She's been a nurse for nearly a hundred years. She has to have experience with babies," Silas said. "Tony Salazar can handle all the legal documents we'll need. And we can homeschool."

They spent the rest of the night making plans for their child's future, confidence growing with every topic they discussed. Except for one thing.

How *would* they get Kiara back?

Stebbins choked back the vomit rising in his throat as the burned and skeletal creature moaned in agony. A stake protruded through its heart, and a disturbingly scant amount of blood pooled beneath its emaciated body.

A guard stood stoically by the door, and a white-coated scientist—possibly Holmes's replacement—watched with avid interest and jotted down notes.

The vampire had been staked three hours ago. The object of this study seemed to be to see how long it took for the vampire's body to stop trying to heal itself before it died. Stakes clearly weren't the best way to kill a vampire. This one had lasted much longer than expected, considering how starved, injured, and weakened it was.

And Director Bowers had armed Lillian with one of these ineffectual pieces of wood before sending her off to face an ancient vampire. If she'd gotten so far as to be able to stake the creature at all, she likely only would have angered it.

Her memorial service had been the day before yesterday. Stebbins couldn't forget the mournful gazes of the agents who were unaware that Lillian had been purposefully set up to die. Or the fear in the eyes of those who suspected something was awry with the circumstances of her death, so soon after her father's.

Guilt gnawed at him like a parasite invading his bowels. Although he hadn't played a direct part in the fatal deception, Stebbins had still contributed by remaining silent. Now his only hope was that her death had been quick.

Not this slow agony that the creature before him endured. Now the vampire reminded him of a dog struck by a car, scrabbling on useless limbs as life bled from it in painfully stretched minutes. It even whined like one, a light, high-pitched keening that was quickly driving Stebbins to madness.

Unable to take it any longer, Stebbins stepped toward the scientist, about to demand that the creature be put out of its misery.

A shadow fell across his path.

Stebbins turned around to meet the cold gray eyes of Director Bowers.

Stebbins froze with a guilty flush. "Sir," he managed in what he prayed was a steady voice.

"It's finally almost dead, I see." The director's gaze looked past him at the dying vampire. He licked his lips, almost looking lustful.

Stebbins looked away, feeling dirty for just seeing such an expression. "Yes."

"You're quiet today," Bowers remarked, not looking away from the macabre spectacle through the glass.

"I...um..." Stebbins fumbled for an excuse.

Just then, he was saved by the approach of Agent Merrill, who Stebbins had appointed the duty of overseeing the search of Agent Holmes's personal effects. "Director Bowers, Agent Stebbins," Merrill said respectfully. "I think we might have found something useful in Holmes's effects."

"Which Holmes?" Bowers asked, still watching the vampire.

Merrill blushed. "Holmes Senior, Sir."

"Very good. What did you find?"

"We found a charge for a safe deposit box in Apache Junction in one of Holmes's bank statements." Merrill's brown eyes glittered with excitement. "We haven't found a number or a key, but we'll keep looking."

"Don't bother," Bowers said. "The Director of the Violent Criminal Unit owes me a favor. He can get me a warrant in a matter of days." His mouth twisted in a scowl of irritation that the AIU was unable to apply for warrants in places such as banks and post offices. "But by all means, please keep searching. There's bound to be other useful evidence."

"Yes, sir." Merrill nodded again at Stebbins before fleeing in a power walk that verged on a run.

"Agent Stebbins?" Bowers said softly. "How goes the next phase of Operation Wrangler?"

Stebbins swallowed. "A target has been selected, and a team will be dispatched at dawn tomorrow to secure the vamp—ah, specimen."

"Wonderful." Bowers smiled, strangely resembling Jack Nicholson when playing the role of a psychopath.

As if hearing that his turn was up, the vampire in the cell finally died.

Chapter Twenty-one

Radu and Lillian stepped out of the back of Razvan's Charger on shaking legs. Radu sighed with relief to be back on solid ground. Two abrupt jolts from the brakes and one near-collision proved that his brother was not as skilled a driver as Lillian. Jayden cast them both a sympathetic look before heading up Silas's flagstone walkway. Radu vowed to apologize for calling the woman a witch at the soonest opportunity.

His relief at escaping the car evaporated when he met the cool gaze of Silas McNaught. The Lord of Coeur d'Alene looked stern and resolved. Radu put a protective arm around Lillian. They had better not hurt her for her father's actions.

Silas greeted them each in turn. "Lord Nicolae, Ms. Gray, Mr. Nicolae, Miss Holmes. Please, come in. Bryan is looking at the AIU database right now to see what they know about… well, all of this, and I would like to speak with Miss Holmes further about her strategies for getting our daughter."

"Of course," Lillian said softly, squeezing Radu's arm.

A wave of pride rushed through him at her bravery.

"There is one thing I wish to ask Lillian as well," Radu said.

She looked up at him with a slight frown. "What?"

Gently, he brushed a lock of hair behind her ear, the feel of her warm skin deepening his resolve. "What is the name of the man who told you I killed your father and sent you to my father's castle?"

"Director Bowers."

Silas raised a brow. "That's right. You had said there's a new director. What happened to Director Carson?"

"Heart attack." Her frown deepened. "Or so we were told. Now I'm not so sure."

Before the two could launch a discussion on that topic, Radu cleared his throat and met Lord McNaught's gaze. "Can this Bryan learn where Bowers lives? Where he spends his time when he is not at the AIU headquarters?"

Silas nodded. "Yes. Why?"

"Because I mean to kill him," Radu growled.

Jayden gasped, and Razvan burst out laughing. "That's my brother."

"I see," Silas said mildly. "And suppose I told you that, during your long nap, the Elders decreed that killing mortals is forbidden?" Radu remained silent, and Silas's lips curved into a smirk. "Of course, maybe you plan to take advantage of our people's assumption that Razvan's and my immunity extends to you, as you did to gain passage out of Europe and across the States to come to me."

Radu's jaw dropped before he narrowed an accusing stare at Razvan. His brother must have told McNaught everything Radu had told him about their journey. Whose side was Razvan on anyway?

Before he could pose that very question, Akasha approached them, a cigarette tucked behind her ear. Radu kept hold of Lillian as the abnormally strong woman stepped closer to her. "I want to apologize for freaking out over what you told us last night."

"No need," Lillian told her. "It was completely understandable under the circumstances. I'm lucky you didn't strangle me." Her light laugh sounded forced.

Akasha's gaze softened further. "I also want to thank you for telling us about Kiara and offering to help us get her home."

Lillian nodded. "I will do everything I can."

"I believe you." Akasha held her gaze for a moment longer before pulling out her cigarette and turning to Silas. "Anyway, I'm going out for a smoke while Bryan does his thing."

Silas nodded and bent down to kiss her.

"I'll join you," Razvan said, withdrawing his pipe from his pocket as he met Radu's glare with a mocking grin.

Radu returned the smile, silently promising to pummel him later for talking to McNaught about him behind his back. Jayden sighed, clearly exasperated at the prospect of the brothers fighting again, and remained behind as well.

Lillian and Radu followed Silas up the stairs into a large office where a young blond vampire typed furiously on a laptop.

The vampire looked up at them, his pale blue gaze resting on Lillian longer than Radu would have preferred. "Junior!" he said with a wide grin that revealed his fangs. "Lord McNaught told me you'd be here, but I didn't believe it."

"Junior?" Silas and Radu echoed.

"It was my nickname at the AIU," Lillian explained. "They couldn't call both Dad and me 'Agent Holmes' without people getting confused." She turned back to Bryan with a confused frown. "Have we met?"

The vampire shook his head. "No, but I know all about you. I've been in the AIU database for years. Their systems think I'm one of their IT people." He held out his hand. "I'm Bryan."

Lillian shrugged and shook his hand. "So while our department has been observing vampires, the vampires have been observing us?"

"*Them*," Radu corrected. "You're not one of them anymore."

Her features contorted into a mask of bitterness before she sighed. "You're right. I'm not."

"Anyway," Bryan brought their attention back to him. "I have good news, bad news, and worse news."

"What's the good news?" Silas asked sharply.

"The good news is that, just like last time we checked, they still don't know about Agent Holmes's—Senior's—extracurricular activities with your wife. And they don't seem to be aware of your...baby so far." A dopey expression crossed his face along with a big grin when he said, *baby*. "They also don't seem to know about Junior's—I mean Miss Holmes's—survival of their attempt to assassinate her." He smiled at Lillian. "They had a beautiful memorial service for you yesterday. I read about it in a department email. Such a nice eulogy."

Lillian made a pained sound in her throat, and Radu pulled her into his arms. God damn this AIU. Somehow, he would kill them all.

"I see why the AIU's favorite murder weapon spared your life," Bryan said with a wink.

Radu bared his fangs, ready to throttle the insolent youngling until the rest of Bryan's words sank in. "So, it is true? They used me like this before?"

Bryan nodded. "At least three times by my count. But I had no idea that you were Lord Nicolae's missing twin! And they have documentation of at least four other ancients hibernating in Europe. For some reason, they haven't discovered any of in the States, otherwise, they'd use them. I look forward to the day the SIS catches on."

"SIS? Radu asked.

"Supernatural Investigations Services," Silas, Bryan, and Lillian answered all at once, making Radu feel ignorant and backward.

"They're an offshoot of Interpol," Bryan said. "Lucky for us, they don't get along with the AIU."

"Back to the matter at hand," Silas said, vibrating with impatience. "What's the bad news?"

"Oh, right." Bryan looked down in embarrassment. "The bad news is that although the AIU doesn't know about Holmes's other experiments, they definitely suspect something." His gaze shifted to Lillian. "All of yours and your father's personal effects and everything in your house has been collected, with a team appointed to search every scrap for clues. They're bound to turn up something."

"I'm sure they will," Lillian said, though she didn't sound as worried as Radu would have expected. "Thankfully, I have the keys to both our safe deposit boxes and my gym locker."

"Gym locker?" Silas inquired with a frown.

She nodded. "I wanted the most unobtrusive place possible to hide my research, in case I couldn't get to Dad's and my lab. The locker came with my gym membership. My stuff is all on a thumb drive, hidden under a giant wad of gum stuck to the inside of the locker, behind my Dracula poster."

Both Silas and Bryan now gazed at her in admiration. Another burst of pride swelled in Radu's heart for his woman's brilliance. The thought made him pause. She was his...at least for now. But would she continue to be?

"Where are these safe deposit boxes and the gym?" Silas asked.

"The boxes are in Apache Junction, where our lab is located. We'd go there when pretending to visit our summer lake cabin in Roosevelt." Lillian's tone quieted with foreboding before she continued. "The gym is in Mesa, only a few blocks from our house."

"That's going to be the most dangerous part of our trip," Silas said. "They'll likely still be keeping an eye on the area, either waiting to see if you show back up or if your father had any partners in his activities." He shrugged and tapped his pen on the edge of his seat. "Either way, I'll have to contact the Lord of

Phoenix—he oversees Mesa as well—and then call my pilot to get us a flight out there first thing tomorrow night."

"You have a pilot?" Lillian asked.

Silas gave her a tight smile. "Yes, and if you two would have contacted me, we would have fetched you instead of having you drive almost three thousand miles."

"I enjoyed our road trip," Radu retorted, using the term Lillian taught him. "And weren't certain what sort of welcome we would receive."

"*And* you wanted to prolong the time before we found out about you two," Silas added. "While I understand such reasoning, that doesn't change the fact that you cost us valuable time."

"I'm sorry," Lillian said with downcast eyes.

Lord McNaught sighed. "No need to fret about it. So far, it appears that we still have time. Unless…" He turned back to Bryan. "What is the worst news?"

Bryan held up his hands as if to placate him. "Nothing that would affect your mission, at least I hope not. But it's still really bad."

The Lord Vampire's eyes glowed in warning. "What is it?"

"The AIU has seemed to have changed their operating methods under the new director. I found something called 'Operation Wrangler.'" Bryan took a deep breath before pressing on. "They are now capturing vampires…intending to discover the best ways to kill them."

Silas slumped in his seat, his face pale as milk. "Oh my God," he breathed. "I have to tell the Elders."

Lillian stared at Bryan in horror. "That is so wrong! The AIU's mission is supposed to be to observe and study preternatural beings and phenomena, not kill them."

"Oh?" Silas said in a suddenly sarcastic tone. "Then what were you supposed to be doing with that stake that they gave you when they sent you to Castle Nicolae?"

"We only dispatched Hunters to slay vampires in extreme circumstances," Lillian explained levelly. "Like when we had proof that they were killing humans."

"Killing humans is against our laws," Silas told her. "And it is a Lord Vampire's job to police his people."

Lillian's frown deepened. "Forgive me if I do not trust your people to look out for the wellbeing of mine. I've already heard of the loopholes your kind use to get around that law."

"And humans have loopholes of their own to commit despicable acts," Silas returned. "Don't forget that vampires used to be humans…and in many ways, we still are. Besides, we do agree on the fact that the AIU deciding to directly target vampires for the purpose of killing them is definitely a bad thing."

She, Radu, and Bryan all nodded.

Silas continued. "Therefore, I need to notify the Elders, so a notice can be dispatched to all Lord Vampires to do what they can to protect their people…They may wish to deal with the AIU themselves."

Radu bared his fangs in disapproval of the prospect. "I want to kill Bowers."

"Wait," Lillian squeezed his arm. "Maybe *I* want to kill him. After all, he murdered my father."

"Maybe we can kill him together," Radu suggested with a grin.

Silas shook his head in bemusement. "After your defense of humans, now you want to kill one. You're a contradiction, Miss Holmes." Rising from his chair, he strode to the door. "I will call the Elders now and book our flight to Mesa. You will stay here for the day's sleep."

The door closed behind him, and Lillian turned back to look at Bryan.

"Do you know why they killed my father?" she asked. "And tried to kill me?"

Bryan shook his head. "There isn't any documentation for those incidents that I've found, though I'll keep looking. Nor do I think there would be, given the potential repercussions for what they did. You might find the reason in that safe deposit box."

"I hope so," Lillian said sullenly. "Not knowing why he was murdered just makes everything even more unresolved. I mean, nothing is ever going to make me feel better about his death, but I just hate the unknown factors, y'know?"

Both Bryan and Radu nodded, and a pensive silence shrouded the room.

"Why didn't he make those phone calls in here?" Radu asked to break the choking quiet.

Bryan swiveled in his chair to face him. "Typically, only Lord Vampires are to speak to the Elders. And we all should be grateful for that. They're scary."

Radu nodded in agreement. Even his father had been afraid of the council of a dozen vampires who ruled over their kind. And due to his ambiguous state from being in hibernation all these centuries, Radu may have to face them himself. Especially if Silas's and Razvan's immunity didn't extend to him.

His heart seized in his chest. If he didn't have immunity, that meant that he had broken the law by allowing Lillian to know about vampires and live. He would be punished...but Lillian would be in even more danger unless they permitted him to Change her.

Chapter Twenty-Two

Wiping sweaty palms on her jeans, Lillian walked beside Akasha into the Arizona Trust bank. Jayden remained outside, her psychic shields lowered so she would be the first to detect a threat. Akasha was there as the muscle. Disguised with her hair in a bun and a cap shading her face, she'd hopefully not be recognized by the cameras while she stood outside the safe deposit box room, ready to beat the crap out of anyone who tried to follow Lillian. After seeing the way Akasha had lifted logs that were pretty much still whole trees, Lillian was confident she'd out-muscle anyone who came after her.

The men, of course, were unhappy with this strategy, but there was nothing they could do about it since the bank would close long before dark. It was up to the women to complete the first two phases of the plan: clear out the safe deposit boxes and the gym locker. The vampires wanted to wait until dark and accompany them for the last, but Lillian thought they'd be more unobtrusive when the gym was most crowded.

At nightfall, the vampires would decide the best way to approach the next two phases: cleaning out Holmes's secret lab and recovering Silas and Akasha's baby.

Ricardo, the Lord vampire of Phoenix, had been welcoming enough, granting them sanctuary in his Hacienda just outside

Mesa. Still, he was clearly nervous having two Lord Vampires under his roof and especially disturbed by the news that the AIU was hunting vampires. A representative of the Elders and vampires from neighboring territories were supposed to come next week to discuss the matter.

But right now, the first priority was to get to those safe deposit boxes.

The keys to both boxes felt like lead weights in Lillian's pocket. Her original ID poked its plastic corners in her thigh with every step. What if the bank had received word that she and her Dad were dead? Them knowing about Dad wouldn't be as big of a disaster since Lillian was signed up jointly with all his accounts. But if she was dead? Would they arrest her? Or just deny access.

On the heels of those terrible prospects, another more terrifying possibility flitted through Lillian's mind. What if the AIU had been able to get to it?

By the time she made it to the teller at the counter, Lillian's mind was so jumbled that it took her a moment to remember what to say. "I need to access both my personal safe deposit box, and the one for J & L Research LLC."

She was tempted to clear out the joint account as well, but didn't want to risk triggering an alert to the AIU. Anyway, there likely wouldn't be enough money in there to pay back Ivan, much less what she and Radu were bound to end up owing Silas and Razvan. Especially since most of hers and Radu's travel money was gone. As for their regular bank accounts at Phoenix Credit Union and Dad's insurance policy and IRA, she supposed she'd have to forget about it. On the bright side, she could also forget about her student loans, the mortgage, and her car payment. Hooray for silver linings.

"Lillian!" the blonde teller favored her with a bright grin, instead of looking at her like she was seeing a ghost.

Marci, Lillian thought with a smile, glad to see a familiar face.

"It's been a while since we've seen you in here. And I'm sorry to hear you and your dad will be leaving us. He didn't say anything about it when he was in here last time."

A measure of Lillian's tension eased from her spine. "When was that?"

"About a month ago," Marci said with a warm smile. "I asked about you, but he was in a hurry, so we didn't get to chat much."

"Oh." She didn't remember Dad taking a trip out to Apache Junction alone right before he was murdered. Had he put something new in the safe deposit box? Or taken something out? Marci gave her a polite nod, encouraging her to continue. "He got a job transfer, so we're moving back east."

Marci nodded sympathetically as she typed on her keyboard. "I hear that. My late husband got bounced across the country by his company. Hopefully, you'll get settled quickly. Now let me call the manager to take you to your box."

"Thank you." Lillian said.

Dad's safe deposit box was also more stuffed than Lillian expected. Aside from eight overstuffed manila envelopes and six flash drives, she also found his and her mother's wedding rings and the keys to their lab.

And thick stacks of cash secured with rubber bands.

Dad must have cleaned out his other account and deposited it here. A ball of ice formed in her chest. Had he known he was going to die?

Her box contained no surprises, just a notebook, flash drives containing her personal research on vampires, and the rest of her mother's jewelry, which Dad had given her on her eighteenth birthday.

The items barely fit inside the leather bookbag she'd brought to hold them. As she and Akasha walked out of the bank, Lillian silently thanked whatever higher powers there were that the AIU hadn't beaten her here.

Jayden met them outside. "I didn't feel any threats outside. How did it go inside?"

"Fine," Lillian told her. "Everything was where it was supposed to be, and then some." When they got in the rental car, she continued, still lowering her voice, "I think my father might have known he was going to be killed. There was a ton of money in the box, so he must have moved it all out of his regular bank account."

"Wow," Akasha said. "Does that mean you're buying us lunch?"

Only then did Lillian realize she was hungry. Her stomach had been too knotted up until she successfully got everything out of the bank. "Of course I will!" She'd also pay back Ivan and Donovan for helping her and Radu as soon as possible. "But we need to drop off the stuff with the guys. There's no way I'm going out in public with that much money."

Her new friends nodded.

When they reached Ricardo's hacienda and headed to the underground lair, the vampires were out cold. Lillian looked at Radu's peaceful sleeping face as tender heat flowed through her. His sleep had been broken throughout their travels. Finally, he was getting some rest. She placed the leather satchel beside him and tiptoed out of the room.

"So, where do you want to go?" Jayden asked when they got back in the car.

"I don't care," Akasha groaned, "As long as it has air conditioning."

"I recommend *Rojo Caliente*," Lillian said. "Dad took me there for my college graduation. The food is amazing, and they have live mariachis."

"Ooh," Jayden waggled her eyebrows. "Mariachis are sexy."

Akasha's lips screwed up like she'd tasted a lemon. "Jayden, *really*?"

During lunch, as if in silent agreement, Akasha didn't even ask her about the files, even though she had to be dying to find out if there was any information about her baby in there.

Instead, they exchanged stories of how each of them had met their vampires. Lillian was stunned when Akasha revealed that Silas had originally been her legal guardian because the state authorities had assumed she was two years younger than she really was.

Tears formed in Lillian's eyes when Jayden told her that she'd met Razvan when she'd been homeless and suicidal from the intensity of her clairvoyant power. She'd offered her life to Razvan, but instead of killing her, he'd taken her to Coeur d'Alene so Silas, who'd also been a psychic since his mortal days, could help her control her ability.

When Jayden then told her about the vampire cult leader who'd been the Lord of Post Falls, and how she'd abducted Jayden as part of a plan to take her people to another world, Lillian's jaw dropped.

Akasha picked up the story of how she, Silas, and Razvan had assembled a team to rescue Jayden and defeat the crazy vampire, Selena, and her cult. When put that way, Lillian understood why they had wiped out the Post Falls vampires. The other vampires had made Silas and Razvan sound like power-hungry murderers rather than the heroes they truly were.

"That's crazy that they believed they could go to another world," Lillian said with a chuckle. She frowned when they froze, staring at her like she was the loony one. "Wait, *is* there another world?"

Jayden nodded. "I *saw* it. Two moons and all. But it wouldn't have been possible for Selena and her cult to go there, from what Delgarias told us. Yet somehow, she almost stopped Xochitl from being able to save the world."

"Xochitl?" Lillian raised a brow. "Why does that name sound familiar?"

Akasha heaved a sigh, sadness welling up in her violet eyes. "Did you hear the reports of the missing heavy metal band, Rage of Angels?"

"That's where I heard that name," Lillian said...then the implications of Akasha and Jayden's story struck her. "Wait, you're saying the band is in that other world?"

"Yup," Akasha said, taking another long sip of her beer. "And they better get back soon, or I'm going to hunt down Delgarias and make him take me there. Jayden saw him there, standing next to Xochitl."

Delgarias. She'd heard that name too. "The Thirteenth Elder?" Lillian asked, going further down the rabbit hole.

Akasha took another bite of her enchilada. "Yeah. Weird guy, but he's saved our asses a couple times. Apparently, he was a friend of Xochitl's mom."

"And does this world have to do with the Prophecy?" Lillian emphasized the word the same way the other Lord Vampire dud.

"Uh-huh," Akasha spoke between bites. "Well, one of them anyway, that Xochitl would save that other world. The other one, Jayden recited when Delgarias spoke it through her mouth."

Jayden shivered. "That was so weird. How did it go?" Closing her eyes, she recited, "*And the queen shall seek seven nightwalkers with seven brides to lead their brethren to battle the unholy father. And they will be joined by kin of the queen and those from allied worlds that hear her call.*"

"Seven nightwalkers must mean vampires." Lillian picked at the remains of her tamale, unable to believe they were talking about some mystical words that allegedly predicted the future. "But who are the queen and the unholy father?"

"Xochitl's definitely the queen," Akasha said. "Delgarias addressed her that way. I mean, he *bowed* to her, man. And her father is the creator of vampires. You'll have to ask Silas more about him when we get back to Ricardo's house."

"Okay." Lillian's head spun at the casual way these women talked about a rock star saving another world and destined to fight a war against someone who'd actually created vampires. Another thought brought heat to her cheeks. "And you two are brides."

Jayden nodded and sipped her margarita. "We're pretty sure, anyway."

"Do you think I'm one?" Her blush deepened.

Akasha shrugged, but Jayden's green eyes turned speculative. "You very well could be," she ventured. "Radu seems like he's madly in love with you."

"We've only known each other for a few weeks." Lillian took a generous gulp of her own margarita. "And up until then, he's been in love with that hideous ex of his."

"Uta?" Jayden inquired mildly, oblivious to Lillian's cringe at the name. "Somehow, I doubt that. His grudge against Razvan for killing her seemed to be more about the principle of the matter than anything else. From what I've seen, he only has eyes for you. You should have seen him when he thought Razvan intended to hurt you." The psychic's eyes suddenly seemed deep and penetrating. "Anyway, how do *you* feel about him?"

Now Lillian's face was on fire. She finished her drink in one long gulp. "I don't have a lot of experience with guys, so I might be really naive about this. But Radu has been kinder to me than any man I've met. I mean, he's such a sweetie. And when I'm with him, all my worries, sadness, and other negative emotions just go away."

Jayden and Akasha looked at each other and nodded. Akasha finished her beer. "Yup, she's got it bad. And Radu Marked you, which is a big fucking deal for vampires."

Lillian shivered, remembering the taste of Radu's blood, the heat of his kiss, and the intensity of his words. *With this Mark, I give you my undying protection.*

"Speaking of big deals," Jayden said, "We better head to that gym and then get back to the Lord of Mesa's place. Our vampires are probably worried sick."

"Right." Lillian bit back a sigh of relief. Girl talk was hard.

As if on cue, the server brought the bill. Lillian paid and left a generous tip before following Akasha and Jayden out of the restaurant.

"Damn, it's so hot and dry," Akasha complained as they got back in the car. "How did you stand living here?"

Lillian shrugged as she turned on the AC before pulling out of the parking lot. "It's all I knew. Though I must say, I'm really liking Idaho."

Akasha nodded. "It's great in the summer, but just wait until winter. You might change your mind.

The venture into the gym went even quicker than the bank, with Lillian only having to get a guest pass for Akasha and Jayden. They flanked her as she used her pocket knife to work the gum free from the wall of her locker, behind the Dracula poster. Then she popped out the little plastic case holding the USB drive and put it in her pocket.

"So that holds the key to making vampire hybrid babies," Akasha said.

"That, and Kiara's health records and baby pictures," Lillian told her.

"Awww!" Jayden squealed as they saw tears well up in the new mother's eyes.

As they passed the weight room, Lillian paused and tapped Akasha on the shoulder. "Can you really lift five hundred pounds?"

"Sure can." She headed inside, loaded a barbell, and making sure no one was looking, lifted the thing high above her head before putting it down just before a guy glanced their way.

"Whoa," was all Lillian managed, still not comprehending how such a feat was possible.

On their way out, a hulking muscle-bound man came in, eyed the barbell, and tried to lift it. His face contorted painfully, and he let out a grunt that sounded like he was suffering the world's worst case of constipation. The barbell didn't budge. The man strained again, and a high-pitched fart squealed through the weight room. Akasha, Jayden, and Lillian covered their mouths and jogged out of the room before letting their laughter roar out.

Their amusement bled away by the time they returned to the Lord of Phoenix's home an hour past Lillian's estimation of how long her mission would take. Sure enough, they checked their phones and saw countless missed calls and messages. Lillian inwardly cursed herself for letting Akasha play the radio so loud.

"Oh man, the guys are going to give us a hard time," Akasha muttered as they used Ricardo's key to open the door and headed down to the underground chamber.

Sure enough, the three women were greeted by six pairs of narrowed eyes, muscular arms crossed over broad chests as the three vampires glared at them. Lillian wondered how long they'd been up.

"What took you so long?" Razvan demanded sharply.

Radu didn't say anything, just pulled Lillian into his arms and rested his chin on the top of her head. She'd never been greeted in such a way before and couldn't help but enjoy it.

Akasha glared at Razvan as she leaned against Silas's chest. "We had to get lunch. Anyway, we made it back safe and got everything we needed, so you guys can chill."

Silas looked over his wife's shoulder to meet Lillian's gaze. "Were you seen?"

She shook her head. "I don't think so. Really, it was an uneventful trip." To dissuade the vampires from further scolding, she went into the room she shared with Radu and emerged with the satchel full of the contents of Joe Holmes's safe deposit box. "Now, should we see if my father left us any information about where your daughter is?"

Both Silas and Akasha nodded in emphatic agreement. Silas pressed a finger to his lips and gestured for everyone to follow him into the guest room he and Akasha had been given. Clearly, he did not want Ricardo to know about the baby either.

Once they were all seated cross-legged on the king-size bed, Lillian pulled the mass of the manila folders from the satchel, fighting a smile as everyone ogled the cash. Flipping through the envelopes, she made a small triumphant exclamation as she found a really fat one with "S-A" scrawled on the back. "Subject Alpha. That's Kiara," she whispered as she carefully slid the sheaf of papers out onto the bedspread.

The first thing they saw was a birth certificate with Kiara's footprints and date of birth filled in, but the rest was blank. Paperclipped to the certificate was an envelope with Silas and Akasha's names scrawled on the front.

With shaky hands, Lillian handed those to Akasha. "It seems my father did listen to me in the end and decided to tell you the truth. And he gave you a birth certificate to fill in."

As Akasha ripped open the letter, Lillian found her own letter and tore into it just as fast.

"Dearest Daughter," her letter read,

"If you're reading this, that means that my worst suspicions have come true, and I am dead, betrayed by my own agency. Before I explain my reasons for believing this, I must warn you to get away before Director Bowers tries to kill you too. Make no mistake, that man is dangerous and will stop at nothing to pursue his corrupt agenda.

Take everything you can, and leave. Go to that lake city I told you about and seek out my Scottish friend. Tell him everything, and perhaps he will shelter you. Tell him I am sorry about my role in what happened with his wife. *Give them everything in the Subject Alpha file.*

"Director Bowers is changing the AIU's directives. *Instead of only observing the preternatural, he wishes to kill everything that falls under that classification—especially vampires. He's made a list of all documented vampires in the database and intends to capture and eventually kill them. If you hear of Operation Wrangler, that is the objective.*

I cannot in good conscience allow that to happen. I've shredded almost all my personal files of the vampires I'm familiar with, and I intend to warn them. However, I believe the agency has been following me and has intercepted the first message I dispatched.

I also wonder if they might have figured out that you and I have been working on our own side ventures. If so, I doubt they've come upon any substantial evidence of what we've been doing, or we would have been taken in for questioning by now. Still, the mere assumption might be enough to damn us.

If my suspicions are true, then I am a dead man. I'm enclosing this note in the safe deposit box, along with all of our liquid assets that I could get my hands on. I lost my tail before doing this, so at least I can be assured that our secrets are safe and you'll have enough money to get away and start a new life. I hope I can evade them long enough to warn you, but I don't have high hopes since you were on assignment today and your phone is off.

I wish I had more time to tell you how much you mean to me and apologize for placing you and countless others in danger for my actions. I only hope you can understand and forgive.

"*Always know that you are my pride and joy and I love you.*
"*—Dad.*"

The letter was dated May 15th. Dad had been out of town, supposedly on a classified field mission, and Lillian *had* been on an assignment that day, running a test at the Biosphere out in Oracle. When she'd returned to the AIU compound, Bowers had called her into his office to inform her that her father had been killed in Romania by Radu Nicolae. A horrific lie that not only kept her from thinking clearly enough to check for a note from her father, it also set up the orchestration of her own assassination.

Droplets of tears fell on the page, blurring the letters. Lillian ground them from her eyes with her fist and took a deep breath, grief burning her lungs. For the past few weeks, she'd been able to shunt her mourning to the side, but no longer.

Now memories bombarded her in an endless fusillade. Her at age six, crying from a skinned knee until Dad distracted her by telling her about epidermal layers as he cleaned and bandaged the wound. The countless science projects he'd helped her create. His proud smile as she graduated at the top of her class with a Doctorate in Biophysics.

Working beside him as a valued equal as they discovered new and exciting cells and the potential of harnessing the supernatural as a force for good.

The last time he'd given her a hug after she'd had one of those disaster-laden days at the lab.

As if sensing Lillian's raw heartache, Radu's arms wrapped around her waist as he gently pulled her back to lean against his strength. She sank into the haven of his arms. Eventually, she'd have to come to terms with handling her problems herself since Dad was gone, but for now, it was nice to draw from his strength.

Still, under her grief, anger at her father for leaving her ignorant for so long before dropping her into an impossible situation boiled in her gut. She hadn't even remembered him telling her about Coeur d'Alene, also known as "The Lake City."

Silas met her gaze, eyes soft and inquiring. "What did your da' have to say, lass?"

"He thinks they killed him because he knew about Operation Wrangler," Lillian said. "He was trying to warn your kind, but one of his messages was intercepted. He wanted me to tell you about Kiara and to tell you that he is sorry for keeping her from you, and sorry for his involvement in Akasha's abduction." She looked down for a moment and took a deep breath before facing him again. "And he told me to ask you to shelter me."

The vampire regarded her with a smile. "That was the gist of our letter from him." He took the letter Holmes had written for them and scanned the contents once more before setting the paper in his lap. "We have about five hours to plan our next move."

Lillian nodded in emphatic agreement. Movement would be good. Action and motion to chase away her grief and stave off her worries for the future.

Chapter Twenty-three

The hot sun made sweat bead across Stebbins's back beneath his suit as he quickened his pace to follow Bowers's rapid strides into the Arizona Trust Bank. Once inside, he released a blissful sigh at the cool air conditioning even as it chilled the sweat on the back of his neck, making goosebumps prickle his flesh.

The pretty young teller watched them approach with wide, nervous eyes either because their suits and poise indicated authority or due to the cold, determined look in Bowers's eyes. Stebbins bet on the latter.

When Bowers reached the counter, he held up his badge. "I'm Agent Bowers of the FBI, and this is Agent Stebbins. We have a warrant for the contents of the safe deposit boxes belonging to Joseph Holmes and Lillian Holmes."

He withdrew a piece of paper emblazoned with the FBI's official seal from his front pocket. How it remained so flat and crisp, Stebbins would never know.

The teller gasped as her eyes scanned the warrant. "I need to get the manager." She scurried off and returned with a balding, rotund man in a designer suit. The two were whispering frantically until the manager gave a stern nod at the teller.

"Miss Holmes was in here earlier today," she said with reluctance. Her eyes flicked to Stebbins. "Is she in trouble?"

Bowers's face went white as an eggshell. "What time?" he demanded.

Stebbins struggled to breathe. *Junior was alive?*

"A little after we opened. I think around ten?" The young woman's gaze darted back at the manager as she spoke. "She just visited her safe deposit box. Mr. Holmes had authorized her with full access, so it was perfectly legal." She lifted her chin defensively.

"Her father died nearly a month ago," Bowers snapped. Before the teller recovered, he tapped his index finger on the warrant. "The boxes, please. And have someone bring us your security footage for the day."

When the manager asked them to come to his office, Stebbins followed him and Bowers in a daze. Could it really be true?

To their disappointment—well, mostly Bowers's—the boxes were cleaned out. Stebbins's heart swelled with relief that Lillian was alive. She was a nice, bright young woman who'd deserved a promising future.

But how had she survived after facing an ancient, feral vampire? Surely she couldn't have succeeded in staking him.

Even after hearing that Lillian had been here this morning, Stebbins was still astonished when they watched the surveillance video in the manager's office. Sure enough, despite the graininess of the black and white picture, there was Lillian, bold as brass, walking into the bank and emptying two safe deposit boxes, then leaving.

Bowers stopped the video and rewound it. "Someone was with her." He pointed. "*That* woman came in behind her and followed her out." She appeared to be shorter than Lillian by at least four inches and wore her hair in a large bun. But the woman's features were obscured by the shadow of a cap, and she seemed to purposefully remain out of direct view of the cameras.

"Damn this low-quality picture! How do they expect to identify criminals with such shitty surveillance?"

The bank manager glared at him, red spots bright on his sallow cheeks. "We're just a smalltown bank. We don't have the money that the fancy ones in the city do."

Bowers's fists clenched until his knuckles whitened. Then he sighed. "It will have to do." He gave the manager his card. "If Miss Holmes happens to make another appearance, or if you or any of your employees spot her in town, call me immediately."

As they left the bank, Bowers scowled. "How did she survive? That vampire killed every man we sent in there, like the monster it's supposed to be."

"Maybe because she wasn't a man?" Stebbins ventured.

Bowers paused with a hand on his Escalade. "Are you suggesting that it decided she suited its other needs?"

Stebbins inwardly cringed at the director's leer along with the thought of what poor Junior had been subjected to. "Maybe," he admitted grudgingly. "Or maybe he—it—was too soft to kill a female."

"They're not human, Stebbins," Bowers snapped as they climbed into the vehicle. "Especially not that one. Yet it allowed her to live, and I'll be damned if I know why. It didn't transform her into one of them. Otherwise, she wouldn't have been out in daylight. Maybe she escaped and found her way back here." After starting the engine and leaving the door open to let the hot air escape while the AC was running full blast, Bowers pulled out his phone and ordered a team to watch Holmes's house. Then he called the team overseas to send a drone into the ruins of Castle Nicolae and, if it was empty, to send in a group of men and perform a forensic investigation.

All of Stebbins's relief at Lillian's survival quickly morphed to dread as Bowers pocketed his phone and grinned. "If she is in the area, it's only a matter of time before we find her."

And whatever Bowers planned to do to her would make her wish the vampire had killed her instead, Stebbins thought.

Radu scowled after Lillian finished outlining her plan for how they should next proceed. "Absolutely not. I will not leave your side."

Before she could argue, Razvan faced him with a narrow gaze. "While I understand your reluctance to part from the lovely Lillian, she does have the most practical idea, Brother." He paced in front of Radu while he lectured like he had when they were younger. "You were the first to point out that she needs to be as far away from here as soon as possible. Her accompanying Silas and Akasha to Flagstaff to retrieve their daughter accomplishes exactly that."

"But—" Radu began, but Razvan held up a hand.

"Furthermore, it is equally crucial to clean out that lab before the AIU discovers it. For that, Jayden and I will need you, especially since Ricardo won't offer us any more help aside from renting a U-Haul trailer and loaning us a truck." His brother smirked in mockery of the Lord of Phoenix's fear of being involved with anything to do with the AIU. "And while it would be nice to have Lillian with us to instruct us on how to safely dismantle and pack everything, surely you agree that it would be dangerous for her to return to Apache Junction a second time."

Radu nodded reluctantly. "Once was dangerous enough."

Lillian stepped closer to him and grasped his shoulders. "I promise I will be careful, and we will meet quickly and safely in Kingman and be on our way back hom—to Coeur d'Alene—in no time."

Radu knew what word she'd almost said. *Home.* But they didn't truly have a home. Silas and Akasha would soon be occupied with their baby, and Razvan would soon wed to

Jayden. It would be wrong to intrude while they built their new lives.

Yet, as Radu studied the face of the woman who'd given him the will to end his self-imposed penance, taught him how to navigate this new world, and reunited him with his brother, hope and determination filled his being. Perhaps Lillian could buy a house with the money her father left her. And maybe she'd invite him to share it with him.

But first, they had to retrieve this baby and recover Lillian's research equipment before it ended up in the hands of those who would use her knowledge to harm her and his kind.

Resignation weighted his shoulders as he pulled her into his arms. "Fine," he sighed. "We will do it your way. But I will be connected to my Mark with you the whole time."

Lillian rested her head against his heart for a moment before looking up at him. "Speaking of, I have an idea about how I can help with the lab. What if you feed on me while I concentrate on how all the equipment should be handled?"

Resisting the urge to lick his fangs at the thought of her taste, Radu considered her reasoning. That was how he'd learned the English language and saw how the world had changed over time. "I think that will work very well," he said.

"Hey," Jayden said to Lillian. "May I hold your hand while he feeds from you?"

"Why?" Radu and Lillian simultaneously asked.

The redhead smiled. "I'm a clairvoyant, remember? I'll be able to see your memories of the lab if you're concentrating on them hard enough. That way, two of us will go in knowing what to do."

Razvan cleared his throat. "What about me?"

Jayden grinned up at him and squeezed his bicep. "You'll be the muscle, of course."

"Of course." Razvan flexed his biceps, clearly placated, though Radu supposed his brother would only be satisfied if he was leading the expedition.

Silas looked at his watch. "Is everything settled then?"

Radu fixed him with a piercing stare. "Promise me you will keep Lillian safe."

The Lord of Coeur d'Alene surprised him by sinking down on one knee and placing his hand over his heart. "Upon my honor as the last member of Clan McNaught and a Lord Vampire, I vow that I will do everything in my power to protect Lillian as if she bore my Mark."

"Thank you." Radu experienced tightness in his own heart at this vampire's acceptance and immediate offer of help and protection. Razvan had chosen well when he'd decided to Change Silas McNaught.

Akasha took the rental car out to be refueled while Razvan and Silas went out to hook the U-Haul trailer to the truck Ricardo had loaned them, granting privacy to Radu, Lillian, and Jayden.

Radu took Lillian in his arms, a touch of distaste roiling through him with another person's involvement in such an intimate act.

Jayden seemed to sense his apprehension, for she avoided looking at him and turned all her attention to Lillian. "Before you take my hand, close your eyes and take three deep breaths. Then, don't just think about your lab. Really place yourself there. Walk around every corner of the room, stop at every item we need to take, and explain everything you think we need to know about it."

"Okay." Lillian's red-gold lashes swept her cheeks as she closed her eyes. For a moment, she was still, except for the gentle rise and fall of her breasts as she breathed. Then she tilted her head to expose her neck for Radu and reached out her right hand for Jayden.

Doing his best to ignore their witness, Radu brushed aside Lillian's hair and sank his fangs into her neck. With the hot, sweet taste of her blood came a rush of detailed images, each with a torrent of information.

By the time he withdrew his fangs and licked his lips, Radu knew the building as if he'd lived inside of it.

As he healed the puncture wounds on Lillian's neck, Jayden released her hand and glanced up at Radu with a slight blush, then quickly looked away. Had the experience also been awkward for her, or had she seen something about him in her visions? There was no comfortable way to ask.

Suddenly, they all heard the rapid thump of footsteps charging down the stairs before Silas burst into the room with Akasha at his heels.

"I received a text from Bryan," Silas said. "The AIU has discovered that Lillian is alive and went to the bank. They're searching all of Mesa, Phoenix, and Apache Junction for her. They also have a vague description of Akasha."

Cold fear wrapped icy tendrils around Radu's lungs. "Then we must go now."

"Do they know about the lab?" Lillian asked, seeming unnaturally calm about the situation. But Radu sensed her anxiety through the Mark that bound them together.

Silas shook his head. "Bryan doesn't think so."

"Then we still need to clean it out." Lillian stood and faced the vampire with steely resolve. "They can't get their hands on Dad's and my work. And after you get everything, I want the place burned to the ground, with no evidence left."

Radu nodded. "And you must go with Silas and Akasha." He choked on the words as his chest constricted. "Go far, and go fast."

Razvan came down then. "We are ready."

"So are we," Akasha said.

Radu grasped Lillian's hand and held it as they went up the stairs and headed out of the hacienda. Ricardo waited outside between Akasha's rental car and the truck with the U-Haul trailer. He wished them all good luck, but Radu hardly heard the Lord Vampire.

All he saw was Lillian, the exquisite shape of her face framed by sunset hair. Her crystalline blue eyes held him enthralled.

This would be the first time they would be voluntarily separated. The invisible grip on his lungs tightened. For an endless moment, they stood, gazing into each other's eyes. A car door shut, and the truck's engine roared to life, breaking the spell.

Radu pulled Lillian into his arms, holding her tight for a moment. The heat of her body seeped into him. A desperate kind of hunger raged through him as his lips closed over hers. The moment their mouths melded, the world fell. He conveyed all his need and passion for her in that kiss, claiming her as his. When at last they broke apart, both were breathless and gasping.

The car horn honked, catapulting them back to the present.

"C'mon," Akasha said from behind the wheel of the rental car. "We need to get on the road."

Radu cupped Lillian's face in his hands. "Stay safe until I return to you."

She nodded, and slowly they separated, invisible threads pulling painfully tight with each step they took away from each other.

Climbing into the truck and shutting the door was the hardest thing he'd done in a while.

"You're in love with her," Razvan said softly as Jayden pulled the truck out of the driveway.

Radu looked at him sharply, ready to retort. Then he sagged against the seat. "I just awoke from a seven-hundred-year sleep. I don't know what I feel."

"That doesn't sound anything like the Radu who left a trail of broken hearts and a line of swooning maidens from village to village...the Radu whose confidence—and arrogance—never faltered," Razvan said quietly. "You've changed, Brother."

Despite a twinge of embarrassment at the reminder of the fool he'd been, Radu held his brother's gaze. "I've had time to think."

Laughter roared through the truck cabin. "Yes, I suppose you have."

For the first time all night, a smile spread across Radu's face. It was good to be back with his twin. That much at least felt right. And perhaps, when he managed to put his chaotic emotions into words, he would seek out Razvan's advice on what was to be done with Lillian. After all, Razvan clearly possessed wisdom and deftness with women to have such a warm, stable relationship with one as lovely as Jayden. Even though the red-haired witch—clairvoyant, he inwardly corrected—looked nothing like her, somehow, she reminded Radu of Ihrin, their birth mother, who the twins had later learned never wanted to give them up.

The truck made a turn on a bumpy dirt road, and suddenly Radu and Jayden shared a mind, as the path became as familiar as if they'd taken it a thousand times.

"We're almost there," they both said.

Unused to being left out of a bond, with either his mate or his twin, Razvan leaned back in the seat with a scowl. Radu was tempted to tease him...until he imagined their situations being reversed. Instead, he leaned closer to his brother as a ramshackle cabin came into view, giving and receiving solace from their closeness.

"What if the AIU already found out about this place?" Jayden asked worriedly.

Radu and Razvan exchanged eager, feral grins. "Then we'll kill them."

Their shoulders slumped in disappointment as they reached out their senses and detected nothing. Then Radu tamped down his bloodlust. No men here meant that Lillian's lab remained safe.

Jayden turned the truck around in a smooth arc then backed the trailer up almost to the front door. While Razvan opened the trailer, Jayden opened the cabin door with the key Lillian gave her. Radu unloaded boxes from the U-Haul and carried them in. Passing by the rustic furnishings, they came to a closet, pushed a mass of jackets and flannel shirts out of the way, and opened a secret panel that revealed another door locked by a keypad.

Radu recited the code as Jayden punched it in. The door swung open soundlessly, and they made their way down a flight of concrete steps and into the high-tech laboratory. As Lillian's memories flared through his mind so strongly that it was as if she stood at his shoulder, Radu followed her instructions on shutting down and dismantling the equipment.

Razvan helped lift the heavier items, and together, the three of them packed everything up.

Radu touched each beaker and petri dish, the centrifuge, and the electron microscope that she'd first used to discover vitochondria and other things in vampire blood. Awe overcame him.

Once again, his twin joined his wavelength. "Your woman is astounding," Razvan said as they hefted the incubator system which had held the embryo of Silas and Akasha's baby. "She may know more about our kind than we do. And then there's the miracle she accomplished."

Jayden looked at the incubator and frowned. "Just because she could, doesn't mean that she should."

The twins fell silent as a multitude of unknowns and hundreds of worrisome consequences of the existence of a half-vampire hybrid danced in their minds.

Razvan sighed. "What's done is done. Besides, if we leave these things here, the AIU will find them and use them with far more terrifying intentions."

Radu nodded and changed the subject. "Where is your little devilish beard, Razvan? You used to be so proud of it." *And Lillian wouldn't have mistaken you for me.*

"Akasha ruined it," Razvan grumbled.

Jayden giggled at her fiance's chagrin. "She didn't do it on purpose."

By the time Razvan finished telling the story, all three of them laughed. Long after the amusing tale, Radu couldn't hold back his smile. It felt so good to work with his brother again. And once the lab was cleaned out, the U-Haul packed tight, Razvan did what he was best at.

Hefting six gas cans and two propane tanks from the truck, he placed each in the corners of the empty cabin and connected each with wicks and wires, setting one propane tank at the top of the stairs.

"Pull the truck forward at least a hundred feet," he called to Jayden.

After she did as bidden, Razvan grinned at Radu and pulled a flare gun from his pocket. "When I say 'go,' fly up as high and fast as you can."

With a boyish grin, he fired it at the first propane tank. "Go!"

The first explosion rocked Radu backward even as he took to the air. One after another boomed, each more deafening than the last. The sky lit up like the dawn as orange flames flared up from the cabin and boards and chunks of concrete rained down in a deadly hail.

Swerving around the debris, Radu flew to the retreating truck and landed in the bed, brushing a burning ember from his pant leg. Razvan landed beside him, laughing like a giddy child. Radu shook his head. If his twin had access to explosives when they were children, they wouldn't have lived long enough to become vampires.

They were halfway out of Apache Junction before the trill of sirens reached their ears. Likely, the AIU would rush to the scene as well. But all their fingerprints and stray strands of hair were obliterated. The whoresons would find nothing but ash.

The first mission had been carried off. Had Silas and Akasha safely recovered their baby? Radu closed his eyes and counted the miles before he and Lillian would meet again.

Chapter Twenty-Four

Akasha's heart pounded in her ears as she pulled the car into the driveway leading up to the cozy, suburban house. At last, they were at the place where their baby was held. The two-hour drive had taken forever, her knuckles white on the steering wheel, her foot cramped with the effort not to slam down harder on the accelerator. As it was, she'd risked over the speed limit to get here as soon as possible. To get her baby. To hold her in her arms. To bring her home.

Silas placed his hand over hers. Only then did Akasha realize that she still held the wheel in a death grip.

"It will be alright, lass," he said in a gentle yet confident voice that made her relax.

"What if they don't give her to us?" She let out the worry that had plagued her throughout the drive. "What if they call the cops before you can hypnotize them?"

Silas's eyes glowed emerald flame. "They *will* give her to us, and I will not give them a chance to do anything but what I tell them to do."

Akasha released the wheel and took his hand, drawing from his strength. For the hundredth time, she thanked the fates that she had been blessed with this powerful, noble vampire who was capable of miracles, the biggest being that he loved her.

However, his ability to hypnotize humans into thinking and doing whatever he commanded was also a big plus.

Suddenly, a different kind of terror engulfed her so thoroughly that Akasha nearly threw the car in reverse and sped away from the placid suburban house. "What if I'm a bad mom? I couldn't relate to kids when I was one. And I'm not a good role model. I drink, I smoke, I cuss, I hate almost everyone, I break stuff, I—"

Silas placed his finger across her lips. "And you're smart, determined, driven, and will teach our daughter to be the same. And if anyone tries to harm her, you'll break every bone in their body."

Lillian's laughter echoed from the backseat. "The last bit is true."

Cupping Akasha's cheek, Silas leaned forward and brushed his lips over hers. "Are we ready?"

Once more, Akasha's throat was too tight for words to emerge. Instead, she nodded and got out of the car. Standing on wobbly legs, she clung to the frame of the car and took deep breaths. Lillian got out of the backseat, still clutching her phone to check for word from Radu and the others.

"It's going to be okay." Lillian patted her shoulder. "I have all the files that prove she's yours."

Gratitude welled up within her at Lillian's brave honesty in telling Silas and Akasha about their child and then taking countless, dangerous risks to get her back.

Akasha clung to Silas's hand as she made her way up the manicured walkway, her gaze scanning the flowers and lawn gnomes lining the path as if searching for hidden threats. The pounding in her ears grew louder as they walked up the steps under the covered porch. She looked at the cushioned porch swing and thought, *Silas and I should get one of those. It looks good for rocking a baby.*

Then Silas rang the doorbell, and Akasha froze like a scared rabbit. Silence fell over her world as she strained to see through the dark curtains and listened for footsteps. What if no one was home? What if they'd gone out? What if the baby was sick and had to go to the hospital? What if the AIU found her? What if—

A light came on from somewhere inside, followed by the sound of someone walking downstairs. Black spots danced in her vision as she heard the swish-swish of approaching slippers in the foyer.

The door swung open, and a middle-aged woman in a blue bathrobe blinked at them with sleepy eyes...which suddenly widened as she did a double-take.

"I *thought* you were coming!" the woman gasped. Then, to Akasha's shock, she grinned at her. "You must be Akasha. I am so glad you woke up! When your Uncle Joe told us about the coma, he just about had me in tears!"

Coma. Right. Akasha remembered the fake story Holmes had outlined in his letter. "Yes. I am so glad to be back. My husband says it's a miracle."

The woman nodded in agreement. "And you were finally able to get back home to your wife. Silas, right?" Silas was supposed to be a truck driver, working long hauls to pay Akasha's medical bills. The woman looked back at Akasha, then back at him with a radiant smile. "Oh my, she has your eyes."

Fidgeting with impatience at this play that she didn't have the script for, Akasha cleared her throat. "May we?"

"Oh!" The woman's cheeks flamed. "I'm so sorry! Of course you want to see her for the first time. Please, come in. I'm Miriam, by the way. I was a friend of Joe's late wife."

Lillian gasped behind them. "You knew my mother?"

Miriam's eyes widened as if noticing her for the first time. "Oh my! Little Lil' how much you've grown. Yes, Laura and I were almost inseparable since college. I used to babysit you until I joined the Peace Corps."

"Wow," Lillian breathed. "I—" She froze and looked back at Akasha and Silas. "We'll have to catch up some other time."

Still trying to breathe, Akasha kept a death-grip on Silas's hand as they walked inside a cozy home that looked like something out of *Better Homes and Gardens*. Every surface was pristine and dust-free. She once more thanked the God Silas believed in that her husband had a cleaning service. There was no way she'd be able to keep her home this spotless and germ free.

Pictures of older children, a boy, and a girl, hung on the walls. Were they Miriam's? Or other foster children? A baby monitor sat on an end table next to a beige suede couch that held a knitting basket.

Miriam followed Akasha's gaze. "She only now got settled down, but I'll go get her right now."

"Thank you," she whispered.

After Miriam headed down the hall, Lillian leaned closer to them and whispered, "I can't believe Dad had a cover story for you. One that would explain any length of absence, or even if you never came back for her." She put a finger to her lips as they heard a bedroom door open.

First, Akasha heard Miriam's soft voice cooing, then the most precious sound in the universe reached Akasha's ears. The whimper of a baby—*her* baby. Then the door opened, and Akasha saw her, a tiny pink form with a crown of black hair in Miriam's arms.

She didn't remember holding out her arms. But when Akasha felt the slight, warm weight of Kiara in her embrace, she'd remember that forever. The rest of the world vanished as she studied those plump cheeks, tiny nose, puckered lips, and green eyes staring up at her. Her vision blurred with tears, but Kiara was still the most beautiful thing she'd seen. Akasha wanted to hold her close, to smell her curling black hair. She also wanted to hand the baby back before she dropped her, or hurt Kiara by holding her too tight with her unnatural strength.

"She knows her Mama, all right," Miriam said.

"She's so beautiful, isn't she?" Silas's deep voice rumbled in her ear.

Akasha hadn't noticed him leaning over her. She looked up to see the tears running unchecked down his cheeks. "Do you want to hold her?" she whispered.

His voice cracked. "Aye."

Holding her breath, Akasha carefully transferred Kiara to her father's arms. The wonder in Silas's eyes as he gazed down at his daughter made Akasha bite her lip to keep from bawling. Kiara seemed to know him too. Her tiny fingers curled around Silas's thumb as she stared at him.

Miriam sniffled and grabbed a Kleenex box, passing out tissues before dabbing her own eyes. "This is the moment I'd been dreaming about ever since Joe placed that little bundle in my arms. Of course, I will miss the dear little munchkin, but this made it worth it." Suddenly her gaze darted to Lillian. "You're the spitting image of Laura.

Lillian bit her lip. "Thank you. I wish I had more time to talk with you, but—"

"Of course!" Miriam said. "I do wish Joe had called and told me you all were coming. I'd have all her things packed."

"He died last month. He...had a heart attack," Lillian said quietly. "We would have called, but he only left your address, not your number."

Miriam's eyes widened. "Oh my God! I'm so sorry! He was a good man. At least he's back with Laura now."

Tears glittered in Lillian's eyes at the mention of her mother. Akasha's heart clenched in sympathy. She missed her mom too.

"Well," Miriam said. "I'll get Kiara's things together."

Lillian followed her. "Do you have her special formula?"

"Yes, but I'm down to only six tubs, so I'm glad you're here. Your father, God rest his soul, neglected to give me the recipe." Her voice faded as she headed down the hall.

Akasha wanted to go into the baby's room to see what an ideal nursery looked like, but she couldn't bear to let Kiara out of her sight. Already, her arms ached to hold her again. As if sensing her need, Silas handed her back.

"Oh, Silas," Akasha whispered, running her fingers through Kiara's silken hair. "She's so perfect!" She had an undeniable urge to take off the baby's little purple booties and count her little toes.

Miriam and Lillian emerged with two overflowing diaper bags, which Silas took. They then went into the kitchen and packed up the formula. Akasha remained oblivious to the conversations until one word made a lead weight drop in her gut.

"Car seat? Oh sh—I mean, darn! I completely forgot." Humiliation scorched her alive. She was the worst mother in the world. Maybe she should give Kiara back and—"

Miriam laughed. "I understand. You were in such a hurry to see your baby. Of course you wouldn't think of anything else. Just take the one Joe brought her in. My kids are too big for it."

Akasha resisted the urge to hug the woman as she brought out a small infant's seat, complete with a pillowed head-supporting arch.

"May I say goodbye to her?" Miriam asked.

"Of course." Even relinquishing her baby for a second made Akasha's chest ache. Still, she carefully transferred Kiara back to Miriam's arms.

"Bye, little munchkin," the woman cooed. "You're finally going home with Mommy and Daddy now. You be a good girl now, you hear?" With that, Miriam placed her in the car seat and buckled her up with expert hands. "Her binky is in the front pocket of the diaper bag, and I'll make her a bottle for the road. I changed her when I first got her out of her crib, so she should stay dry for another hour or two."

Akasha picked up the car seat and rocked Kiara, unable to stop looking at her.

When Miriam came out of the kitchen with the bottle, she blinked at Akasha. "Goodness, dear. You'll throw out your back, holding that heavy thing like that. You're so tiny. If you set it back on the floor, you'll see that it will rock by just moving the handle.

"Oh." Once more, Akasha felt like a total idiot. First, for forgetting to hide her strength, and second for not knowing even how a baby seat worked.

Miriam handed her the bottle and bent down to kiss Kiara on the top of her head before Silas suddenly captured her with his gaze. "You will not remember Lillian. You will not remember our names. We told you we were heading to Texas."

"Texas…" Miriam nodded. "I can't remember their names."

Hefting the baby and the bags, they left her, and Lillian showed Akasha how to buckle in the car seat. "Do you want me to drive so you can sit in the back with her?"

Akasha nodded gratefully. Silas also opted to sit in the back. They held hands, counted their baby's fingers and toes, and smiled.

Chapter Twenty-five

Lillian peeked in the rearview mirror at the happy couple. She'd done it. She'd found their baby and helped them get her back. All her worst fears...that the AIU had already tracked down the baby and taken it, that Kiara had gotten sick and died, that the woman who had her had moved away...none of them had happened. Retrieving the baby had gone easier than she ever thought possible. They had plenty of formula, and they were almost to the little airstrip in Kingman, the closest private airport to Flagstaff.

She should be relieved. She should feel triumphant. She should be damn exuberant.

Instead, she was terrified.

Now that her task was complete, what would become of her?

Would she stay with Silas and Akasha and be a live-in nurse to Kiara? Other than taking vitals, drawing blood, and feeding and changing, she didn't know anything about taking care of babies.

Or maybe she'd buy a home in Spokane or Coeur d'Alene. Would Silas and Razvan still be willing to protect her from the AIU? Director Bowers and the rest were aware that she was alive now. Agents would be hunting her. She'd have to spend the rest of her life looking over her shoulder. Would Silas and Akasha want to risk sheltering her when it could pose a risk to their baby? She wouldn't blame them if they wanted her as far away as possible.

The prospect of being kicked out of Coeur d'Alene prompted a more troublesome question. What about her and Radu? True, he had Marked her and thus forged a bond that would last until her death, but would he follow her into exile if Silas decided to make her leave? Even though Radu clearly cared for her, that didn't change the fact that they hadn't known one another long enough for him to abandon his brother for her. Nor would she want him to.

Instead of triumph as she pulled the car into the airport lot, a touch of moroseness overtook Lillian. Especially when there was no sign of the truck Razvan and Radu had taken to clean out the lab. She tried to tell herself that even though Radu's team had two hours' less driving time, cleaning out the lab probably took longer than retrieving a baby.

But as the minutes ticked by like seconds, her worry intensified. Bowers had the AIU agents searching Mesa and Apache Junction. What if they'd intercepted Jayden and the twins? What if they'd captured them? If their new objective was to kill vampires…Radu and Razvan might be in danger. Her stomach gave another lurch. If they'd been taken, it would be all her fault for insisting they clear out the lab. After getting Radu to the United States and reuniting him with his brother, she may have gotten them, and Razvan's kind fiancé, killed.

After Silas and Akasha struggled through their first adventure in diaper changing, Silas joined her by the fence that separated the boneyard from the live planes. When he looked at his watch and frowned, another worry bubbled to the surface. She peeked at the clock on her phone, seeing the ominous confirmation. The flight would take two and a half hours. If the truck didn't arrive soon, they'd be stuck here for the day, and in even more danger of being discovered. She tried to send a text, but the damn thing wouldn't go through. The reception was null out here.

Shoving her phone in her pocket, Lillian leaned against the cold chain link fence and watched the road. In the flat desert terrain, headlights would be visible from miles away. Yet the landscape remained dark.

Come on, Radu, she pleaded silently. If anything happened to him, she didn't know if she could bear it.

A hand landed on her shoulder, making her jump.

"My apologies, lass," Silas said. "I only wanted to ask if you are all right. You look troubled."

"I never should have sent them to the lab," she said quietly, even though Akasha was still by the car, feeding Kiara with such intense concentration that if the rest of the world caught on fire, she wouldn't notice.

"Don't be ridiculous," the vampire scolded. "As the senior Lord Vampire, it was my call, and I'd do it over again, given the research and equipment you and your father kept in that lab. You spoke truly when you said that the AIU cannot get their hands on those things."

Lillian sighed. "You're right, but that doesn't make me worry any less."

Silas smiled tightly. "I know."

Fighting her agonized worry, she changed the subject. "How can you be the 'Senior Lord Vampire' when Razvan is the one who made you?"

"Because I've been a Lord longer. Razvan only took Spokane five years ago when he'd given up his search for Radu. As I have more experience, I make the calls in matters such as this." Suddenly, Silas chuckled and shook his head. "What am I saying? There's never been anything like this. You and your father irrevocably bent the rules for my kind."

Her shoulders slumped. "I am sorry. I told Dad that it was a bad idea to tamper with…ah…your reproduction…especially without your knowledge and consent, but he was determined to see if it was possible. Most of all, I shouldn't have helped him."

"Yes, yes. I met the man, and I am well-aware of how focused he was with his studies. I mean it when I hold you blameless." Bending lower, he smiled and whispered. "Besides, I've always wanted a daughter."

"Thank you," Lillian said with gratitude at his absolving her. She looked back at the road. "But what if something happened to Radu?" She blushed and quickly added, "And Razvan and Jayden?"

From the corner of her eye, she saw Silas study her with an intent, unreadable expression. "As you pointed out before, Razvan Changed me into a vampire. Because of that, we have a sort of bond. If aught happens to him, I will know it. So far, there is no sense of danger. Besides, the Nicolae twins are over a thousand years old. Which means they are incredibly powerful. And Jayden has a certain talent of her own. She doesn't like to use it, but she will if she needs to."

Relief flowed into her like she was soaking in a warm pool. Like Jayden, Silas was a clairvoyant. He would be able to tell if Razvan…and by default, Radu and Jayden, were in danger.

A measure of her fear abated, and she dared to venture to another concern. "Jayden and Akasha told me a little about the Prophecy. Do you think that Radu is part of it, or…" She swallowed, hoping she didn't sound presumptuous. "Me?" Her face flamed as she was unable to bring up the mention of the "seven brides."

Silas tapped his finger on his chin. "It would not surprise me in the slightest if you both are involved, but I think that should wait until we return to Coeur d'Alene. With all that has transpired, it is hard for me to focus my attention on other matters. Ah." He pointed at the road. "There they are."

Lillian whipped around, pulse rising at the sight of approaching headlights. Even though she lacked a vampire's night vision and couldn't make out anything more than two dots of light off in the distance, she knew it was Radu. She sensed it deep in her heart. Was it an effect of the Mark he'd placed on her or something else?

Heart in her throat, she remained still until the truck pulled up next to the rental car. She didn't even notice Akasha walking up to them until she handed the baby to Silas. "You take her a bit so I can help with the heavy lifting."

Silas raised a brow. "I can lift as much as you."

Akasha grinned. "Yeah, but you've been glancing at Kiara every other minute. I know you want to hold her."

Just then, a small cry erupted from the baby. Silas visibly melted as he lifted her to his shoulder, gently rubbing her back and murmuring to her in his soft, Scottish burr.

Love flowed from their gazes to each other, encompassing the whimpering baby.

Lillian's chest tightened as she wondered what it would be like to experience love like that.

Then Radu emerged from the truck, and her pulse accelerated with joy at the visible proof of his safety. Razvan came out behind him, but she sensed nothing except friendly relief that he was okay. Strange how, even though the two vampires were identical in appearance, the responses they evoked in Lillian were vastly different.

His lips curved in a smile as his gaze lit on her. She started to jog to Radu, then slowed awkwardly. What if everyone thought she was desperate? Radu's smile dimmed, but he didn't break his stride toward her. As his arms enfolded her, she no longer cared if she looked silly.

She didn't know what it was about him, but he made her feel safe. In his arms, she experienced security that she never fathomed could exist.

Her worries fled as she helped the vampires transfer the lab equipment from the U-Haul to a hand truck to be loaded on the plane. All their bags were already aboard, and Silas's pilot paced back and forth, eager to get in the air.

Everyone let out a collective sigh once they boarded the plane and headed down the runway. Lillian watched the lights of the small airport shrink out the small window, seeing herself slipping out of the AIU's reach. Kiara began to fuss again as the air pressure changed, but Lillian barely noticed as she laid her head on Radu's chest and slipped into her first peaceful sleep in days.

Seemingly seconds later, Radu awoke her with a kiss on the forehead. "We've landed."

"Already?" she murmured sleepily.

After that, everything was a rush. Aside from their bags, the rest of the cargo would remain on the plane for now, as there was no time to unload everything. They piled into Silas's and Razvan's cars and raced back to Silas's home as the sky turned gray with the impending dawn.

When Jayden pulled into the driveway behind Silas's Barracuda, Lillian saw a black-robed figure seated on the stoop. She blinked and rubbed her eyes. Was it the Grim Reaper?

Razvan's answer was more terrifying. "Delgarias." His dry and nervous laugh echoed hollowly inside the car. "Of course he chooses now to drop in."

Delgarias. The Thirteenth Elder. The one who other Lord Vampires talked about with fearful eyes and hushed whispers.

Lillian shivered. What would he think about her? And how would he react to what she and her father had done? Her heart stopped as she saw Silas and Akasha get out of the car and walk around it to stand in front of the doors as if to block the backseat from view. Oh God, what would he do about Kiara?

Razvan and Jayden got out of the car, opening the back doors for Lillian and Radu with impatient looks. *Can't we just hide back here?* She wanted to ask. Radu looked like he was thinking the same thing, but with a sigh of resignation, he scooted out of the backseat and held out his hand for Lillian.

Just as she emerged from the car, Delgarias stood and removed his hood, and looked right at her. "Ah, here you are at last!" His face split in a wide grin. "The Engineer and third Bride!"

Jayden glanced over at her and murmured, "He did the same thing to me when I came here, except he didn't give me any titles. Just dropped in to see how I was doing."

Lillian nodded, though she only half paid attention to Jayden's words. It was impossible not to stare at Delgarias. His luminous skin, glittering blue eyes, and pointed ears marked him as something not human. Most astonishing was his hair. Each waist-length strand was translucent, with a black inner core, so it shimmered like midnight held captive in glass. In all of her studies, she'd never seen hair, fur, or scales formed in such a manner.

Delgarias winked at Jayden. "You were so overwhelmed by me that I saw no need to compound it, Inner Healer, second Bride. Oh, and am I invited to the wedding?"

Jayden bit her lip and looked up at the graying sky. "Of course."

Bride. Lillian shivered. And he'd called *her* the third one. The muscles in her neck tightened with the effort not to look at Radu to see his reaction. Did he want their relationship to go that far? Did she?

Delgarias turned those otherworldly eyes on her once more. "And you've recovered the lost brother. Very good."

Radu inclined his head respectfully but remained silent. So far, Delgarias didn't seem mad at them.

But once the Thirteenth Elder glanced back at Silas and Akasha, Lillian supposed she'd thought too soon.

"You all returned home rather late." His piercing gaze roved over the Lord of Coeur d'Alene.

"Aye." Silas maintained eye contact, but the tightness in his shoulders betrayed his nervousness. "Perhaps if you would return tomorrow? Dawn approaches, and we must retire."

Ignoring the request, Delgarias stalked closer to the car as Silas and Akasha visibly tensed. "What are you hiding?"

Lillian sucked in a breath. Silas hadn't told the Elders about the baby. Fear raced up her spine in an icy path. And now they were facing the big boss Elder. What would he do to Kiara?

Her legs tensed, ready to bolt to the car, but Radu's hand clamped on her arm, holding her in place. "You'd die," he whispered.

Akasha and Silas certainly seemed ready to. They moved closer to block Delgarias's path to the car. Akasha's fists rose like a boxer ready for a match, and Silas bared his fangs.

Delgarias moved forward, and Silas charged him with a snarl. The Elder sighed and muttered a word as his unnaturally long fingers flicked in their direction with a graceful gesture. Both Akasha and Silas froze, completely immobile. Even their faces were still twisted with silent battle cries.

Razvan and Radu moved in front of Lillian and Jayden but otherwise made no move to defend the baby. Instead, they all watched with slack-jawed horror as Delgarias brushed past Akasha and Silas and opened the car door.

"What have we here?" he asked, though no one was capable of a reply.

Lillian's throat tightened to hold back a scream as she heard the baby gurgle. Delgarias's expression was out of view as he leaned inside the car. Through the pounding of her heart, she heard him unbuckle the seatbelt and another sound from the baby that she couldn't decipher.

Then Delgarias emerged, holding the baby with those odd fingers cradled gently around Kiara's tiny body, supporting her head with practiced care. For the longest time, he simply stared at her. The baby gazed back with wide, alert eyes. Then she reached up and curled her chubby fingers around a lock of his glistening hair.

Delgarias smiled a second before his lips turned down, looking grave. His gaze darted to Silas and Akasha, and then to Lillian, then back at the baby. His brows drew together, and his eyes once more met Lillian's, stealing her breath. For a moment, he opened his mouth to speak to her, but then he returned his attention to Akasha and Silas. "It seems something is missing from your report."

A small croak escaped Silas's frozen lips as he remained trapped in a half-lunging position.

Transferring the baby to a one-armed football-carry, Delgarias strolled to Akasha and patted her drawn-back fist. "Now, there was no need to attack me, little General. We can accomplish so much more with a civil discussion. If I release you, will you behave?"

Akasha made a small squeak that Delgarias seemed to take as assent. With another soft word and swipe of his hand, Akasha and Silas stumbled forward, gasping as they grasped each other for balance.

For a moment, it looked like Akasha would attack Delgarias anyway, but then her shoulders slumped before she reached out for the baby, eyes pleading.

With one last, lingering glance at Lillian, Delgarias handed Kiara back to her mother. "Silas is right. We had best go inside."

Silas lowered his head in assent, but mingled wariness and hostility swirled in his still-glowing eyes as Akasha got the diaper bag. Staying between the Elder and Akasha, the front stoop crowded while Silas unlocked the door.

Razvan and Radu strode forward, shielding Akasha from either side as Lillian and Jayden glanced at each other and took the rear guard.

Two by two, they headed down to the basement. But as Silas reached to open the secret panel to the chamber beneath the basement, Delgarias held up a hand. "I need to stay in here, if you do not mind. The egress windows are sufficiently covered."

Silas nodded, but checked the windows anyway.

Delgarias sat on a raised platform in the corner, leaning against a dusty amplifier. A drum kit sat behind it, and a microphone stand stood off to one side, gathering cobwebs. When she'd first stayed there, Lillian had been confused as to why this stuff was down here, then she remembered. The missing band, Rage of Angels, had been friends of Akasha's. They must have practiced down here.

The Elder vampire placed both hands flat on the platform and closed his eyes like Jayden had when seeking a vision. But somehow, Lillian didn't think that was what he was doing. When he opened his eyes, he looked somehow more alert and refreshed.

"Pull up some of those bean bag chairs," he commanded, gesturing to another corner of the large basement room.

Silas sighed and grabbed two bags, and Radu grabbed two more while Razvan kept watch over Akasha and the baby. Lillian got the last bag, noting that there were five. One for Akasha and one for each band member.

Once they were seated like kids awaiting storytime, Delgarias leaned forward and eyed them all. "These reports about the AIU's change in agenda are very disturbing, especially now. A national council meeting for all the U.S. vampires will be arranged as soon as possible." His gaze encompassed Lillian.

"You will tell me everything, and I mean *everything*, that you know of the AIU, and the events that led up to your father's death, and about your coming to be here with Radu Nicolae." His brows drew together, and he leaned forward. "And I also want to hear about this baby."

Licking dry lips, Lillian told him everything, growing more nervous by the second as Delgarias remained expressionless. Would he snap her neck as soon she finished talking? Radu's grip tightened on her hand. Would he get himself killed trying to protect her?

Her fear increased when Delgarias didn't immediately respond.

Jayden patted her on the shoulder. "Want me to get you a glass of water?"

Lillian nodded gratefully, and at last, Delgarias smiled. Maybe that meant that she wouldn't die.

When the Thirteenth Elder finally spoke, it was to Razvan and Silas. "I informed the Elders that I will be handling all cases in the Northwestern United States for the time being. Given that Lillian is one of those I've foreseen in the Prophecy, it was easy to determine what to do with her."

"Which is?" she dared to ask.

"Why, you will stay here, naturally. Whether in Coeur d'Alene, Spokane, or somewhere in between, I do not care, so long as you remain under either Lord McNaught's or Lord Nicolae's jurisdiction." His piercing gaze shifted to Radu, lingering there before moving to the other two vampires. "However, just like with the General and the Seeress, she is not to be Changed until I decree it."

"Earlier, you called me the Engineer," Lillian said, bringing the Elder's attention back to her. "But I'm a biophysicist, not an engineer."

Delgarias raised a brow and then looked at the baby, who was squirming in Akasha's arms. "Aren't you?"

She shook her head. "That was mostly my father's doing. And all his idea."

"Be that as it may, you've contributed to an...interesting situation."

Kiara let out a cry, and Akasha held her close. "I won't let you take her away from us."

Delgarias eyed her coolly. "You couldn't stop me if I were so inclined." His features softened. "But I would never dream of parting a child from its mother. Even if..."

"If it's a baby that's not meant to exist?" Silas cut in. "You didn't *see* her in your visions, did you? So she may muck up your precious Prophecy."

The Elder shook his head. "There's no such thing as something that's not meant to be. People and events that serve the random are to be expected. And just because I did not see her does not mean she does not have an important role to play. I did not see Martin Luther King. I did not see Marie Curie. I did not have a vision of the day any of you were born. I only became aware of your existence when I knew what you would do. Thus far, none of your paths seem to have changed." He paused and swept them all with a scolding look. "So please, stop looking at me as if I'm going to denounce your daughter as an abomination and burn her at the stake."

His expression softened. "The only thing I am concerned about is how the rest of our people will react to this knowledge. I will have to tell the Elders, of course. Only to avoid another ludicrous trial, like the one four years ago. Other than that, I recommend keeping her existence quiet for the time being. If other vampires discover that it is possible for them to have children, they might want one for themselves." His eyes darkened. "And I am not certain that is a good idea."

Suddenly a rank smell permeated the air.

"Um," Akasha said, "Is this meeting done? I need to change the baby."

Delgarias nodded. "For now. We can discuss the rest tomorrow." He rose and strolled to the couch.

As Akasha rummaged through the diaper bag, she looked up at him. "How is Xochitl?"

The Elder stretched out his long frame and closed his eyes. "She had a few ordeals herself, but last I saw her, she is well."

"Do you know when she is coming back?"

"No." The word was clipped with finality.

A hand fell on Lillian's shoulder, making her jump.

"I did not mean to frighten you," Radu whispered. "I only wanted to help you carry that bag so we may retire."

Lillian needed no further urging. She handed her beanbag to Radu and grabbed another to put them away. Razvan and Jayden seemed to have had the same idea. Once the bags were stowed back in the corner, the four of them left Silas and Akasha and headed down to the lower guest rooms, eager to put some distance between themselves and that vampire who had clearly been something else other than human before he was Changed.

Chapter Twenty-six

Hours before sunset, Radu rose from the bed. Despite all the stressful things he'd endured and the monotony of travel, he found he couldn't sleep much. Perhaps it was because he'd spent the last seven centuries asleep. Or maybe, it was the overwhelming sense of power radiating from the Elder vampire upstairs. A power so deep and cloying that it crawled over his flesh. Or maybe it was the vast chasm of the unknown that threatened to swallow him...and Lillian. Though Delgarias and Silas had agreed that Lillian would be welcome here, nothing was said about him. Except that Delgarias called Lillian a bride. Surely that meant Radu was to wed her, but...a stone of dread sank in his belly. What if she didn't want to be his bride?

Sitting on the edge of the bed, Radu gazed down at Lillian. Even though her features were relaxed and her body composed in slumber, the dark circles of fatigue under her eyes and a fine crease between her brows reflected the unceasing travails she'd endured the past three nights...and days.

Between securing her father's information and hours of driving to help Silas and Akasha recover their baby, she'd had barely a moment's rest.

The AIU was still out there, looking for her. And now they knew she was alive. The infant may be safe, but Lillian was in more danger than ever until Radu could fulfill his original promise: to help her destroy those who had murdered her father and sought to kill her.

And now that Silas and Akasha's baby had been safely delivered home, Silas and Razvan would now decide which of their territories he and Lillian would reside in and what their roles would be. With the Thirteenth Elder already here, waiting for them, it seemed that had already begun.

Radu's frown deepened. Delgarias had been expecting Lillian, and with his talk of her being a bride and an engineer, he clearly anticipated that she would play a role in this Prophecy. But as for Radu, the Elder hardly acknowledged him, aside from calling him the lost brother, which was a fact. Nothing prophetic about it, nothing that carried weight for the future.

Lillian made a soft murmur in her sleep and burrowed deeper under the blankets. Radu felt a tug on his heart so sharp that it hurt. Why did he care so much? He'd only known the woman for a few weeks. And yet that meager time had awakened him, made him feel more alive than he had in centuries. Somehow, Lillian had come to mean more to him than Uta had. Yet even if she wanted to continue to share her future with him, what *was* his future?

Restless with countless unknowns, Radu quietly left the bedroom and paced back and forth in the hall. Delgarias's power radiated from above, making it impossible to forget the Elder's words.

Engineer, Bride. But who was Radu?

The door next to his opened and Razvan came out into the hall with an inquiring look. Radu cursed inwardly. Of course, his twin would sense his anxiety.

Razvan refrained from launching into an immediate inquiry. Instead, he flicked his gaze upward and scratched the stubble of his regrowing beard. "Hard to sleep with *him* upstairs. Even if he does tone it down for Jayden's sake."

"He's *shielding?*" Radu asked incredulously. "I can feel his power like an itch all over my skin."

Razvan chuckled and withdrew his pipe from his robe pocket. "Usually, it vibrates in your bones and teeth."

Shuddering at the thought, Radu leaned in close and lowered his voice. "Back when we were younglings, the Thirteenth Elder was believed to be a myth. When did he make himself known?"

"From what I've heard, he's paid visits to a handful of Lord Vampires over the centuries, paying particular attention to Silas. But his real return was when Silas was summoned to a farce of a trial before the Elders." Razvan grinned, lighting his pipe. Cherry scented tobacco wafted between them. "You should have seen the looks on their faces."

Radu frowned at the pipe. "Put that out. Akasha said no smoking with the baby here."

Razvan quickly tapped out the pipe in a little brass ashtray he carried in his pocket. "That will take some getting used to."

Radu found himself smiling back at his brother. "From what I understand, Delgarias has been visiting more frequently."

"Yes."

"So that means that whatever this Prophecy is, it's going to happen soon." He looked down at his bare feet, trying to ignore the shroud of dread cloaking him.

"I assume so." Razvan studied him intently, cocking his head to the side. "Why does that upset you? You used to be up for an adventure."

Radu sighed. "He called Lillian a Bride, but he didn't say whose bride she was. I mean, I'm fairly certain that she is to be mine. But for one thing, would Lillian want marriage? For another, what else am I supposed to do?"

Razvan arched a brow. "Is that all? He never specified that Jayden is mine, though it is clear that she belongs to me. As for what we're supposed to do, I'm pretty sure it will involve fighting some enemy."

For the longest time, Radu remained silent, but his brother's dark eyes were like invisible hooks digging into him, ripping out the truth. Radu shoved his hands in the pockets of his borrowed robe. "I love Lillian. I can imagine how foolish that sounds as we've only known each other a short time, but there it is. Yet I do not feel right to ask for her hand until I've established my place in this world as well as resolved everything with you."

Razvan grasped Radu's shoulder. "You can't keep wallowing in guilt about what happened with Mother and Father. It was not your fault. We've been through this. You are my brother, and one of the eldest, most powerful vampires in the world. You are honorable. You—"

"You won't think so when I tell you one more truth." Radu's shoulders slumped as he braced himself for another damning confession. "I lied to you, Razvan. When I said that you were the one left out to die by our birth parents and I was the one who was chosen by Father, by both sets of parents. I lied. Mother told me that it was me who was left outside to the wolves. It was you who the *Voivode,* our father, chose to take from your cradle. *You* were the one who was wanted."

Razvan blanched, face tight with shock as if he'd been slapped. "Why did you lie to me?"

"I was jealous," Radu choked out the bitter words that had been festering inside him for a millennium. "You were Alexandru's true heir, destined to follow in his footsteps in everything. You were the most clever, the bravest, the most confident. The first to embrace the Change, the first to develop your powers. I could not compete, so I lied to hurt you. I just wanted to be first in something. I suppose I succeeded in that. I was the first to be a petty fool."

Silence hung over them in a leaden pall. Radu closed his eyes, waiting for his brother to denounce him, to banish him from his side for all eternity.

Unable to bear the heavy quiet, Radu opened his eyes to see Razvan smiling and shaking his head.

"And all this time I'd been envious of you," Razvan chewed on his unlit pipe. "You had the lion's share of our mother's love. Both of them. Crina always held you first, and Ihrin greeted you with the most smiles."

Radu's brows shot up to his hairline. "You were envious of me?"

"How could I not be? Be it our mothers' affection or the adoration of every female in the village, you stole the heart of every woman who crossed our paths. Against you, I never stood a chance." He laughed. "To be honest, I'm happy you were not around when I found Jayden. Else you likely would have stolen her heart too."

"I have no interest in your witch, I mean, clairvoyant," Radu corrected himself. "Lovely as she is."

"Yes, it is clear to the world that you only have eyes for the lovely Lillian," Razvan said, pocketing his pipe. "And though I want to throttle you about your lie, I forgive you. That was centuries ago." Suddenly, he moved forward and embraced Radu. The twin bond enveloped them like a healing balm. "Anyway, tomorrow will be soon enough to learn where we go from here. Good day, Brother." Razvan clapped him on the back before releasing him and returning to his room.

Radu decided to do the same. Willing his worries to abate for at least a few hours, he enfolded Lillian in his arms and breathed in the scent of her hair, savoring the heat of her body tucked against his.

The peaceful solitude ended too soon. Shortly after dusk, Silas's house filled with strange vampires. First was a doctor, accompanied by a nurse. Both marveled over the baby before they whisked little Kiara off to examine her. Lillian and Akasha followed at their heels. It was apparent to all that what had been her father's pet project, Lillian saw as a great responsibility. Radu longed to follow her, but Razvan shook his head and gestured that he should remain beside him in Silas's office.

The next visitor was Silas's vampire attorney, Anthony Salazar. When he'd recovered from his shock at Kiara's existence, he opened his briefcase and launched into a nearly incomprehensible diatribe of what sort of paperwork was required for the infant.

All the while, the Thirteenth Elder sat quietly in a corner, his pale, unnatural blue eyes surveying everything and everyone. Radu wasn't the only one whose hackles rose at the presence of the strange and powerful vampire. Just what had he done to suspend Silas and Akasha in mid-attack? And what was he?

Just when Salazar finished his legal monologue, gathered up his papers, and departed with a bow, Lillian and Akasha returned with the doctor. Silas held out his arms for Kiara, and after taking his daughter, he gestured for Lillian and Radu to sit before his desk. "Razvan, Jonathon, you stay too," he addressed the doctor.

Akasha gave Lillian one of those mysterious looks of female solidarity before she bent down and kissed her husband on the cheek. "Jayden and I are going shopping for baby stuff."

"Aye, lass. Kiara and I will eagerly await your return."

When the women left, Silas's gaze flicked between Radu and Lillian, looking no less ominous despite the chubby, gurgling infant he dandled on his knee. "I may as well come out with it, Miss Holmes. I need you to remain in my territory rather than Spokane. First, because your knowledge is essential to my daughter's health and wellbeing. Second, you will be invaluable in Jonathon's clinic. Tomorrow, you will move your lab equipment there and start working with him and his nurse,

Jessica, in explaining your experience so they may decide what your job will be. Do you have any objections?"

Lillian glanced at Radu, then shook her head. "I thought my chances to use my degree ended with my fake death. I'm relieved that I'll be able to continue my work." She swiveled her seat to face Delgarias and continued with the same clinical tone. "I would very much like to study your genome."

Everyone sucked in a breath to hear her speak to the Thirteenth Elder like he was a specimen.

Delgarias laughed. "And I would be interested to see the results. Let's schedule an appointment once you're settled in." Rising from his seat, he grinned at everyone. "I see that everything is well in hand, so I will take my leave for now."

With that, shadows swirled around him, enveloping him until he vanished.

A collective sigh of relief echoed through the room at the intimidating creature's departure.

Except for Radu. His hands gripped the arms of his chair so tightly the wood creaked. Lillian seemed overjoyed to join McNaught's ranks and work with the doctor. His gaze narrowed on Jonathon. The vampire doctor was entirely too handsome, with his pale blond locks and eyes as blue as Lillian's. What if Lillian was to be Jonathon's bride instead? They certainly had more in common.

Just as Radu opened his mouth, whether to argue or plead, he didn't know, Silas turned his flaring green gaze on him. "And now we come to you. With your age, power, and being the brother of Razvan Nicolae, you should be a Lord Vampire in your own right. But since you've been hibernating for so long, you have no experience in ruling in this modern world. Furthermore, you must establish your power among the other vampires, earn their respect, and prove yourself capable of leading. Now Razvan and I have done a lot of talking…"

Razvan cut in. "With the impending Prophecy, we've decided to keep our territories united. For that, a third Lord Vampire would be beneficial in securing the Northwest and ensuring we have the right vampires running things if or when we have to leave. Eventually, we hope to consolidate the Inland Empire in a triumvirate of sorts."

"Precisely," Silas said as he handed his daughter a paperweight, which she gnawed on with her pink gums. "You may be a viable asset to this plan, Radu. But first, we must determine what to do with you. Common sense dictates that you belong with your brother, and you will indeed go to Spokane with him to learn how he runs things."

Blood roared in Radu's ears. Of course he wanted to be with his brother, but what about his relationship with Lillian? Would he be permitted to visit her in Coeur d'Alene? He looked at her. She sat stock-still, staring ahead. He couldn't read her expression, and when he reached out with the Mark, he encountered such a chaotic cacophony of thought and emotion that he was unable to discern whether she was dejected or jubilant.

When he looked back at Silas, he saw that both he and Razvan watched his internal struggle with calculated interest.

Razvan continued announcing his fate. "Yet there are other factors to consider. The first is your Mark on Lillian. We wouldn't dream of interfering with such a sacred covenant, so naturally, you may see her when you wish. Also, it would be beneficial for you to spend time in Coeur d'Alene, training under Silas. We both have different ways of managing our respective territories, and you should see what works best for you."

A measure of panic slowed its rapid fluttering in his chest. He wouldn't be parted from Lillian. At least not completely.

But from the sound of things, he would be spending much of his time learning lessons in lordship from Razvan, while she would be spending most of hers with that damned doctor. Radu saw that Lillian was pleased to be using her talents once more, and he was happy for her. Truly he was. But did Dr. Jonathon Greenbriar have to be so damned comely?

The pages of the report shook in Stebbins's trembling hands as he read to Bowers. "The bank records under the Holmes's J & L Research account at that small bank Lillian visited reveal something extremely strange. There were several purchases from New Life Medical Supplies. I checked them out, and they specialize in equipment for in vitro fertilization."

Bowers scratched his chin. "They were setting up a fertility clinic? What were they trying to breed, I wonder?"

Stebbins shrugged. "Maybe Junior—I mean, Lillian—was infertile and wanted a baby."

"Why didn't she just visit a fertility clinic?" Bowers countered. "It would have been quicker and more cost-effective than setting one of her own up. Besides, she wasn't married or even dating."

"Many women these days will voluntarily become mothers without a man in the picture," Stebbins argued half-heartedly. "Or maybe she and her father were preparing to go into business for themselves and leave us."

"The AIU is for life," Bowers snapped. "Holmes Senior was well aware of that, and he should have informed his daughter." He ticked off each point with his fingers. "Holmes Senior was, ah, retired because of his insubordinate attempts to stop Operation Wrangler. He wanted to protect those monsters. He was infatuated with them. With all the IFV equipment purchases, I think they were trying to breed the things. We'll know for sure when we do a complete search of that building they'd leased under their other company name."

Stebbins wiped a rime of sweat from beneath his collar. "About that. The building was burned to the ground last night before the team arrived."

A surge of anger contorted the director's features before he took a deep breath through his nose. "And the remains of the equipment?"

"There were none. The place was reduced to ash." When he'd heard the news, Stebbins had inwardly cheered, despite himself.

"Then she recovered the equipment and tried to erase her tracks," Bowers said through gritted teeth. "There is no way she could have done that herself. She had help. As she did to leave Castle Nicolae and Romania in the first place. And speaking of..." His tone shifted to something more airy and speculative. "The drones discovered that the vampire is no longer beneath the ruins. It has left hibernation. You know what that means?"

"What?" Stebbins asked, though he had a pretty good guess.

"Those creatures have taken her under their wing. They are helping her, just as her treasonous father attempted to help them." Burning fury returned to Bowers's cold gray eyes. "And I don't suppose your team has picked up her trail?"

Stebbins hunched his shoulders, trying to hide his relief in delivering the news. "No, Sir. She's vanished without a trace." Attempting to divert the director from Junior, he forced a mild tone. "Why don't we just let the vampires have her? They keep themselves secret, so the chances of her revealing classified information are null. And we're still making headway on Operation Wrangler." He shuffled his papers in an organized stack. "In fact, I'm due to dispatch the recovery team for our next subject. And the vivisections will be scheduled—"

"The vivisections can wait for now," Bowers interrupted. His teeth bared in a horrific parody of a smile. "Perhaps we can combine the objectives of Operation Wrangler with our mission to recover Miss Holmes. Vampires have a tightly knit communication network, as we've observed. If some have been aiding her, others will have heard."

Chapter Twenty-Seven

Four weeks later

Lillian looked up from the skin sample she'd been observing, and wrote down more notes before rubbing her lower back and trying to ignore the screams of pain in the operating room. Dr. Greenbriar's latest patient was a vampire who'd been nearly decapitated in a car accident. Lillian had asked to be allowed to observe how the vampire's tissue knitted back together with the aid of blood transfusions, but the doctor had refused, saying her presence would increase the vampire's stress and delay the healing. Also, since she was human, there was the risk of him attacking her in a fit of bloodlust. Dr. Greenbriar did, however, allow her to take a scrap of the patient's ragged flesh back for analysis…which didn't go as well as she'd hoped, since the tissue deteriorated so quickly.

Since vampires seemed immune to illnesses and aging, the majority of Dr. Greenbriar's cases were broken bones and severed limbs. And since there were only seventy-six vampires living in Coeur d'Alene, he wasn't very busy. The majority of their time had been spent exchanging information on vampire physiology.

With his CT scanner, Jonathon was able to look into a vampire's brain. Lillian was interested but not surprised to learn that they altered upon transformation. The sensory cortex expanded, the number of cortical folds increased, and the gray matter became denser. The only thing that appeared to shrink was the adrenal gland and the pituitary gland. And the hypothalamus appeared to be altered, but she hadn't gotten a chance to dig more.

Her fascination with the brain scans rivaled the doctor's enthusiasm for her Electron Microscope, photoactive probes, and gene chips.

It was quickly decided that her first task would be to see if there was a way to better preserve vampire blood for transfusions, which were the primary ingredient in every treatment, but broke down at a dismal, rapid rate. Lillian already had a plan in mind, which would utilize synthesizing recombinant DNA.

She should be happy. She was back doing what she loved, learning the mysteries of the paranormal. Hell, she now had access to multiple vampires, a psychic, and two different sorts of mutants. And tomorrow, Delgarias would come in to allow her to take blood and tissue samples. She was dying to observe what was in his DNA.

Instead of fulfillment and jubilance, a sense of emptiness gnawed a hole in her heart. She missed Radu. After spending four weeks practically glued to his side, being without him made her ache like her entire skin was a raw wound.

At first, she tried to tell herself that it was simply her mind adjusting to the lack of stimulus his presence had provided, and likely her sex drive reacting to no longer being indulged every single night. But her heart screamed the truth until she could no longer deny it.

She'd fallen in love with Radu. She'd gone to Romania to stake his heart. Instead, he'd claimed hers. Never mind the fact that she'd only known him for a little over a month. Her college friends were right. Love gave the finger to logic.

With her in Coeur d'Alene working with Dr. Greenbriar while monitoring Kiara's development, and Radu in Spokane with his twin, they'd barely seen each other.

Even worse was the fact that ever since Delgarias had called her a Bride, Radu had been quiet and pensive. Was he upset with the news? Did he not want to marry her? She understood that such a sudden commitment would be off-putting. Hell, Lillian wasn't sure if she was ready for marriage either, but she hadn't considered that he might be repulsed by the idea. She hoped he wasn't. After all, Radu hadn't given her a clear reaction to her prophesied title. And she was too scared to ask.

So Lillian kept quiet about the subject, hoarding each moment with him like precious jewels. To break away from Silas and Razvan and all the vampire politics, they often went out to the movies, then dinner. Her heart melted at Radu's sometimes over-the-top bliss when he tasted her food. She'd gained a few pounds thanks to that, but it was worth his reactions.

During their little movie dates, Lillian almost felt normal, going out with the guy she loved and savoring every touch and heated glance until they'd either end up at Silas's or Razvan's place, making love like it was their last day on Earth.

But those times were too few and far between. And with everything else going on, it was getting harder to pretend. From what she'd seen of Razvan's handling of the Spokane vampires, he was like a mob boss, infusing his leadership with an undercurrent of fear. Silas, on the other hand, was more like a big corporate CEO, meticulous that everything was done by the book and with the proper paperwork keyed in their secret code.

Only last night, after having dinner at a fantastic Vietnamese restaurant, Radu had told her that he didn't think he wanted to lead like either of them. "Before he'd lost interest in ruling, my father was feared and respected among his vassals. But he was also loved. They knew he would keep them safe from invading enemies and that if they had a grievance, or committed a crime, he would listen to each case and make the fairest judgment he could decide. I think I will try to be more like him."

"I think you will be a great leader," she said before taking another sip of her *pho*. And that just made her love him more.

But as Radu was finding his place amongst the vampires in the Inland Empire, Lillian continued to feel like an outsider. The other vampires clearly regarded her as one too. First off, she was human and thus not even supposed to know about them. Even more damning was that she was a scientist, something they'd been taught to fear ever since they'd been Changed.

Jayden and Akasha had attempted to comfort her on the day they went out to sample wedding cakes.

"They used to give me the cold shoulder too," Jayden said after taking a bite of a cake with lemon curd filling. "Vampires used to kill psychics on sight in the old days. But now that they've heard that Razvan will Change me as soon as he's allowed and that I'm getting my degree to help them, they're getting used to the idea."

Akasha grinned and grabbed a piece of cake with cream cheese frosting. "I think they're all still scared shitless of me since they know I could rip their heads off with my bare hands. That, and I've never been much of a people person."

As Jayden nodded in emphatic agreement, Lillian concurred. Akasha was an abrasive one and definitely reluctant to let people in. Yet she'd befriended Lillian rather quickly.

"You've been kind to me ever since I showed up here," Lillian told her. "And I can't thank you enough for that."

"Yeah," Jayden said in an odd, musing tone. "You were nice to me right away too. Hell, you broke Razvan's jaw the night you met me just because you thought he was holding me against my will. I think you're more of a softie than you let on."

"Maybe," Akasha grumbled. "But honestly, I think it might have more to do with the Prophecy."

"What do you mean?" Lillian asked, picking at her cake.

"Something Silas and I figured out about Xochitl. She's not human, and other humans naturally sense that and avoid her. But when she met her band, they didn't react that way. Instead, they instantly clicked. Silas and I think that was because of all the things they were destined to do together. And she and I became friends because Silas was destined to guard her and the band. And apparently, I'm supposed to help her lead a war." Akasha shrugged and swiped a blob of frosting from Lillian's plate. "Anyway, I figure that since you and Jayden are involved with the Prophecy too, it makes sense that we'd get along right away."

Lillian blinked at her nonchalant tone. "You both seem really calm about this Prophecy stuff."

Jayden shrugged. "Well, I am a psychic. I'm used to omens and portents."

"And I'm married to one," Akasha added. Then she blushed. "That and, well, it's nice to finally have friends, so I don't really give a damn about how I got them, I'm just happy to have you guys."

Warmth filled Lillian's heart. "I never really had friends either. And I am glad to have you both."

Friends made her feel like she was building a new life, more than her work. Which was a change from her previous life in the AIU. But there was still something missing.

And now, as she put away her microscope slides and wiped down her corner of the lab, a black hole was expanding in her chest. Radu hadn't called her last night or during the day.

What if he'd already tired of her? Razvan had said he was popular with the ladies. What if one of the Spokane vampires had caught his eye? What if—

Suddenly, the air heated around her, and an almost imperceptible breeze flitted through her hair.

Dr. Greenbriar's voice echoed in the hallway. "Mr. Nicolae, if you would wait in the lobby, Miss Holmes will be out shortly."

Lillian's heart skittered. Radu was here.

"Mr. Nicolae!" Jonathon's protested.

And he wasn't going to wait outside for her. She reached up to remove her surgical scrub cap just as the lab door opened, and Radu strode into the lab.

Normally she would have scolded someone for coming in unannounced in case she was working with something that required a completely sanitized environment, but instead, she remained frozen, gazing raptly at him, his presence making her nerve endings sing, his dark eyes sending ripples through her belly.

"H-hello," she said dumbly, wishing she was wearing something more attractive than her scrubs, lab coat, and poofy cap. "What are you doing here?"

Radu stalked toward her with sinuous grace, those sinful, dark eyes holding her captive. "I sensed your distress. What is hurting you?"

Heat flooded her cheeks. *The Mark.* She'd been pining for him so badly that he felt it. "I...um...It's silly. It's..."

"Something you don't want to tell me." He stood inches from her now. Slowly, he reached up and brushed his knuckles along her cheek. "What is it, Lillian? What brings those shadows of pain to your eyes?"

His will washed over her in an irrefutable tide, compelling her to bare her soul. But sharp barbs of insecurity dug into her as well.

"I'm um, not exactly dressed for this," she stalled. "Can I at least get out of my scrubs so I don't look so…nerdy?"

His husky laugh vibrated through her, tightening things in her lower body. "You look…ah, that word my brother uses…adorable." His fingers slipped down from her cheek to graze her collarbone. "Though I do agree that we should get you out of your clothes. But first, tell me what hurts you."

"Do you still want me?" The question tore from her throat. "I mean, not just for sex."

Her face flamed as he tilted his head with a mute inquiry for her to clarify further. She took a deep, shuddering breath and pressed on. "It's just that you've been so distant ever since Delgarias showed up and called me a Bride. Like you're averse to the idea of sharing your life with me. I know it's stupid for me to be bothered. We haven't known each other that long, but—"

Radu's arms locked around her with dizzying speed. His lips closed over hers, cutting off her words. He kissed her until her legs turned to jelly, and liquid heat pulsed between her thighs.

Dragging his mouth from hers, his eyes glowed as he gasped raggedly, "I will show you how much I want you."

One hand swiped off her cap and grasped her hair while the other cupped her ass, pulling her against his hardness. Lillian gasped as his lips trailed down her jaw before closing over that deliciously sensitive spot on her neck. She writhed against him as her core throbbed with need.

Then he was pulling down her pants, smiling wickedly as she helped, kicking off her shoes. Her fingers frantically unbuttoned his shirt, eager for the heat of his skin.

Before she knew it, they were both naked. Radu lifted her in his arms and carried her towards the exam table.

"Wait," she gasped. "Not there." Even though she sterilized the surface after she so much as touched it, the idea of making love where she worked with blood and tissue wasn't appealing.

Radu nodded and turned, walking purposefully to the left side of the room. For a moment, she thought he was going to press her up against the wall and take her there, but then he sat on her stool.

Lillian wrapped her legs around his waist. A deep moan flowed from her lips as he lowered her onto his cock. She watched him throw back his head and clench his teeth as she sank down all the way to the base of his shaft.

His hands cupped her ass, shifting her at an angle that reached all her tender spots. Lillian arched her hips, riding him in an undulating rhythm that reached all her tender spots. Clinging to his shoulders, she cried out as he gripped and moved her in a quicker pace, stoking the fires of her mounting pleasure.

The ecstasy built and built until it peaked with such intensity that her orgasm roared through her entire body, not just her pulsing core. Mercilessly, Radu kept up the intoxicating thrusts, taking her climax yet higher. With a low growl, his fangs sank into her throat as he came, overwhelming her with sensation, his pleasure feeding hers in a neverending loop.

When at last he stilled, Lillian went limp in his arms, his heart pounding against hers.

I love you. The words froze against her lips. Instead, she said, "We should probably get dressed. Dr. Greenbriar probably heard everything, but that doesn't mean I have to give him or Jessica an eyeful."

With an endearing groan of reluctance, Radu lifted her from his cock, and set her on her feet. "Someday, I will make love to you so fiercely that I will banish all sensibility from that brilliant mind of yours."

Heat filled her cheeks as she scrambled to put her clothes back on, unable to form a response. Radu heaved a melodramatic sigh before grabbing his pants and pulling them on.

"Are you hungry?" he asked with such a hopeful note that she laughed.

"As a matter of fact, I am. I always seem to work up an appetite after we…" She paused and narrowed her eyes. "Is that why you pounced me?" she teased.

"No. I did that because you're irresistible." His wicked grin made her feel like she was still naked. "Though I cannot deny the benefits of giving you an appetite. Would you like to have ice cream again?"

Her laughter increased until her belly hurt. "I suppose. But we need to stop by Silas's place first. I am not going out in public in my scrubs."

Lillian led Radu from the lab and locked the door behind her. With flaming cheeks, she explained to Dr. Greenbriar that she didn't need a ride home after all. He gave her a knowing smirk before going back to his charts.

When she and Radu exited the clinic, he pulled her into his arms, and they rose up high in the air. Her belly dipped at the sudden altitude. Radu hadn't flown with her since Romania. Clinging to him tighter, she wrapped her legs around his waist, savoring the solid heat of his body against hers. With him, nothing could hurt her.

Too soon, they landed in front of the modern castle. Lillian made an attempt to straighten her sex touseled and then windblown hair, but to no avail. It would be obvious to everyone what they'd been doing.

As soon as they entered the house and saw Silas pacing through the living room, his features drawn and grave, Lillian's euphoria dissolved. Was something wrong with the baby?

Silas turned to face them. "The Lord of Phoenix has called in the favor I owe him."

"Which is?" she prodded softly, trying to tamp down relief that at least Kiara was still okay. Because whatever had happened seemed just as dire.

"The AIU has taken one of his people. He wants one of us to rescue him."

Chapter Twenty-eight

"I will go," Radu said firmly. Finally, here was an opportunity to do something useful. "You have a wife and a baby to look after." His lips peeled back to bare his fangs. "And I already vowed to kill Bowers."

Lillian gripped his arm. "I'm going, too."

"You can't," he growled in fury at the thought of her returning to such danger. "The risks are too great."

"Getting inside the compound will be impossible without me," Lillian countered with a stubborn lift of her chin. "Besides, your original promise was to help me take him down. We will do this together."

Radu's growl deepened at the thought of her being anywhere near Bowers. His eyes bored into hers, willing her to defer to his will, but her gaze held his, not backing down. Her will beat against his through the Mark they shared.

"You know I'm right." Her voice rang with an implacable challenge. "I know the layout of the place, where the holding cells are, where Bowers's office is. I'll know the best place to get in, the best place to get out. If the captive vampire needs medical attention, I'll be best suited to administer it. Furthermore," she grasped the collar of his shirt and pulled him down until they were face to face. "I have the right to avenge my father."

Razvan laughed as he stalked into the living room. "And don't think I will allow us to be separated again either, Brother."

Radu turned to him with a frown. "But you are to be wed in a week."

"So?" Razvan shrugged. "We'll be back with plenty of time."

"Yeah," Jayden said from behind her fiancé's shoulder. "I'm coming too."

As the vampires' gazes whipped to her in immediate protest, she held up a hand and addressed Silas. "You know what I'm capable of," she said with her hands on her hips. "Tell them that I'd be useful."

Radu frowned. What was the psychic capable of that would aid in this situation?

"Aye," the Scottish vampire said with obvious reluctance. "But I'm not sure if the benefit of your talent outweighs the danger."

Razvan also frowned, but did not immediately refute Jayden. Instead, he kept his gaze on Silas. "Either way, my brother is right. You must not go."

Silas's jaw tightened. "But the Lord of Phoenix is calling in this favor from me."

"Yes, but you will be the one sending us. Two ancients and a woman who's familiar with the inside of the AIU headquarters."

"And a powerful psychic," Jayden added, crossing her arms over her chest. "You know, the prisoner may need counseling when we get him out." She reached up and caressed the point of Razvan's growing beard. "Just like Lillian said to Radu, we will work together. After all, that is what marriage is about."

Radu bit back a smile. Jayden had his brother there. Then his mirth faded as he realized he hadn't gotten the chance to ask Lillian for her hand in marriage as he'd planned to do tonight. Damn this disaster for interrupting.

We'll do this together. Lillian's words echoed in his mind. At least there was that. And he would do everything in his power to keep her out of harm's way. If any of those AIU agents so much as touched her, he'd tear out their throats. Except for Bowers. He had something a little more…thorough planned for him.

"Radu?" Lillian's voice brought him back to the present. "Are you okay?"

"Yes." He bent and kissed the top of her head, breathing in the sweet scent of her hair. "Why do you ask?"

"You were smiling, but not in a good way."

His savage grin broadened. "I am looking forward to killing our enemies."

Silas laughed. "You make me wish I was coming along."

Razvan leaned against his desk and withdrew his pipe. "So you are seeing sense?"

"Aye. I can't go leaving my bairn." His green eyes lit up at the mention of Kiara before narrowing on Razvan's pipe. "No more smoking in the house, remember?"

Razvan twitched and gave him a guilty look before tucking the pipe back in his breast pocket. "Sorry." He swiveled to face Lillian. "What is our best plan for getting into the building?"

Lillian paced a few steps back and forth in front of the fireplace, her mind racing so intently that Radu felt her thoughts like rippling waves. "I know which entrances don't have metal detectors, and if Bryan can access the shift logs, we'll see who is working and where they should be. If we could just get past the gates and I found a way to open the door, you guys could rush in with your super-speed." She sighed and trailed a finger along the shining black marble hearth. "Too bad my badge is inactive."

Silas leaned forward. "Wait, you still have it?"

"Yeah, it's stuffed at the bottom of my backpack somewhere, but I'm dead, or at least they thought I was until our trip to recover Kiara. Now I'm on their wanted list, so there's no way that badge will work." Waves of frustration emanated from her taut form.

"Bryan might be able to change that. I'll call him now, and then I'll call my pilot." Rising from the recliner, he pulled his cell from his pocket.

Razvan once more withdrew his pipe. "I'm going to step outside while you do that."

In mute agreement, they all followed him. Instead of walking down the flagstone porch steps, Razvan jumped off into the grass. Leaning against the stone wall of the castle, he lit his pipe and looked up at the stars. "We might die on this venture."

Radu leaped down beside him. "We could have died on the last one." Tentatively, he reached out to clasp his brother's shoulder. "Are you afraid?"

"Afraid?" Razvan laughed before taking a deep draw on his pipe. "No. Like many others, I've been arguing for the AIU to be taken down ever since its incarnation. It is too dangerous for mortals to know about us. And it was inevitable that they'd take a more hands-on approach to their studies and eventually seek to kill us. I am eager for the opportunity to stop them." The embers of his pipe reflected in his eyes, which remained solemn. "However, that doesn't change the fact that we've just been reunited, and I only found the love of my life less than a year ago. It would be a shame for my happiness to end so soon."

Jayden walked through the grass and wrapped her arm around Razvan's waist. "I think we're going to make it. Delgarias seemed pretty sure that we have other things to do."

Lillian nodded as she stepped beside Radu. He grinned and seized her, pulling her back against his chest, unable to get enough of her warmth. She tilted her head backward to look up at him, a plethora of emotions in her bright blue eyes. "Every vampire we've talked to believes he's omnipotent. I don't believe that is the case, but I do believe that we can succeed in rescuing that vampire. The trickier part is getting away with it without being traced back here."

Razvan blew out a cloud of smoke. "You're right. We may have to leave the state for a time. Perhaps even the country." His forlorn expression echoed Radu's. "A pity. I really like it here."

"I do as well," Radu said. After all that he and Lillian had endured on their journey to make it here, and after being welcomed so readily by Silas and his wife, having their help in finding a place and a purpose, the prospect of finding someplace else to call home made his heart sink in despair.

The iron gate at the bottom of the hill swung open, and Akasha's Roadrunner roared up the driveway and pulled to a stop in front of the garage. She got out of the car and eyed them curiously. "What's with the meeting?"

Jayden explained while Razvan watched Akasha warily as if expecting her to demand to accompany them.

Instead, the woman's shoulders visibly relaxed with relief. "You guys better be careful. Don't make me come down there to rescue you. I've dealt with government goons before." She shivered before she turned and got Kiara out of the car.

Lillian's gaze swept over Akasha's disheveled hair and coveralls. "Did you bring her to the shop with you?"

"Yup. Silas had some of his people sterilize part of it and overhaul the ventilation system, so there's no fumes or anything." She bounced the baby on her hip. Kiara gave her mother a slobbery grin, an emerging tooth glinting in the moonlight. "She hung out in the playpen for a while and then in her swing while we listened to music. She really likes Tool. The only thing I'm having trouble with is getting used to wearing gloves so my hands don't get covered with grease. Anyway, does anyone want to hold her for a minute? I haven't had a cigarette in hours."

The concern bled from Lillian's eyes. "It will be good for her to see her mom work."

"Yeah," Jayden reached out and took the baby. "A lot better than her being stuck at some daycare— or night care, in this case."

Kiara gurgled something at Radu and reached out with chubby arms. Jayden gave him a questioning look. He nodded and held out his arms.

The baby was light as goose down, warm as sunlight, and wriggly as a fish. Radu adjusted his grip and gazed down at the wonder that Lillian had helped to create. It had been centuries since he'd held an infant— the last had been one of his birth sisters' babies— and his heart once more tightened at the experience. Peering into Kiara's green eyes that were so like Silas's, a thought whispered in his mind before he managed to stop it. *Lillian and I could make a baby.*

Shaking off the thought, he cursed himself for a fool. Aside from the fact that a vampire hybrid child may be detrimental, and that it would be foolish to have a child when they were embroiled in a multitude of hazardous situations, one thing remained a larger barrier to any plans for the future.

He had not yet asked Lillian to share his life. What was holding him back? A foolish desire for the right moment? Tomorrow they would be risking their lives.

And yet, as he looked down at the little baby who had grabbed fistfuls of his hair, Radu was unable to find the words.

Chapter Twenty-nine

Lillian took a deep breath and crossed the parking lot of the AIU compound. The skin between her shoulder blades itched the moment she got in range of the surveillance cameras. Even though night had fallen, the heat from the Arizona desert sun radiated up from the asphalt, making her sweat beneath the Kevlar vest she wore under her clothes. Razvan had been in a shootout or two and had a stash of vests that he insisted everyone, even the vampires, wear.

Her badge thumped across her vest with every step. She resisted the urge to grab it to still its motion. Funny how she'd never noticed the thing in the two years she'd spent working here. Now that Bryan had reprogrammed the magnet with another employee's ID, the lanyard scratched her neck, and the incessant thumping drove her mad.

Even more irritating was the gun holster at the small of her back, under her Kevlar vest and lab coat. The damn thing chafed, but without any special powers like the vampires, she needed some sort of weapon, and every AIU agent underwent lessons at the gun range.

Behind her, Radu, Razvan, Jayden, and four other vampires from Phoenix waited. They were loaded for bear as well, with backpacks full of welding torches from Akasha's garage, grappling hooks, a first aid kit, and a variety of weapons.

If everything worked, she would use the badge to get past the gate, then open the door at the south end of the building, closest to where the holding cells were located. Bryan had sent out a memo that locks on the north gate would be temporarily disabled and would need extra guards there. In reality, he would shut down *all* of the gates.

The vampires would knock out the remaining guard at the south gate, dash in the building with their preternatural speed, get past the staff, break down the holding cell door, and whisk the captive to safety. It was a simple, slapdash plan, nowhere near the idea of rappelling down the air ducts Mission Impossible-style, with Bryan guiding her through a Bluetooth earpiece, but it would have to work.

And at least she did have Bryan on the line, but he was only able to tell her who was working tonight and which department they'd last badged into. Though he could take care of the gates, there was no way for him to disable the security cameras without activating an alert that would send armed agents to the compound in minutes.

They would have to suffer being seen and pray that hers and Jayden's brown wigs, the vampires' caps, and their blurring speed would make them harder to identify. The only thing going for them was that fewer staff worked the graveyard shift. But twenty employees and eight armed guards were still a lot.

Their talk of leaving Coeur d'Alene and going into hiding became more likely every moment. But she would bear it as long as Radu was with her.

That is…if they got out of here alive.

Five feet from the door, Lillian whispered into the little Bluetooth piece. "I'm going in." She didn't need to signal Radu and the others. With their preternatural senses, they could see and hear her.

"Okay." Bryan's voice sounded slightly crackly in her ear. "Jones just logged into break." Jones was one of the guards assigned to the holding cells. "And the lab tech is entering data on one of the computers in Lab D."

"Perfect," Lillian said with a confidence she didn't feel. But Bowers was in there. Bryan had confirmed that much to her. And he had to pay.

Now was the moment of truth. Grasping her badge, she swiped it through the reader on the door. When the little light blinked green, and she heard a click, the breath she was holding slowly trickled from her lungs.

At first, the door didn't give. Then she realized it was because her hands were slippery with sweat. Wiping them on her pants, she turned the handle and pushed the steel door inward. Immediately, the cold AC blasted her, making goosebumps rise all over her skin.

A trickle of cold sweat ran beneath the gun holster, making her extra aware of its presence. Lillian prayed she wouldn't need to use it on anyone but Bowers.

Actually, she didn't want to shoot him. An evil smile that was more of a grimace stretched her mouth. She had something else in mind for Bowers. That is if Radu didn't kill him first.

As if conjuring Radu with her mind, a black blur seized her, jolting her where she stood before her feet left the tiled floor. Another black blur with a patch of brown went by. Razvan and Jayden. Just like when outlining the location of her secret lab, Radu had fed from Lillian to gain the layout of the AIU compound with Jayden holding her hand.

Lillian's blurry vision from the rapid motion made her stomach lurch with nausea. She closed her eyes until Radu set her back on her feet a second later. In front of her, Razvan and the other vampires surged back in one breath, and in the next, a metallic clang rang out so loud she winced. They hurled themselves at the door, trying to force it open.

Radu stood beside her, eyes darting up and down the halls, in wait for AIU agents to come running. He wasn't disappointed.

A stocky man in a lab coat burst out of the door to D Lab, eyes so wide the whites showed all over. Radu growled, fangs bared and eyes glowing, but the man's attention remained on Lillian. His gaze scanned her white lab coat and brown wig before moving back up to her face. His cup of coffee—which he wasn't supposed to have in the lab—fell from limp fingers.

"Junior? You're alive?"

A lump formed in her throat at the nickname even as she drew the pistol and pointed it at him. "Get back in the lab, Craig," she said with the most authoritative voice she could muster. "Now! And you never saw me."

"I—okay!" But before Craig turned to flee, Radu seized him.

Lillian grabbed Radu's shoulder. "Don't hurt him! He's not part of this."

Radu snarled something in Romanian before capturing Craig's eyes with his glowing gaze. "You will go back to what you were doing. You will lock the door and stay in there until morning. You will not remember any of this."

He released Craig, who stumbled and nearly slipped on his spilled coffee before scrambling back into the lab and locking the door.

Another crash reverberated through the corridor as the other vampires attacked the door. This time, the walls shook with the force, but still, the door didn't give. Lillian had been afraid of that. After all, the thing was designed to hold vampires captive.

Footsteps thundered through the hall. Three agents rounded the corner, and shots rang out.

Lillian raised her gun as a bullet whizzed past her shoulder. These guys wouldn't show any mercy. She recognized them as Bowers's personal thugs.

Firing, she dropped one man before Radu thrust her behind him. Razvan roared and charged them with blinding speed, his brother at his heels.

It was like watching a horror film on fast forward. Screams tore through the hall as blood, guts, and chunks of flesh went flying all over the place. Lillian blinked and stepped closer to Jaden, who had her back pressed against the wall to avoid gunfire.

The Phoenix vampires charged the door again. There was a sharp crack as part of the frame gave way, but the door still held. One of the vampires cried out in agony as his shoulder caved in.

After the two men collapsed in bloody heaps, Radu and Razvan returned. Radu gently nudged the wounded vampire away before thrusting himself at the battered door. The frame made another cracking sound. Radu leaped back and then forward, slamming the dented steel with a kick.

The door still refused to give.

"The torch!" Jayden said. "Maybe we can melt the hinges."

"What hinges?" One vampire snapped. "I can't see any."

Lillian's heart sank. "We're running out of time. Someone had to have activated the alarm by now. We're going to be overwhelmed by a SWAT team any minute."

Suddenly, a voice called from around the corner. "Junior!"

Radu and Razvan jerked their heads in the direction of the voice, fangs bared.

Lillian frowned and kept her gun pointed down the hall. "Who is it?"

"Agent Stebbins."

Her frown deepened. Stebbins had always been kind to her, but... "You mean, assistant director?" Accusation dripped from her voice. The assistant director didn't do anything without the director's command.

"Not by choice," he said. "I only found out what really happened to your father afterward. What Bowers tried to do to you."

"How did my father die?" she spoke past the bile burning her throat.

Silence filled the corridor before Stebbins answered. "Bowers shot him in the back of the head execution style."

Radu uttered a curse in Romanian.

"And why did you stay after you found out?" Lillian demanded. She glanced at the door to the holding cell. "As assistant director, you oversee all of our operations. How could you go through with Operation Wrangler?"

"Because I was afraid!" Stebbins said. "Bowers made it clear that I'd get the same treatment as your father did if I didn't cooperate."

Rage boiled through her at his cowardice, along with a bitter dose of self-disgust as she realized that she wasn't sure what she would have done if she was put in the same situation.

Dad tried to stop it. That's why Bowers killed him. Lillian reminded herself. *And they believed I would have tried to stop this too. Otherwise, they wouldn't have tried to eliminate me as well.*

"Why are you here now, talking to me instead of trying to kill me?" she asked, maintaining her grip on the gun.

"I want to help." Stebbins's voice lost its tremor, filled with resolve. "What Bowers is doing is *wrong*. Murdering our own agents, torturing and killing living things. I didn't sign up for this. I should have tried to stop it sooner, but by the time I realized what was going on, I was already in too deep." They heard him sigh, remorse imbuing the sound. "But now that you're here with a team of rescuers, the least I can do is open that door so you can free the vampire."

"How do we know this isn't a trick?" She'd trusted Stebbins and her fellow agents before. Never again.

"You don't have any reason to." Sorrow and regret dripped from his tone. "But I'm alone and unarmed. Your vampires should be able to hear and smell that. Ask them."

Radu and Razvan glanced back at her and nodded in confirmation.

Breathing deeply through her nose, Lillian nodded back at them. They didn't have any other choice. They were running out of time. "Come out slowly. Hands on your head."

Agent Stebbins emerged, fingers laced atop his short black hair. Beads of sweat trickled down his forehead, despite the cool of the air conditioner. "I am happy to see you alive, Junior. I mean that. I always admired you and your father."

Lillian couldn't form a response for that, but she didn't have to. In the blink of an eye, Razvan seized Stebbins and thrust him in front of the door to the holding cell. "Open it. Now."

Looking up at the vampire, Stebbins's jaw clenched. "If I do, you must promise to take me with you. I'm a dead man if I aid you and remain here."

Razvan's lips curved in a sinister smile. "Deal."

Somehow, she sensed that Stebbins would come to regret that bargain. But Stebbins seemed satisfied.

With trembling fingers, he punched the code in the keypad. "You must hurry. Bowers has already called for backup."

"Where is he?" Lillian asked.

"Holed up in his office." Stebbins stepped away from the door. "With four guards waiting at the entrance."

The door made a clunking sound as the locks discharged, but it didn't budge. The frame was warped.

Razvan charged the door with a savage kick until it flew open with a metallic shriek.

As the vampires charged in, Lillian and Razvan turned around and backed in, guns trained at the doorway.

Suddenly, the most piteous bleating whimper reached her ears. Lillian turned and immediately wished she hadn't.

The captive vampire hung suspended from chains, completely naked. His entire body was covered in angry red burns and blisters. One eye had been gouged from the socket, leaving a scabbing hole. Runnels of dried blood coated his face. The vampire squirmed and whimpered in his chains, a plea that couldn't be ignored.

Lillian had never seen someone so broken, so mindless with agony. One of the Phoenix vampires froze, face bone white with shock at the sight of the captive's piteous state.

The horror in Stebbins's eyes matched hers. "I don't have the key to the restraints. I'm sorry."

The Phoenix vampire tried to break the chains with his hands, but they were crafted to withstand a vampire's strength. Cursing, he pulled a torch from his backpack and attempted to hold it to the chains, but the vampire screamed and thrashed so wildly that there was no way to aim the flame.

Radu seized the captive's shoulders and spoke to him so softly that Lillian couldn't hear what he said. As he spoke, the Phoenix vampire heated up the upper links on the chains until they glowed red. Then he pulled them apart. The molten metal stretched, looking like goopy glue.

The captive collapsed in Radu's arms, sobbing and clinging to him for dear life. Lillian's heart ached for the poor guy. Waves of guilt pelted her that she had been part of an organization that would inflict such monstrous torture upon a living thing. If she made it out of here alive, she vowed to use her Bioengineering only to help others.

Radu gently stroked what was left of the vampire's hair and muttered soothing words to him, promising safety, promising an end to his pain. His eyes met Lillian's over the vampire's shoulder, full of rage.

She studied him for a second. "I love you."

Radu's lips curved in a tender smile, and he opened his mouth to respond, but Razvan cut them off. "We must go now, before—" He broke off as one of the Phoenix vampires shouted, and the sound of multiple heavy boots thundered down the hall.

It was too late.

Gunshots erupted, and the vampire guarding the door collapsed as his head exploded. A dozen men burst into the cell, dressed in armored suits, and armed with machine guns, rocket launchers, and what might have been a flamethrower.

Lillian had a split second to relive the short, blissful time she shared with Radu before they opened fire again.

Chapter Thirty

Radu had a second to place himself in front of the captive before the first barrage of bullets took him in the chest. What felt like a million giant balls of hail slammed into his ribs and sternum, the impact stealing his breath. He nearly tumbled to the floor but managed to keep his footing.

Lillian wasn't so lucky. She collapsed before he could reach her.

Diving down, he yanked her into his arms, curling his body around hers to protect her from their attackers. "Are you all right, Lillian?" He spoke past the ringing in his ears. If she was killed, he didn't know if he would survive it.

"Ow," she groaned. Her wig had flipped in front of her face, and she tore it off. Since Radu was half deaf, her reply was mostly inaudible. Radu mostly read her lips. "These vests might be bulletproof, but getting shot hurts like hell." Still gripping her own little gun, she held it up and aimed over his shoulder.

Her shot took one of the men in the face of his glass helmet. The glass cracked, but the bullet didn't pierce the shield. Still, the web of cracks obscured the man's vision.

Two vampires rushed the attackers but could not find purchase with their fangs through the armor. One vampire was shot in the head, but the other managed to throw the man across the room, slamming him into the steel-reinforced wall.

Razvan remained on his feet, firing a larger gun at their helmets as well, though it looked like he was aiming for the exposed inch of flesh on their necks. One went down, a gout of blood sprayed from the wound.

The vampire they'd released groaned with hunger and crawled forward.

"No!" Radu yelled even though the prisoner likely couldn't hear him. "Stay hidden, or they'll kill you!"

The captive must have discerned Radu's intent, for he made a mewling sound of protest before reluctantly crawling back behind the meager shelter of a steel cabinet.

One of the other men shot a weapon that had a barrel like a cannon. A metal canister clattered on the floor with a thunk. One of the Phoenix vampires seized it and threw it back. A deafening explosion shook the room and tore three of the men to shreds. But still, eight remained.

Lillian fired her gun again, cracking the helmet of one of the men who aimed another explosive cannon. The shot went wild, clattering in the corner of the cell before anyone tried to catch it and lob it back. A second explosion erupted, tossing them back like rag dolls. Radu clung to Lillian and ducked, shielding her from the worst of the impact of slamming on the concrete floor. Chunks of debris hailed upon them like stones from an angry mob.

From the corner of his eye, he saw Jayden scramble to her feet. She stood facing the men with a look of fierce concentration. Some alien power radiated from her as one of the men dropped his gun, clutched his chest, and immediately collapsed.

"Drop your weapons," she commanded in a voice that was deeper than her usual soft cadence.

Two obeyed, and a machine gun and the grenade launcher clattered on the floor.

Lillian and Radu gaped at her in shock. Jayden had been right when she said there were things she could do.

But she didn't vanquish them all. The third man instead raised his weapon as more guards poured into the room to protect him. Fire blazed from his weapon's black tip in a deadly spray. Radu rolled himself and Lillian out of the path of the flames. "Get the prisoner and get out!" He shouted to no one in particular.

Two of the Phoenix vampires scooped up the captive and darted to the doorway, knocking the three of the men on the floor, but missing the one with the flamethrower. One of the Mesa vampires remained on the floor, a chunk of shrapnel protruding from his heart. The other noticed his dead friend and let out a deafening roar before launching himself at the men.

As the man with the flamethrower tottered from the impact, his weapon went off again in a sweeping, upward arc, covering both the vampire and the men with fire. The reek of burnt flesh and hair stung in Radu's nostrils. For a moment, he was transported back to that fateful day when he returned home to see his castle aflame. The sound of his mother and father screaming, the smell of them cooking to death in the flames.

Then his heart lurched. Not this time. He would save the ones he loved. Lifting Lillian in his arms, he nodded as Razvan did the same with Jayden.

"Wait," Lillian coughed. "Stebbins."

Radu looked to see the man on a bloody heap on the floor. He was more inclined to leave him there, but Lillian's pleading eyes undid him. Heaving a sigh, he reached down and grabbed Stebbins's ankle, unceremoniously dragging him out.

Razvan reached into the wall of flame and seized a man, flinging him to the other side of the room as Radu elbowed the others aside. The moment Radu and Lillian passed through the doorway, Razvan and Radu forced the warped steel slab shut, muffling the screams somewhat.

For a while, they slumped against the wall coughing uncontrollably. Radu rubbed Lillian's back as she hacked. Tears streamed down her cheeks from the choking smoke. Slowly, she recovered her breath. "Are you okay?" she mouthed.

He nodded. "I have a bullet in my forearm, but I'll heal." He gestured with his words in case she was as deafened as he was. "What about you?"

"Just some bruises," Her lips formed the words as she cupped her ears. "Also, I'm deaf from all the gunfire and explosions, but I consider myself lucky." She smiled and squeezed his hand before they both turned to survey the rest of their party.

Razvan limped alongside Jayden. She appeared unharmed, but Razvan had a gaping wound in his shin. The two remaining Phoenix vampires sat slumped against the wall next to the prisoner. They both had a multitude of cuts on their faces but otherwise seemed fine. The prisoner thankfully hadn't sustained further injuries.

Her gaze traveled to Stebbins's prone form. Disengaging from Radu's embrace, she clambered to the AIU agent's side.

Her trembling fingers reached out to press against the side of the man's neck. "He's still alive." Radu faintly heard her say.

"Not for long," Stebbins croaked as his eyes opened. "They got my lung." In confirmation, blood splattered from his mouth as he coughed. Slowly, he reached for his chest. "Take my badge. It will open Bowers's office." His bloody lips grinned in his ashen face. "I paid. Now it's his turn."

Lillian's fingers curled around the badge, though she didn't yet unclip it from his pocket. "Thank you."

He coughed again, another clot of blood flying out of his mouth. "I don't deserve your thanks. But at least I died doing the right thing." One more cough, another splatter of blood, and Stebbins went still.

Smoke curled from the cracks of the cell door, triggering the fire alarm. Water rained down on them from the overhead sprinklers.

Lillian ground her fists against her teary eyes and gingerly removed the badge. "Let's go get Bowers."

Radu waited to hear an objection from Razvan or the Phoenix vampires. Surely more men would be on their way.

Instead, they all nodded.

Just then, the captive vampire barreled into Stebbins. His fangs latching onto the corpse's neck, throat working as he guzzled the remaining blood.

Lillian made a small sound of protest, but Radu held her back. "The man has no more need for his blood. And this one needs to regain his strength before he goes feral and tries to attack you or Jayden."

After the vampire finished, he grasped Radu's ankles, pressing his head against his legs, babbling incoherently. Radu's heart constricted with pain for the poor defeated creature, and even though he needed to conserve his strength, he lifted his wrist and slashed it with his fangs before lowering the bleeding wound to the broken vampire.

The vampire fed with eager gulping swallows until Radu's head swam with dizziness. "Enough," he growled, and wrenched his wrist away, ignoring the pain as his flesh tore further. Turning to the Phoenix vampires, he commanded them, "Take him to the van and return him to his master. We will meet up with you as soon as our last bit of business is concluded."

The Phoenix vampires nodded and took the freed captive away, ignoring his pleas to stay with Radu. Why the vampire had formed such an attachment to him, he didn't know. But what he'd suffered was yet another crime to lay at Bowers's feet.

Radu pulled Lillian into his arms and claimed her lips in a devouring kiss, savoring each taste and sensation as if it was the last. Because it very well could be. Who knew what surprises Bowers had in store for them?

With a tight grip on Radu's hand, Lillian marched resolutely down the hall and to the elevator, with Razvan and Jayden following behind. Cursing as the elevator door refused to open, she gestured for them to take the stairs.

The reek of smoke and gunpowder had risen to the top floor of the building, though it wasn't nearly as strong.

Two more thugs waited in the hall, but Razvan and Radu made short work of them.

"This one." Lillian pointed at a door with Bower's name engraved on a brass plaque.

Crouching on either side of the door, Lillian once more withdrew her gun before swiping the badge at the electronic lock. Just as Stebbins had promised, the control panel blinked green, and the door unlocked with a click.

Still hunkered down in case of gunfire, Lillian pushed the door open, training her pistol forward.

A shot whizzed past her, narrowly missing Radu as well before he bolted forward and knocked the gun from Bowers's grip. Razvan stormed into the office with equal swiftness, pinning the man's other hand.

Radu got his first look at the man who killed Lillian's father, who tried to use him to kill Lillian.

Though Bowers was slight in build, balding, and with birdlike narrow shoulders, a trickle of ice seemed to race down Radu's spine at the sight of the man. He'd never seen a human with eyes that cold and merciless.

Lillian, however, was undaunted. "You killed my father."

Bowers nodded. "He was trying to stop me."

"So I heard." She stalked closer to him, like a mongoose facing a cobra. "Why did you launch Operation Wrangler?"

Bowers craned his neck upward to regard Razvan and Radu with a look of blazing hatred that turned his gray eyes molten. "Vampires are monsters. I've known that since one killed my mother."

If he'd been expecting sympathy, he was courting the wrong woman. Lillian laughed, bitter and dry. "There are monsters in every species. If it had been a mortal man, would you then want to exterminate the human race?"

Instead of answering, Bowers regarded her with a petulant scowl. It was too late for him to see reason.

Lillian shrugged and tapped the gun on her hip. "I suppose it doesn't matter anyway. You're through, Bowers. You'll never kill anyone ever again because I'm going to exterminate you."

Radu found his voice. "No. Let me kill him. Let me avenge you, your father, and all those of my kind that he's destroyed."

Razvan nodded. "He's right. Taking a life can sometimes leave a stain on your soul. Let us take that burden."

Her lips curled in a rueful smile. "That is kind of you to offer, but I swore an oath to kill the one who murdered my father. That burden belongs to me."

Razvan opened his mouth to protest, but Radu silenced him with a squeeze on the shoulder. Bowers took that opportunity to try to lurch out of his chair, but Radu seized his wrist and slammed it on the desk, smiling at the crunch of breaking bones. "No. You will take your payment for what you've done."

Lillian reached the desk, eyes intent on her prey. Radu stared, enraptured. She looked like an angel of vengeance, descended from heaven to pass judgment on the unworthy.

He thought she'd shoot Bowers in the head with her pistol, but instead, she set the gun on the desk, just out of reach, and bent down to reach inside her boot sheath. She rose, holding a gleaming scalpel.

Bowers thrashed further. "You fucking bitch! You're just as monstrous as they are!"

Radu seized the man's head with his other hand, tilting it back. "I saw what you did to that vampire we pulled from your cell. You're the monster. She's giving you a quicker death than you deserve."

Leaning across the desk, Lillian pressed the scalpel to his Adam's Apple. "He's right. And you should be thankful we don't have enough time to make you suffer as your captives did."

With that, she dragged the blade across his throat. Blood poured out in a crimson parody of a smile.

Lillian's composure dissolved as she flinched and gagged at the wet, gurgling sound that passed through Bower's lips. His cold gray eyes stared at her as the blade slipped from her fingers and fell in front of him with a clunk.

Radu was only too happy to finish the job. With a roar, he sank his fangs into the wound, drinking the lifeblood of his enemy. Razvan's head bumped his as he too closed his mouth over the other side of the gash.

The twins drank and drank, for once letting go of their usual restraint to take only a little, instead, sucking down their fill.

Once Bowers was reduced to a bloodless husk, they let the body thump face-first onto the desk.

Wiping his mouth, Radu crossed the office and pulled Lillian into his arms. Her face was pale, and her slight body was trembling, but a smile of utter peace made her radiant. "Let's leave this place."

Suddenly they heard a man clearing his throat.

Radu whipped around, and his heart lodged in his throat at the sight of Delgarias leaning against the door frame. The Thirteenth Elder's strange eyes surveyed the bloody scene before him and shook his head. "I have never seen such reckless, indiscreet behavior. You infiltrated a government building, killed federal employees, and murdered the director of one of the branches of the FBI. One of the lower branches, but no matter."

Lillian's shoulders slumped. "We had to."

"We'll leave the country," Razvan said coolly. "Go into hiding."

Delgarias shook his head. "That's not good enough. I can't risk this escapade interfering with the Prophecy. You need to go home."

"But won't they track us down?" Jayden argued. Just like Lillian's, her wig had long since become dislodged.

The Elder gave her an inscrutable smile. "Not if I can help it." With that, a ball of white light formed in his palm. He lobbed it at Bowers, and the corpse vaporized into a pile of ash.

Razvan gasped, his face white as chalk. "What are you?"

"There's no time for explanations. For all I know, more men might be on the way. Follow me."

In the elevator, Lillian stammered out an explanation to Delgarias as he rubbed the bridge of his nose. "I understand. Believe me, I do. And the AIU *will* be dealt with before they can kill any more of our people. But that does not lessen the danger and inconvenience you've caused."

Once on the main floor, Delgarias strode to the center of the lobby, his pale glittering eyes glowing like sapphire flames. His arms rose, and lightning crackled from his freakishly long fingers.

The lightning blazed up in the air, shooting out in multiple bolts in every direction. Pops and cracks echoed throughout the building as the sharp tang of ozone permeated the air.

"Shit!" Delgarias suddenly cursed and threw out a hand towards them. A clear, rainbow-tinged bubble formed in front of Radu, Lillian, Razvan, and Jayden just before a bolt of blue lightning skittered against the barrier.

The shield vanished as quickly as it appeared.

"I'm terribly sorry," Delgarias said with a short bow. "I'm afraid I'm not as good at that as my nephew-in-law."

Before they could absorb the mind-boggling concept that this being had equally deadly relatives, the Elder beckoned them forward. "Now that I've fried every camera and electronic device in the building, it's time we head off. You have a plane to catch."

"Wait," Radu said, even as his instincts quailed at the prospect of arguing with one so powerful. "There is something I must do."

Instead of turning that deadly lightning on him, Delgarias regarded him with a smug smile as if he knew what Radu intended. And perhaps he did.

Slowly, Radu down on his knees and took Lillian's hands in his and gazed up into her eyes that were blue as the morning sky.

"We may have only known each other a short time, but I think it's still been long enough to know my heart." He took a deep breath in an attempt to calm that heart, which was now threatening to burst from his ribs. "Lillian Holmes, will you marry me?"

Epilogue

Lillian clutched her bouquet of lilies and gardenias and smiled nervously at Jayden. "Are you sure you don't mind?"

Jayden laughed. "It's a little too late now. Honestly, I'm happy to not be the only one being stared at. Besides, we may as well get used to things like this. Radu and Razvan are twins, so they like to do things together."

"Yeah...but even sharing a honeymoon?"

Jayden didn't have time to respond to that, for the string quartet had started the first strains of Metallica's "Nothing Else Matters." Both Radu and Razvan originally wanted to hire the actual band, but Lillian and Jayden put their respective feet down. Though they both liked heavy metal and rock music just fine, neither was inclined to walk down the aisle to electric guitars.

All of the vampires of both Spokane and Coeur d'Alene sat in folding chairs alongside the aisle. Except for Delgarias. As if not wanting to frighten the others, he stood off to the side in the shadows but with a clear view. He met Lillian's and Jayden's gazes and smiled, looking like a proud father.

Akasha faced them with a grin. "Showtime."

With that, she headed down the aisle with Kiara in her arms. Both mother and daughter looked resplendent in matching blue satin gowns. Adjusting her grip on the baby, she awkwardly scattered flower petals on the length of white cloth spread across the sand. Kiara was crawling now, and everything she could reach ended up in her mouth. But she was a cheerful baby, and all Silas and Akasha could talk about these days.

"Ready?" Jayden threaded her arm through Lillian's, clutching her bouquet in her other hand.

Lillian nodded. Though her heart ached at not having her father with her on the happiest night of her life, having her new sister at her side dulled the worst of the pain. Side by side, they walked down the beach, the waters of Lake Coeur d'Alene seeming to lap in time with the music. Twins for the night, they both wore simple white silk dresses with silver flowers embroidered on the bodices and hems.

Radu and Razvan awaited their brides, dressed in identical black tuxedos with blue silk dress shirts beneath their jackets. Lilies adorned their lapels. Beside them stood their best men. Silas smiled near Razvan's shoulder, while Angelo, the vampire they'd rescued, remained at Radu's side, looking far healthier than he had when they'd taken him from his cell. He was even a little dashing with the eye patch. He'd insisted on going wherever Radu went, and the Lord of Phoenix hadn't been able to refuse. Though Ricardo was upset at the deaths of two of his vampires, the debt had been paid when they'd saved Angelo. Besides, the near demolition of the AIU earned his reluctant gratitude.

Lillian wondered how long it would take the AIU to recover. According to Bryan, their servers had been down for almost forty-eight hours before they went back online. Unfortunately, they knew better than to believe that the damage to their building and computers was due to a freak lightning storm, but instead of suspecting vampires, they were now looking for witches—actual witches, not psychics. Lillian prayed the incident would never be traced back to her and the vampires who'd helped her.

Forcing all unpleasant thoughts away from her wedding night, Lillian turned her attention to her soon-to-be husband. Studying every line in Radu's sculpted face, she marveled at his savage beauty. Never had she imagined that she would be so happy. With him, she'd never be lonely again.

At long last, Lillian had a home, or rather she would soon. While Radu waited for his approval to become a Lord Vampire, they looked at houses in Sandpoint and Spirit Lake, because the vampires decided they'd like to consolidate the whole Idaho panhandle and Eastern Washington. Razvan was somewhat disappointed that Radu wanted to remain in Idaho, but understood his love for the trees and lakes.

Radu gazed at her with such wonder and tenderness that she could hardly breathe as Anthony Salazar officiated the ceremony. Lillian didn't hear a word that was said until it came time to exchange their vows.

After promising to love and cherish each other for all of eternity, Radu slipped an ancient sapphire ring on her finger. "It was my mother's," he whispered.

Tears filled her eyes, but he brushed them away before claiming her lips in a passionate kiss, heedless to their audience.

The world fell away until all that remained was the two of them, their hearts beating as one.

Applause brought her back to the world. She beamed at Radu as the musicians started playing an orchestral rendition of Dio's "Rainbow in the Dark." Her father had liked that song.

The reception was also held on the beach, with caterers serving champagne and hors d'oeuvres that most of the guests couldn't fully enjoy. Some vampires slipped away to find their own meals while Radu made sure to have Lillian eat her fill, groaning in delight with each dish she tasted.

Razvan frowned at them. "I envy you that power, brother. But at least I inherited the better looks."

Everyone laughed at the joke.

"I can't eat anymore," Lillian said. "Not if I want to save room for cake."

Radu pouted. "Well, perhaps we can open our gifts while we wait for your appetite to return."

Razvan shook his head. "Silas will throttle us if we don't wait for him to come back from his hunt." Suddenly, his phone rang. "Ah, there he is now. I'll be sure to tell him to hurry." Digging the phone from his pocket, he answered it. "What's taking you so long, McNaught?"

Even though the reply was a shout, Lillian couldn't hear what Silas said on the other line, but she could hear the vampire's thick Scottish brogue that he only had when he was upset or emotional about something.

Razvan's smile melted from his face as his features paled. "Oh my God...We're on our way." Ending the call, he returned his phone to his pocket and turned away from his brother. "Akasha!" he shouted.

"What?" She scampered across the sand to meet them.

"Xochitl is back," he told her.

Lillian gasped as a stone of foreboding dropped in her belly. The memory of Jayden reciting the Prophecy echoed in her mind.

The queen had returned.

Keep reading for a teaser of Book 5, PLEADING RAPTURE!

Teaser of PLEADING RAPTURE

Soft grass cushioned Aurora's fall. She struggled to sit up, but her head spun from passing through the portal. Closing her eyes, she counted to ten. When the dizziness passed, she sat up and looked around. Xochitl's car was nowhere to be seen, but the light from the moon and lamp posts made her realize that she knew where she was, the Fort Sherman Park. The wooden fencing and little playground brought back memories of climbing the fort and going down the slide at night with her friends when there were no kids around to point out that they were too big for that. No one was too old for a slide.

She peered around and saw no sign of Xochitl or her Datsun. Had it gone off toward the lake or to the parking lot? She didn't see any tire marks on the grass. Maybe she'd dropped from the portal in a different part of town since she and Xochitl weren't connected when she jumped in after her. Hell, she didn't even know if Xochitl had seen her running behind the Datsun.

Aurora scrambled to her feet and stretched, groaning as her back popped. At least she knew where Xoch' would go. With no family here, Silas and Akasha were all Xochitl had. Well, she could possibly go to Sylvis's parents' place or even to Aurora's family, but that was doubtful. No one tolerated Xochitl's weirdness more than Silas and 'Kash. That's why they all had practically lived with Silas and Akasha until the band moved to Seattle.

Music and laughter from a distance reached her ears. Aurora turned around and saw a glimpse of light from the beach ahead. Was there some sort of party going on over there? She perked up. Maybe someone had a phone she could use. Hopefully, Akasha hadn't changed her number in the last six months.

As Aurora crossed the park and came to the sidewalk and short concrete wall that separated the park from the beach, she had to do a double-take. Instead of bikinis, shorts, and tank tops, the people on the sand were decked out in tuxedos and fancy gowns. Tables were set out on the edges with fancy glasses and plates with slices of a big white cake. Now it made sense. This was a wedding party. She wondered if they'd needed a permit or if you could just head out to the beach and do it. Maybe that was why it was going on at night, so they didn't have sunbathers and kids and swimmers in their way.

Oh well. Someone would have a phone. And maybe they'd let her have a piece of cake and a glass of champagne. The munchies and cottonmouth were kicking in from that doobie she'd smoked with Beau. She hefted her leg over the short concrete barrier and hopped onto the sand. As she neared the party, a man split off from the group and approached her.

Aurora sucked in a breath as he passed under the lights strung up around the area. He wore a tailored suit that clearly did not come off the rack and hugged a fit frame that she knew would be a work of art beneath the cloth. His hair was almost shoulder-length, black and wavy, framing a face that could have been stamped on a Roman coin. Eyes the color of coffee bored into hers.

When he spoke, her knees went weak at the rich timbre of his voice. "What brings you out to the beach at this hour?"

"I...um..." Aurora swallowed, trying to find sensible words. Not only was it impossible to say that she'd been dumped in the park by a portal, but it was also hard to speak to a man as luscious as this. And then came the old wariness as she remembered where she was. A town that was ninety-eight percent white...a town where at least twenty percent of those people hated her race. She peered back up at him, looking for that telltale gleam of scorn or disgust at seeing a Black person. All she saw was mild curiosity and something else that made heat flood her belly. He wasn't exactly checking her out, but there was some sort of interest there. She recovered her voice. "Um, you didn't happen to see a blue Datsun station wagon come by here, have you?"

His inky black brows drew together at the odd question. "No. I haven't seen a Datsun wagon in years. A few Zs and pickups, though, but not tonight." He had a trace of an accent that she couldn't quite place. Somewhere back East, definitely. The hot guy stepped a bit closer, his features growing even more gorgeous as he came more into view. "Are you all right? You look a little disoriented."

She nodded in agreement. "I suppose I am. Would you happen to have a phone? I need to call a friend and see if they can pick me up."

"Not on me, I'm afraid. It ruins the lines." He smoothed his hands down his suit.

"And what fine lines they are," she blurted. Heat rushed to her cheeks. "I'm so sorry. I couldn't help myself."

He chuckled, a low, velvety sound that should be rated for mature audiences only. "Forget about it. I am flattered."

Another wave of dizziness made her knees buckle for a second. Clearly, interdimensional travel and being high didn't mix.

The man grasped her shoulder with a firm but gentle hand. "Hey, are you okay?"

She nodded. "Yeah, just had a dizzy spell. I forgot to have dinner." No way was she revealing to this classy, hunk of sexy that she was kinda baked. Not to mention the whole dropping through a portal into the park.

"Well, why don't you sit down for a moment, and I'll bring you some cake. Would you like some champagne as well?"

"That would be wonderful." Her mouth felt like Death Valley. "And could you…" she trailed off as he jogged back to the party before she could ask him to see if someone had a phone she could use. Everyone here probably had seven-hundred-dollar iPhones. Gone were the days of the cheap but sturdy Nokias.

Mr. Hottie McHotstuff returned with a large slice of cake and a delicate flute of champagne. Aurora thanked him and had to use every bit of her will to not gorge the cake like a stoner. But damn, that was good cake, white and fluffy, with custard filling and cream cheese frosting. Even then, she was subconscious of every crumb that stuck to her lips.

"Are you feeling better?" The man took the plate and handed her the champagne, which she tried to sip as ladylike as possible when she was more accustomed to chugging beers and downing shots.

"Much better, thanks." Aurora looked back at the party that was about thirty feet off. The people were laughing and talking and only casting her occasional curious glances. "So, is this a private party?"

He nodded. "A double wedding. I do not want to offend, but I'd rather not interrupt it."

"Don't worry, I understand," she quickly assured him. "My mom is a dragon when it comes to outsiders at family gatherings. My brother wasn't even allowed to bring girlfriends over until Mom was absolutely certain things were serious." A lump in her throat formed as she realized just how much she missed her family. She took a sip of champagne and closed her eyes, savoring the taste. This was definitely a top-shelf brand. "I should probably head over to the resort and find a phone. My friends are wondering where I am."

"I have one in my car," the man said with a tempting half-smile. "We could head there, and you could use it."

She shook her head. "I know better than to get in a car with a stranger."

"My name's Tony." His smile radiated warmth as he extended his hand. "Now, we're not strangers." His eyes narrowed as he peered at her with an intensity that made her shiver despite the warm summer night air. "In fact, I'm not sure we *are* strangers. I swear I've seen you before."

He probably had seen her on TV or in the papers. The news would have run stories on her band's disappearance. But he clearly wasn't a metalhead, or he would have recognized her immediately. And she wasn't about to tell him she was a missing person. Not before she was reunited with her friends, and they announced their return together.

"I'm Aurora," she replied and shook his hand. His grasp was warm and vibrated with barely suppressed strength. "And I *know* we've never met. You don't seem like the kind of man I'd easily forget." She instilled a flirtatious tone that sounded unfamiliar to her. Damn, why did this man have to affect her so intently? He seemed to be everything a girl could dream of. Handsome, kind, and wealthy. But now was not the time for her to try dating again. Not with all that crazy prophecy stuff going on and her career on the line.

That rich and sinful laugh once more emerged from Tony's lips. "Again, such charming words. Are you a writer?"

She smirked. "Sometimes." She wrote the lyrics to at least half the songs on every Rage of Angels album.

He looked back at the wedding party and then back at her. "I hate to insult this lovely gathering, but you are far more interesting company. I don't suppose you'd want to go for a walk with me during your quest for a phone? And again, my offer still stands to use mine." He pointed at a sleek black sports car in the parking lot under the streetlight. "As you can see, it's near the street and in the light, so you're perfectly safe. Or, we can go to the resort and have a drink, and maybe some dinner, since you mentioned that you missed it. I would very much enjoy getting to know you better." The heat in his eyes promised that if he had things his way, they'd do more than talk.

Damn, a drink sounded nice. A drink and a few minutes not worrying about the chaos of her life. Not to mention the prospect of fun naked times with what was possibly the hottest man she'd ever seen. But she needed to find Xochitl and...*You know what?* Xochitl had her car. She was probably at Akasha and Silas's place by now. Who said Aurora couldn't relax and have a drink with a hot guy for a few minutes? A few minutes of blissful normality after months of weirdness. Then she could just call Akasha, and they'd pick her up. Or, if she decided to take Tony up on his unspoken offer, he could just give her a ride.

"Well," she began.

"Aurora!" Beau shouted from beneath one of the huge pines in the park. Sylvis stood beside him, eyeing the wedding party quizzically.

Her eyes widened. Zareth must have brought them over. She glanced back at Tony. "I have to go. My friends found me."

Tony inclined his head in an old-fashioned way. "While I'm glad that your situation has been resolved, I do regret that our talk has been cut short."

"Me too." She grinned and lifted herself up on her toes and kissed him on the cheek. He smelled like an entrancing combination of vanilla beans and expensive, old-fashioned tobacco. For a moment, she was tempted to wrap herself around him and explore him further.

She turned and hefted herself over the concrete barrier and jogged back to the park before she could gauge his reaction to her stolen kiss. Though it didn't really matter one way or another. She'd never see him again.

Click here to get Pleading Rapture!

About the Author

Formerly an auto-mechanic, Brooklyn Ann thrives on writing romances featuring unconventional heroines and heroes who adore them. Author of historical paranormal romance in her critically acclaimed "Scandals with Bite" series, urban fantasy in the cult favorite, "Brides of Prophecy" novels, the award-winning, "Hearts of Metal Series, and the B Mine series, horror romances riffing on the 1970s and 1980s horror movies.

She lives in Coeur d'Alene, Idaho with her gamer son, rockstar/IT Guy boyfriend, and three cats.

She can be found online at https://brooklynannauthor.com as well as on Twitter and Facebook.

For exclusive updates, sneak peeks, and giveaways, sign up for Brooklyn Ann's Newsletter at https://www.brooklynannauthor.com/newsletter/

Books by Brooklyn Ann

Series by Brooklyn Ann

B Mine

(Horror Romance)

HIS FINAL GIRL

HER HAUNTED HEART

HIS SCREAM QUEEN

HER HALLOWEEN PARTY

~~~~~~~~~~~~~~~~~~~~~~~~~~~~

Brides of Prophecy

(Paranormal Romance/ Urban Fantasy)

Also don't need to be read in order until book 5...kinda

Prequel: Tesemini (Free)

Wrenching Fate (Free)

Ironic Sacrifice

Conjuring Destiny

Unleashing Desire

Unleashing Desire

[Pleading Rapture](#)

[Melding Souls](#)

[Reclaiming the Magic](#)

[Leaving the Shadows](#)

~~~~~~~~~~~~~~~~~~~~~~~~~~~~~~

Hearts of Metal

(Contemporary Romance)

Standalones that intertwine

[Kissing Vicious](#)

[With Vengeance](#)

[Rock God](#)

[Metal and Mistletoe](#)

[Forbidden Song](#)

[Tempting Beat](#)

[Heart Throb](#)

Scandals With Bite

(Regency paranormal romance)

Books do not need to be read in order

Bite Me, Your Grace

One Bite Per Night

Bite at First Sight

His Ruthless Bite

Wynter's Bite

The Highwayman's Bite

For excerpts and special content, visit BrooklynAnnAuthor.com

I love hearing from readers! If you have any questions or comments, feel free to send me an email!

Contact@brooklynannauthor.com

Made in United States
Orlando, FL
04 October 2023